Her Widow's

Peak

To Gloria thank you
for your support.
Ella D. Fleming

A Novel by

ELLA D. FLEMING

HER WIDOW'S PEAK

Printed in the United States

ISBN-13:978-0692352762
ISBN-10:0692352767

Printed by Createspace 2014
Published by BlaqRayn Publishing Plus 2014

Rebecca Durst: Editor
Stanley Newton: S&N Photography

Dedication

This book is dedicated to my Lord and Savior Jesus Christ the author and finisher of my faith.

My dearly departed mother, Mrs. Venie Delestion, thanks for all you've done for me. I love and miss you momma.

To my sister, Dr. Joann Adeogun; Cleo Scott Brown, my mentor; Sandra Daly, my friend and confidant, and Gale Christopher, who pushed me to keep writing. Thank you all for believing in me.

To my Pastor, Rev. Isaac J. Holt Jr. my spiritual leader. Thank you for allowing God to use you to preach and teach with such power and conviction, and for believing in me and helping me grow.

To my husband and best friend, Keith W. Fleming, Sr. who

always supports me in whatever I do.

Thank God for placing you in my life.

I love you.

To my children Tina and Keith Jr. and my grandchildren,

Rhiannah and LaQue.'

Be all God created you to be and put him first.

This book is for you all and the generations to follow.

Ella Delestion-Fleming

Presents:

Her Widow's Peak

A Novel

Introduction

Every good mother wants the best for her child. It doesn't matter if you are the biological, adopted, or grandmother. You want to raise them right, give them a good education, teach them everything you know about life and love, and hope they make the right choices, all the while praying they don't make the same mistakes you've made. That is, if you've shared some of those mistakes and are working on doing better.

"***The aged women likewise, that they be in behavior as becometh holiness; not false accusers, not given to much wine, teachers of good things. That they may teach the young women to be sober, to love their husbands, to love their children...***" Titus 2:3-4 KJV

No matter what decisions your child makes along their journey, we as parents must hope what we have instilled in them will not return void, always praying and hoping that your voice will always be somewhere guiding them through life; all the while learning to let go and trust God.

"***Train a child in the way he should go, and when he is old he will not turn from it...***" Proverbs 22:6 NIV

Growing up in Charleston, SC in the projects, I heard a lot of wives tales and superstitions about a person's appearance, and some were placed on me. For example, if you sweat on your nose that meant you were mean or if you had a **Widow's Peak**, you were going to kill your husband. For the record my husband is still alive after 28 years of marriage.

Since I was a little girl, I've always liked stories with morals at the end. I was also fascinated with words that have more than one meaning to them. When I got saved and started reading my Bible more, I enjoyed the parables. A parable, according to one definition, is **a simple story used to illustrate a moral or spiritual lesson, as told by Jesus in the Gospels**. This story is my rendition of all of this. My "parable," if you will, or my interpretation of these two scriptures.

Throughout this book, you will take a journey with a young woman named Brenda who was raised by her grandmother, who brought her up in the church with Christian values, but as she gets involved with the wrong man, her life takes her on many levels. Her struggle with her relationship between God and man brings her full circle back to her first love, Jesus Christ, the ultimate peak. So sit back, get your favorite beverage, find a nice place to relax, download the play list I have provided, and enjoy...

Her Widow's Peak

Playlist

Sunshine—Roy Ayers

Moments In Love—Art of Noise

Take Everything In—Angie Stone

Love Suggestion—Will Downing

Sit Down—Angie Stone

Album (After Tonight 2007)-Will Downing

Sleeping With The Enemy—Teena Marie

Diamond In The Back—Curtis Mayfield

Find Your Way Back In My Life--Kem

I Who have Nothing—Luther VanDross & Martha

Wash

Love Ballard--LTD

Nothing Has Ever Felt—Will Downing & Rachelle

Ferrell

A Mother's Love--Kem

Summer Madness-Kool & The Gang

What You See Is What You Get—The Dramatics

For the Lover In You--Shalamar

Hey There Lonely Girl—The Stylistics

HER WIDOW'S PEAK

In The Rain—The Dramatics

Yearning For Your Love—The Gap Band

We Both Deserve Each Other's Love--LTD

Zoom—The Commodores

WEY-U—Chante' Moore

Something Special—Will Downing

London Chimes-Paul Hardcastle & The Jazzmasters

Paradise Cove-Paul Hardcastle & The Jazzmasters

It's Working--William Murphy

Broken But Healed--Byron Cage

I Told The Storm--Greg O'Quin

The Battle Is Not Yours--Yolanda Adams

Another Man Is Beating My Time--Barbra Mason

No More Tears--Anita Baker

It Don't Hurt Now--Teddy Pendergrass

ENJOY!

Arrangement of Contents

"THOU SHALT NOT KILL.."

Exodus 20:13

Prologue

Transparent—that's how Brenda felt as she walked down the long corridor to what she thought was the therapist's office. *How could this be happening to me? I'm not crazy.*

"This way, Brenda," the orderly said as he escorted her to the door.

With each step, her body shook with anxiety. All she could think was *what will the church members say if they found out? After all, black folk don't go to psychiatrists; they go to church to deal with their problems*— or so she was told. This time, however, was different. It didn't matter what anyone thought or how she was feeling. It wasn't her decision to make; it was the Judge's.

At the moment, her freedom was the most important thing in her life. For over ten years, it had been her family, or more specifically, Ray.

Ray was Brenda's husband. A tall, bow-legged, chocolate

brother with a smooth bald head that seemed to run on down his perfectly built frame. His eyes drew her in with every blink. How could she resist his smooth words? No matter the lies he told, she wanted to believe—she had to believe. She remembered her mother's words when she was a little girl.

"Brenda you will always have a mean streak," she would say. "Just look at your head."

"What about my head?" she'd ask.

"You have a widow's peak, and that means you are going to kill your husband."

Over the years she grew up believing that her mother's words were just an old wives' tale. How could such an insignificant piece of hair growing down a person's forehead determine their destiny? After all, she was just a child; how dare she predict such a horrible fate for her own daughter.

Every day growing up she resented her peak. She would take the razor and shave it every time it grew back, until she noticed that it grew even longer, so she decided to let it be.

Who knew that her mother's words would someday ring

true? That she would hear a Judge slam his gavel on his desk and sentence her to 15 years, fifteen long years in a mental facility for murdering the love of her life. After all, she couldn't remember anything; it was all a blur…it all happened so fast. She didn't remember grabbing the knife. All she wanted was a romantic evening for two. She wanted to tell him the exciting news: he was going to be a daddy.

As the time passed, and the candles melted, she began to worry. *Where could Ray be?* she thought to herself. It was eleven o'clock; he couldn't possibly still be at the studio at this hour.

Ray was an up-and-coming photographer in the city of Atlanta and was famous with the local celebrities. He also did a lot of work for their church. That night, she remembered trying to call his cell with no success, getting into her car and driving downtown, seeing his car outside in his parking space, standing at the studio door, and turning the knob.

It was dark; playing loud on the CD player was "Let's Get It On," Ray's favorite song by Marvin Gaye. As she walked towards the set, she heard rustling, and as she proceeded closer to the sound, she couldn't believe what she was seeing. *This can't be happening to me,* she thought as her mouth flung open. *This **must** be a bad dream.* They were naked, they were holding each other, they were kissing, and this was an abomination. How could she not know? Why didn't she see the signs? Their entire relationship flashed before her eyes.

If it were a woman she could deal with that—what woman could resist Ray—but a man? Worse than that, her Pastor! Not the man who married them ten years ago; not the man who counseled them through the difficult times in their marriage. Not the person she thought would bless their baby seven months from now. Her heart began to beat as though it were about to fall out of her chest. It was as if legions of demons had entered her body; she became possessed.

With the bloody knife in her hand, and her head pounding as if she were having the migraine of all migraines, she covered her face as the tears began to flow. When she opened her eyes, all she saw was the police officers reading her

Miranda rights. She blacked out again, waking to the sounds of whispers coming from the nurses and doctors in the hospital.

She lifted herself up from the hospital bed with an IV needle in her hand, scratches and bruises all over her body. She turned in the direction of the doctor.

"What happened? What am I doing in the hospital?" she asked. "Where is my husband? How is my baby?" she shouted hysterically.

The nurse and doctor tried with all their might to calm her down but to no avail. The doctor told the nurse to give her a mild sedative to calm her. As she began to relax, the doctor started to explain what had happened to her husband. She couldn't believe what she was hearing.

"No, I wouldn't do that! I love Ray," she insisted. "He was my world; we are going to be parents!" The look on the doctor's face was one of deep regret and sadness. She could somehow read every single worry line and wrinkle on his face, as though they were sending out physic signals to her brain telling her that there was no more baby.

With the IV still attached to her arm, she jumped up out of the hospital bed and began to make a hasty exit to the door, exposing her naked rear.

"I have to see Ray!" she said shouting at the top of her lungs. "Tell me where he is!" No sooner had she reached the door handle, the officer outside stood directly in front of her, blocking her path.

"Ma'am, I need you to settle down and let the doctors take care of you," the officer stated.

Brenda knew she had no choice; where was she going to go? There was no one. Her mother was gone, Ray was gone, and now her unborn child was gone. How could this be? *Why is this happening to me?* she thought. She tried to always do the right thing by everyone. She tried to do unto others as she would have them do unto her. She was faithful in her church and her community. Why was God punishing her? As she laid in the bed waiting, for what she didn't quite know, she began to try—try to remember what happened. Why couldn't she remember?

≈

Seven months later, she was still in a hospital, but not for the reason she thought she would be. No, there will be no delivery of her and Ray's baby, just a 15-year sentence in this cuckoo's nest for something she couldn't have done. Slowly they continued to walk to what she thought was the therapist's office. When the door opened, Brenda was surprised; it wasn't who she expected to see. It was Mrs. Benjamin, the first lady of her church, the Pastor's wife. What was she doing in this office? Why was she here?

"Come in Brenda." Mrs. Benjamin cordially asked.

Brenda was curious and deeply puzzled by the sweetness and calmness of her former first lady. After all, from everything that she had been told, her husband too was murdered by Brenda, and for reasons no woman in their right mind would want anyone to know. Yet everyone did know. Why the pretense? What was she up to? Was she out for revenge? Brenda wasn't having it. She had lost too much. Everything and everyone she had ever cared about was shot to hell. There was nothing left to lose.

"What kind of sick game are you playing with me, Mrs. Benjamin? Are you trying to keep me in here for the rest of my life? Are you trying to steal what little sanity I still have left?"

Brenda continued to bellow out the point she was trying to make.

"Look, I didn't mean to kill your husband; I don't remember doing it. I'm sorry! Please forgive me!"

On bended knees, with tears streaming down her face, she kept begging. Mrs. Benjamin handed Brenda a tissue.

"No forgiveness necessary..." she said to Brenda. "In fact, I am going to help you get out of here. You see, I know what happened that night..."

"I too followed my husband to your husband's studio. I

had been suspecting him of cheating on me for months, but I didn't have any proof. So I waited for him to leave the church one evening, and I found them together. I was so ashamed and embarrassed that I couldn't tell anyone..."

"That day, that dreadful day, I got a call from my physician; you see I had been feeling quite ill for months. I thought it was the flu or a virus, so I decided to get a physical. When my doctor came in the door, it was as if someone had stuck a gun to my head and pulled the trigger...'

"He told me I had AIDS. I was like a zombie; I got in my car and drove around for hours, until I ended up at your husband's studio... "I saw them; it was sickening! I wanted to kill them, but you walked in, so I hid. I saw you jump on them with the knife as you began to stab Ray until he wasn't moving..."

"While you were taking care of your husband, I was taking care of mine with the other knife. He was so busy trying to stop you, that he didn't even notice me behind him. My husband knocked you out..."

As she looked up at Mrs. Benjamin, she noticed something, something she had never noticed before, on Mrs. Benjamin's head. Why hadn't she noticed it before? Maybe because she always wore her nice pretty hats every Sunday, or perhaps it was because she never wore her hair back in a bun before? It all began to make sense; she too had a Widow's Peak...

LEVEL

I

Chapter 1

THIS TALL BLACK TREE

In disbelief and in shock, Brenda did not know what to say. Somehow she seemed frozen in time. Her knees were stuck to the floor. *What is the bitch telling me?* she said to herself. How could she let things get this far? As angry as she was with Mrs. Benjamin, she felt sorry for her and strangely connected to her at the same time. After all, they both had lying, cheating, backstabbing, husbands who were on the D.L. Not only did she have to grasp the fact that the whole marriage was a lie, but that she lost everything trying to save it: her freedom, her baby, and now maybe her life. She thought about the day she met Ray...

HER WIDOW'S PEAK

She was a student at Spelman College in Atlanta studying to be a scientist. It was her junior year. She went to the local club with her roommates, Shannon and Debbie, to blow of some steam after a long midterm. Ray was the bouncer who had a pretty well known reputation with the locals and most of the college students in the area. He did some free lance photography, and he enjoyed taking photos for special events and functions at the colleges in the area.

She remembered getting out of the car, approaching the club, and wanting to change her mind. After all, clubbing wasn't her thing. She would have preferred to have stayed home and watch television or give herself a pedicure. They paid the cover charge and went inside; her roommates immediately went to the dance floor and tried unsuccessfully to convince Brenda to do the same. She refused and began backing away from her friends and into the crowd, not realizing she was backing into to Ray.

As their bodies collided, Brenda turned around and found her face pressed into the biggest, hardest abs she had ever seen.

Slowly, as she began to look up at this tall black tree, she wondered if she could possibly climb it. When she got to the top, there he was: this black Adonis that stood 6 ft 3 weighing about 200lbs with muscle that seemed to reach to the ceiling.

"Hello," he said with a deep powerful whisper. "Are you alone?"

Moving her mouth but barely speaking a word. "No…ooh, I'm, ah, with my friends."

She stuttered. *Lord have mercy, what a beautiful black man* she thought to herself. *I can't believe he is speaking to me. With all these beautiful women in here, why is he wasting his time talking to me?*

Brenda remembered something else her mother used to tell her.

"Bre-Bre," that was the nickname her mother called her, "you are a saved, Christian woman and that means you need to conduct yourself like one. You better watch out for those smooth talking Negroes out there. Just because it looks good and sounds good don't mean it's good for you. They only want one thing and once you give it, you surely can't get it back...

"A man has an agenda and they are always on the hunt for fresh meat. Keep your draws up and your eyes open. Don't be nobody's fool..."

Why is Momma messing with my head right now was her conscious thought. After all, she wasn't here; she didn't see how this man looked, couldn't smell his cologne. *I would be a fool to miss this opportunity.*

They sat and talked for hours; it was as if they were all alone in the club. In the background, she could hear the DJ playing "Love Ballad," an old school joint by LTD. It was as though he was playing it just for them, and Ray was mouthing the words to her. Brenda knew she was messed up, it was over, and that if this man asked her to go home with him, she knew she couldn't, she wouldn't, say no.

After that night Brenda and Ray were inseparable. Brenda would wait for Ray to pick her up for daily coffee and doughnuts after her classes. They would talk about each other's hopes and dreams for the future. She knew it had only been a couple of months, but she was falling head over heels in love with Ray and she wanted to hear that he was in love with her.

How will I know how he feels? she often asked herself. Although they spent a lot of time together, Ray had been very respectful of her feelings; in fact he had never even made a move on her.

Perhaps he thinks of me as just a friend, or maybe he wasn't feeling me in that way, she thought. *He must be getting what he needs somewhere else. There must be some loose girl out there he's making booty calls to. Maybe he's just not attracted to me*. She was driving herself crazy with worry and doubt.

Brenda knew Ray was more experienced, and he would be her first real boyfriend, not that she could really call him that. What if he wanted to get serious? What if he wanted to sleep with her? She was a Christian and a virgin. She wanted to save herself for marriage. Besides, she and Ray never even talked about church, and since she'd met him she hadn't stepped a foot in one. Out of all the things they had talked about, they never talked about what he believed in.

Brenda decided she would take a leap of faith; she was going to tell Ray how she felt. She called him on her cell and asked him to meet her that evening for a quick bite at a local restaurant near campus. Ray agreed, stating he had something important to ask her. *Oh my God! What could he possibly want to ask me?* Brenda quickly ran to her apartment to find something special to wear that night.

As she pulled on outfit after outfit, she'd stare at herself in the mirror. "I am fat!" She yelled out. "I need to lose some weight. Ray wouldn't think of wanting someone my size." Brenda was 20 years old, 5' ft 2 inches tall, 173 1bs, with short black hair and beautiful brown skin. She dressed very modestly for her age and was often teased by her roommates about her fashion sense, or lack thereof, as well as her not wearing makeup.

She called out to Shannon in the next room. "Girl you've got to help me look good for tonight...I have a date with Ray.

I think he is going to ask me to be his woman!"

Shannon started looking through Brenda's wardrobe, mixing and matching until she found something that made Brenda look presentable. When she looked in the mirror, Brenda didn't recognize herself. She was stylish in a black sleeveless dress that stopped about three inches above her knees; it showed off Brenda's shapely curves, along with black sheer stockings, and a pair of black four inch heel boots. She also did Brenda's hair, makeup, and accessorized her outfit with a pair of large gold hooped earrings, bracelets, and a thin chain belt to accent her waist line.

"Wow, is that me? I look beautiful...thanks Shannon."

"Girl, Ray is not going to know what hit him."

Spraying perfume on, Brenda grabbed her purse and ran out to her car. When she arrived at the restaurant, Ray wasn't there. She watched with anticipation, lifting herself from her seat to look outside with every car door slam. Watching the door every time it chimed to see if it was Ray, Brenda became more anxious. "Maybe he's just running a bit late," she spoke softly to herself.

After about fifteen minutes, the waiter asked if she was dining alone. Looking at each table, more specifically the tables with couples kissing and holding hands, the strong aroma of garlic glided through the restaurant. Brenda said no, only asking for something to drink. Another thirty minutes passed, so she began tapping her glass of water with a clean fork she pulled from a neatly folded napkin on the table. Wondering what was keeping Ray, she called him. The telephone rang three times, and then a female answered.

"Hello." Her voice was cracking. "May I speak to Ray?"

There was a slight pause, "He's in the shower...uhm...who is this? The female on the other end exclaimed in a very hostile tone.

"I'm Brenda...who is this?"

There was that brief pause again, "I'm Sheila, Ray's woman and why are you calling my man?" Brenda immediately hung up the phone, paid her bill and ran out of the restaurant. *What a fool, sitting, waiting; I should've known there was someone else...*

That night Brenda cried herself to sleep. Shannon and Debbie tried consoling her but to no avail. Days went by and no word from Ray. The sounds of the apartment complex buzzing with students running up and down the halls, laughing, and blasting music didn't seem to faze Brenda; she was caught up in her thoughts of doubt and anger, analyzing what she could have said or done differently.

Maybe it's for the best, she reminded herself, holding back the tears and mucus buildup in her throat. *I will just focus on getting out of school and starting my career.* She was already falling behind in her classes spending so much time with Ray. Winter break was approaching, and Brenda couldn't wait to go home to see her mother and put Ray out of her mind.

She turned on the radio to drown out her thoughts. It seemed as though every song dealt with a relationship gone wrong.

As she began to pack her things, there was a knock at her

door. Stopping, she wiped her nose with a tissue and dragged to answer it. It was Ray.

"Hi Brenda," he said with an innocent look on his face. Brenda was surprised to say the least. Then anger took over. *How* dare *he show up at my doorstep! What about I'm sorry for standing you up, or for leading you on and not telling me you had a girlfriend,* she thought to herself.

As the minutes ticked away, Brenda stood holding the door open staring at Ray as if she was seeing a ghost. "What do you want?" she asked with attitude.

Ray continued with the innocent act. "I wanted to see you and tell you how sorry I am for the other night. Baby, I wanted to be there but something came up that I had to take care of—"

Brenda interrupted him with a shout. "Yea, I know what came up, and I know who it came up for!" she yelled.

"What are you talking about?" Ray asked.

"Look, don't come to my door a week later and play dumb with me. I may have come from South Carolina but we aren't slow, like you northerners seem to think!" she said with a matter of fact look. "I don't play games...I don't have time to waste on a brother who doesn't know how to appreciate a good woman when he sees one. All you had to do was tell me the truth. Now if you don't mind, I have some packing to do..."

She proceeded to slam the door in Ray's face.

Ray was shocked to hear Brenda be so forceful and straightforward with him. He used his hand to hold the door open, preventing her slamming it in his face.

"Brenda, just hear me out!" he exclaimed. "I don't want to lose you...I— I never met anyone like you before and I got scared. You're smart and pretty and I found myself falling for you. I didn't know how to deal with it. I've always had to keep my feelings bottled up to keep from getting hurt, that is until I met you.

"I was prepared to ask you to be my woman, but my old girlfriend came into town and one thing led to another and I couldn't face you... You mean a lot to me Brenda and I want to make things up to you if you just give me a chance..."

Brenda didn't know what to say. Standing there watching this big black man crying in her room seemed to turn her on.

Suddenly, "Love Ballad," the song they listened to the night they met at the club, came on the radio. She immediately grabbed Ray by the hand and pulled him into her room, kissing him. All bets were off; she knew there was no turning back. *Lord help me*, she reasoned in her mind, *what am I doing*?

As Ray began to undress her and kiss her on her neck, scriptures from the bible began to come to her mind. ***"Be not unequally yoked together with an unbeliever. What fellowship has darkness with light?"*** Still with all she knew from the Bible, Brenda could not resist his touch. With every love song radiating from the radio feeding into her spirit, she wanted more and more.

As she laid there in his arms, she knew Ray was all she would ever want and need. There was this bond between them now that no one would ever be able to break. "Will I ever be enough for him?" she whispered into the night as she watched him sleep. Just then she heard the voice of her Pastor. "Your body is the temple of the Holy Ghost, you don't want to yield it to someone who won't respect it."

"Ray," she gently tried to wake him. "Are you sleeping? Can we talk?"

"Sure baby... what do you want to talk about?" he said, yawning and rubbing his eyes.

"Us..." she replied with hesitation.

"What about us?" he asked.

She continued with even more trepidation, "Where is this relationship going between us?"

At this, Ray turned to face her. "What do you mean where's it going...?" he repeated.

"Ray, I need to know how you really feel about me, especially after what we just did; you know I've never made love before...I wanted... to save myself for the man I was going to marry."

Ray looked deep into Brenda's eyes and smiled as he stroked her hair. "I know you were a virgin baby...that's what makes this so special," he said to her.

"Please don't hurt me Ray; I don't think I could take it. I am not a person who takes sex lightly... I need to know that we are going to have a future together?"

He kissed her tenderly before replying, "Baby, you know I care about you and I will do whatever it takes to make you happy..." At that moment, Brenda's body shook with great desire as she seduced him all over again.

The next morning she woke up to Ray staring at her. He had such a peaceful expression on his face. "Good morning baby, how did you sleep?" He asked serenely. "Do you want to go get some breakfast?"

Next morning shyness crept into her voice, "Good morning...I...I slept like a log. What time is it?"

"Ten o'clock, why?"

Brenda freaked. "Dear God, I am late for my Biology class...I have a test and I didn't have a chance to review my notes!" She was rushing around and throwing things, so Ray knew he was being dismissed.

"Can we see each other later on?" he asked. "I really want to Ray, but I am getting behind on everything, and I have to study for my finals before I go home for winter break. What are you doing for Thanksgiving? Are you going home to see your folks?" she asked.

"No!" Ray said, very sternly.

Brenda realized at that moment that she didn't know anything about Ray's family. In fact, he had never even mentioned them before. Maybe they weren't as close as her and her mother. She wanted to ask more questions, but she was already late for class.

"Tell you what..." she said, "Why don't you come home

with me and meet my momma? Have you ever been to Charleston before?" she asked.

"No, I've never been to Charleston and I would love to meet your mother, but I have to go out of town for a photo shoot with this new rap artist who just signed a deal with Mega Records. They want me to shoot his CD cover."

Brenda brightened. "What if I skip going home for Thanksgiving and go on the shoot with you?"

"Look baby, I don't think I will have a lot of time to spend with you. I will be spending most of my days and nights working. Besides how would it look if I took my woman with me on my first big job? It wouldn't be professional, now would it baby?

"No," she said with a disappointed pout on her face.

"Maybe Christmas, okay...?" he said. Somehow Brenda knew that wouldn't happen for Christmas as she rushed to the bathroom to take a shower, get dressed, give Ray a kiss goodbye, and run out the door.

While taking her test, all Brenda could think about was

the night before. Ten more minutes, the professor announced, papers rattling from the other students in the class. She reflected on everything they said and did. *I'm going to hell*! she thought to herself. *He didn't even propose, what was I thinking?*

Just then the professor told everyone to pass up their papers. Brenda snapped out of her daydream, looked down at her test and realized that she hadn't finished.

"Oh my Lord!" she said.

"Is there something wrong, Ms. Greene?" her professor asked.

"Yes, Professor Jacob," she said as she began to try to come up with a good excuse for not finishing her test.

"I really have a lot going on right now, personally, so I didn't finish..." She gave him an imploring look as she continued, "...is it possible I could take it over at another time?"

Her professor looked at her with his usual unconcerned smirk. "We all have our personal problems, Ms. Greene, but we must learn to work through them and accomplish our goals mustn't we? Why, if I give you a break for having personal problems, I would have to give all my students a break, now wouldn't I?" he said.

Brenda had no rebuttal— after all he was right— so she collected her books and walked out the door.

The rest of the day didn't seem to go so well. In every one of her classes, she just couldn't seem to focus. All day her mind lingered on Ray. Brenda knew she was in trouble: her grades weren't looking good and she was barely passing her classes. She knew she had to focus and buckle down; she couldn't afford to fail. Somehow she had to get a grip and learn how to manage her relationship with Ray and school. After all, she wanted to be a scientist. It was important to her to find cures for diseases.

It was as if God was calling her to do this ever since she was a little girl playing with her chemistry set she'd gotten for Christmas one year. It was important to her mother as well; Momma Greene would always tell her boys and books don't mix.

She didn't know what to do. Praying was the first thing that came to mind, but she knew that she hadn't done it in a long time. She knew it couldn't hurt so she attempted to try.

"Lord," she started. "If you help me pass my classes I promise I will never let Ray touch me again. Amen."

Just as she said those words she heard her mother's voice in her head. "God knows your heart. Don't be making vows to God you can't keep. Once you start having sex you can't stop, not unless you commit your flesh totally to God."

Chills ran down Brenda's spine. *She's right...how can I resist Ray's touch? Maybe I can lead Ray to Christ and we can join the church.*

≈

Tests were over and Brenda was eager to see Ray. It had been a long hard semester, and she just wanted to relax and take her mind off of all the studying. It was a week left before she was to go home and she had to say good-bye to Ray.

They spent every waking moment together. Again, Brenda tried to pry information out of Ray about his family and his childhood with very little success.

All he would say was he didn't want to talk about it. He did, however, tell her he moved to Atlanta after he got out of the Army about a year ago. He served four years in the Army with Special Forces and did two tours in Afghanistan. He decided to join the military after 9/11. He also told her that he was a freelance photographer taking some pictures for a magazine in a building not far from the Twin Towers when they came down.

He said when the towers got hit by the first plane, he ran outside and began to shoot moment by moment until he could no longer see from all the smoke and commotion. He told her that whole experience made him feel obligated to go after those bastards who killed all those people.

Ray's face seemed to change as he reflected on that day.

His eyes began to glaze over with a faraway look. It was as if he was reliving the moment all over again then he just stopped talking.

Brenda was impressed, to say the least, at his commitment to help others, and it did explain why his body was in such good shape. She wanted to know more. With great eagerness, wrapping her arms around his broad shoulders trying to comfort him, she continued with the questions. He explained to her that he couldn't talk about everything that went on because it brought back a lot of painful memories he didn't want to relive. She respected his wishes and changed the subject. At least she had something to tell her mother that might impress her.

"We only have two more days left together...what should we do?" she asked expectantly.

"Look Brenda, I've been meaning to tell you...they moved the shoot up to tomorrow so I need to go home and pack..."

Brenda was stunned! Why hadn't he mentioned this earlier?

"I can come and help you pack and maybe drive you to the airport tomorrow.

"NO!" Ray said abruptly; a little too abruptly "...I got it. I will be up all night trying to put equipment together and stuff like that...the label is going to send a car for me early so it would be best if we just call it a night."

She was confused and a little disappointed. What was wrong with Ray? It was as though his whole demeanor had changed. *One minute he wants to be with me, the next he wants to be by himself.*

"Alright," she said, "will you call me every day?"

"Whenever I get a free moment...I promise," he said as he kissed her goodbye and ran out the door. Brenda had a bad feeling about Ray's hasty exit. Maybe talking about 911 and the war really got to him. *I hope he'll be alright* she thought as she got ready for bed.

Although she was going to miss Ray, she knew she had to tell her mother about him, and knowing the type of woman her mother was, it was probably best that he wasn't coming with her for Thanksgiving. After all, no man that she knew or had ever known was any match for Momma Greene.

Chapter 2

MOMMA GREENE

Brenda loaded her car and headed off to Charleston. She was getting excited about seeing all her friends and church family. As she drove down the long stretch of highway with the windows rolled down and the breeze blowing on her face, all she could think of was her mother. She thought on how she struggled and sacrificed to give her so much.

Momma Greene (Mrs. Elnora Mae Greene) was an independent, strong, Christian woman about 63 years of age, with jet black hair accented by a patch of gray perfectly placed on the right side of her head. Her beauty was strikingly timeless, as if she'd stepped out of the first Ebony Magazine, the issue featuring the first dark complexioned woman. Her tall stature and petite frame made her look elegant in anything she wore.

She had a no nonsense approach about life and she'd tried to instill good moral values in Brenda.

Momma Greene had raised Brenda from an infant. Brenda's biological mother, Momma Greene's daughter Karen, ran away from home at the age of sixteen. Brenda was never told anything about her; in fact, there wasn't even a picture of her in the house nor was there ever any mention of why she left.

When Brenda would ask anything about her, Momma Greene's only reply would be, "I'm your momma." From that point forward, Brenda called her Momma, never asking any more questions.

However, she could still recall a time when she was around four or five years old, hearing Momma Greene yelling over the telephone at someone about coming to "see your daughter." Brenda remembered thinking *it must be my mother...if only I could hear her voice*. She'd gone running to the other extension just so she could listen; they had already hung up.

She also thought about the times she would hear weeping late at night coming from Momma Greene's bedroom. Through their paper thin walls, she could hear her praying, begging, and pleading with God on behalf of her child, who was out there somewhere doing "God only knows what."

It would get louder and louder. "Please protect and keep her and let no hurt, harm or danger come nigh her, in Jesus name," she would hear her say. Then she would thank God for answering her prayers and begin to shout, cry, and moan. The next day it was as though nothing had happened and all was well in the Greene household.

Brenda had a great deal of admiration and respect for her mother. She often reflected on how Momma Greene would work two, sometimes three, jobs to put food on the table and a roof over their heads so she could send Brenda to tutoring, putting her in special programs to help her excel in school. She never missed her recitals or science competitions, making sure Brenda had all the necessary supplies and school clothes she needed throughout the year. She would save extra money so they could take special vacations even if they never left South Carolina.

She'd tell Brenda, "Everyone should travel outside their own city and see the world." Sometimes they'd go to the airport just to watch the airplanes take off, imagining where everyone else was going.

Momma Greene believed in doing what was right in the sight of God. After all the struggles and trials in her life as a young woman, she was determined to give her grandchild a good Christian foundation and support system.

They were often in church five days a week, staying for hours. She had Brenda participating in almost every activity the church offered, from the choir to Sunday school, then youth ministry, vacation Bible school and teen Bible study—and the list went on and on.

Every time there was a contest or a convention, Brenda

was in it; she made sure Brenda was on the bus. Momma Greene took other children under her wing as well, sponsoring them for trips and disciplining them when they misbehaved. Brenda thought about the many times her mother would chastise children in the movie theater, in church, or even in the street.

She would say, "Boy or girl, why don't you pull up your pants, or act like you got some sense and stop embarrassing the black race." She would buy things for families less fortunate, babysit for single parents who had to work; she was even a foster parent to children that no one wanted because they were disabled or uncontrollable. Momma Greene definitely played her part in that "village" of child rearing.

She often told Brenda about her childhood in Charleston, South Carolina. She spoke of how much she loved growing up in the projects with her mother and two sisters because of the sense of community and level of support the neighbors gave to one another. Everyone looked out for the next person, and whenever someone needed anything, the neighborhood rallied together to help out. People had manners and respect; good morning and good evening was said to everyone. The old saying was, "It's due to a dog."

If you misbehaved everyone disciplined you. It didn't matter if it was by a teacher, a neighbor, or a family friend. When word spread to your parents, you would get hit with whatever was available at the time: a belt, an extension cord—you name it. There was no such thing as time out or grounding.

Brenda would say it all sounded like child abuse to her and asked if anyone ever called Child Protective Services. Momma Greene told her, "I got your Child Protective Services! Black parents raised their children the best way they knew how to keep them from having no manners and to keep them out of trouble. The Bible tells you if you don't discipline your child you don't love them: **spare the rod spoil the child**.

However, it wasn't always so pleasant for Momma Greene. Being an adolescent of dark complexion was hard back then because people in the south were notorious for what's called "color struck" even among their own race. She said the children in the neighborhood would tease her, calling her "Little Black Sambo" and telling her she was skinny and looked like a giraffe. They would pick fights with her until she started fighting back; they soon learned to leave her alone.

Brenda was curious about Momma Greene's father and asked what he was like and whether he was present in her life growing up. She told Brenda that he knew who he was, but that he wasn't a full time daddy to her and her sisters and he didn't live with them. He never took any of his Father's day or Christmas gifts with him when he left their house. Momma Greene had given voice to these questions as a child and was promptly told by her mother that it was "none of her damn business." Later she was finally told the truth; her father was a married man.

In years to come, Momma Greene found out it was common in those days for married men to have mistresses that lived in the projects.

Jobs were scarce for black woman with little to no

education, so most worked for white folks, taking care of their children and keeping house. Momma Greene, as a child, resented when her mother brought home the white folks' hand-me-downs. On occasion, she returned home with bras, panties and slips for them to wear, and when Elnora refused to wear the intimates, her mother got very angry with her. She called her ungrateful, considering herself better than everyone.

Despite their varied disagreements through the years, Elnora loved her mother, learning to forgive her for the many things said and done to her with the help of the good Lord; she took care of her mother until the day she died.

Momma Greene had a great deal of experience with men early in her life. Because of the lack of affection from her mother and father, she became starved for attention. She believed by telling Brenda about her life she could somehow keep her from making the same mistakes she had. She confessed to two marriages and a host of relationships that caused her a great deal of heartache.

Her first husband, John Baker, whom she'd met in high

school at the age of fifteen, was her first love; she was madly in love with him and he gave her anything her heart desired. This too made her mother jealous of her.

Momma Greene would tell Brenda, "Don't let a man buy you anything because then they would think they own you...be your own woman and learn to do things for yourself, do you hear me child?"

"Yes ma'am..." Brenda would reply, trying to understand her momma's words.

The two lovers got married after he joined the Army and she graduated high school. They moved to Kentucky and lived there for about two years until he cheated on her with other women and actually fathered two children outside the marriage. It ended after five years, with Elnora deciding to move back to Charleston where she met Alex Chisolm, a local cab driver.

She wasn't really that interested in him, but loneliness and hurt over her divorce from John overwhelmed her reasoning mind, and she found herself in a relationship with this man.

Her daughter Karen, Brenda's mother, was the ending result.

"Watch out for those rebound romances Brenda...those are the ones that will mess your life up."

That relationship lasted about a year, until the day after Karen was born, when Elnora found out he had another woman pregnant. Both women ended up in the same hospital, the same room, going into labor at about the same time. Both were placed in the same recovery room after delivering their babies; the other woman had a boy.

The beds were divided by a large curtain meant to provide some inkling of privacy. Elnora was resting after breast feeding her baby girl, having placed her in her hospital issue bed when she heard a familiar voice talking to the woman next to her. She was a bit drowsy yet sure she heard the woman say, "Alex, come hold our son..."

Momma Greene said she jumped out of that bed, snatched back the curtain, saw Alex and cussed him out on the spot. When he saw her, he put the baby down, trying to explain himself with no success; Momma Greene didn't let him get a word in edgewise.

By this time, the other woman got in on the verbal abuse and both of them caused such a ruckus in the hospital—screaming, slapping and boxing him—that both babies began crying, causing the nurses and staff to come see what was the commotion. She said they both told him they would see him on '**The Green**' for child support (that's what they called the local child support office in those days.) She didn't hear from him again until he called from jail asking her to take him back. But Elnora, with her many colorful expressions, said she told him, "When chickens have teeth! My love is like a faucet: when it's on, it's on, and when it's off, it's off!"

As big and strong as Ray was, Brenda knew he wouldn't be able to handle Momma Greene. Behind all his charm, good looks and smooth talk, she knew her mother would see right through him, giving him the third degree. It was bad enough she would have to answer questions she didn't even know the answers to, but she knew her mother would ask her if her virtue was still intact. It would be the first thing that would come out of her mouth. As she drove down the highway, she started rehearsing what she would and would not say.

The first thing I need to do is get back in church and ask God to forgive me for what I have done. She knew it was the only way. *I know she's going to ask me about school and my grades...I also know she's going to ask me for my password so she could look it all up for herself. So I know I need to be honest about that...I just can't let her think that it was because of Ray my grades aren't good; not that she would believe a word I say anyway...*

HER WIDOW'S PEAK

Momma Greene's second husband, Sam Greene, was a local businessman who owned several restaurants and auto repair shops in the city.

He was a handsome man of about forty who attended church regularly. She met him while working in one of his restaurants as a waitress while putting herself through school for business/accounting.

She said he would come by to check how everything was going just to see her until the day he finally worked up enough nerve to ask her out. With much hesitation and a year of him asking, she agreed to go to the movies with him. They dated for at least six months before she even let him come to her home or meet her daughter.

He was a God-fearing man who treated her like a queen. She began attending his church where he was the head trustee. After six more months of dating, they were married.

Brenda asked her how she knew he was the one for her after so many bad experiences.

Momma Greene responded, "It was because of all the

wrong choices I'd made...the one thing I knew for sure was what I didn't want in a man! I knew I didn't want to deal with any more trifling jokers; I grew up and wanted different things out of life...a man was no longer my focus or source for happiness; it was my child and our future..." She had to learn to love herself and handle her business.

As she grew in the word of God, she knew the qualities to look for. She didn't think there was any such man out there that came close to those requirements until she met Mr. Greene. This time she waited to hear from God and did her homework.

"Something you young girls need to start doing," she added. When Momma Greene talked about him her face lit up. Yet there was a hint of sadness in her eyes. "I sure miss that man," she would say. They were married for twelve years before he died of prostate cancer.

HER WIDOW'S PEAK

Twelve miles to Charleston, Brenda contemplated as she passed the mile marker, changing the radio station from R&B to Gospel. She began to smell the unpleasant order of the paper mill coming through her partially opened window. Turning on to her exit, her thoughts ran to Ray and what he might be doing. *Will he remember to call me tonight?* Just then her body began to tingle.

"Stop this right now!" She commanded her flesh.

As she pulled onto her street, she could see her mother outside sweeping the porch. As she approached the driveway to their two-story, recently renovated old Charleston home, she could smell the chicken. With a smile her mother approached the car to help Brenda unload her things.

"Bre-Bre, how was the trip...did you get the car serviced before you hit the highway?" She asked.

"Yes ma'am..." Brenda said as she carried her bag into the house.

"Take your things on in the room and get settled...I will finish dinner and we will sit down and have a nice meal before we go to bible study."

Bible study! It had been a long time since she had picked up a bible let alone gone to a bible study. *Lord what am I going to do now?* Brenda knew she couldn't tell her mother she didn't feel like going—that would be a dead giveaway—so she got herself situated and they sat down to a nice dinner.

Her mother asked about school and how her grades were coming along. Trying not to lie, yet not giving away too much information, she said that things were getting pretty tough; however, she believed she was passing her classes.

"Well, we will make sure pastor prays for you tonight...I think all your friends are due home today from college as well. You know he likes to lift you kids up in prayer before you go back to school..."

As much as she wanted to see all of her friends and get back to her church, she knew she had backslidden, and the guilt of it all was attempting to consume her. *How am I going to do this*? These thoughts tortured her. *I need to get myself together! Why am I torturing myself; it's not like anyone will know what I've done..."*

As they turned into the church parking lot Brenda's heart began to race. Liberty Hill Baptist Church. The sign flashed like neon lights on the Los Vegas strip. "Take your burdens to the Lord and leave them there" was the word of the month on the sign.

The building was decorated with wreaths on the door and the lobby was graced with an enormous tree beautifully decorated for Christmas. The church was packed with members eager to hear the word from Pastor Hamilton. Momma Greene went to sit by her friends while Brenda made her way to the back hoping no one would see her; at that moment, the Pastor began to speak. His topic was sanctification and holiness.

The guilt was too much for Brenda! She jumped up, running out into the vestibule, tripping over her jacket sleeve. Bracing herself on the table to keep from falling, she felt a strong hand catch her, gently lifting her up. As she glanced upward she saw a man she had never seen before.

"Are you alright?" he asked with a concerned look.

"Yes... thank you..." she managed, barely above a whisper.

"Is Bible study over?"

"No, no..." Brenda responded tightly.

"Are you sure you're ok...you look upset. Is something wrong?"

Why won't this man just leave me alone...I said I was fine. Who does he think he is...my social worker?

Even though she wanted to be angry with him, she caught herself checking him out from head to toe. He was about 5'10, 180lbs, with smooth milk chocolate skin, jet black curly hair, and a neatly trimmed mustache. His eyes were a deep hazel with the most beautiful specks of gold and green. "I'm James Powers; I just joined your church Sunday..." His smooth, large hand was extended out to her.

"Nice to meet you..." she grasped the hand lightly in a flimsy shake, "I'm Brenda Greene... welcome." He smiled;

her heart did a little flip-flop.

"Nice to meet you as well, Brenda...I hope to see you again," he said as he went inside.

Girl get yourself together, she chided. *A man is why you can't sit and hear the word right now.*

Later that night and the rest of the holiday, her mind stayed on Ray. *Why hasn't he called me? Where is he...?*

Chapter 3

IN SICKNESS AND IN HEALTH

Thanksgiving passed, and Brenda went back to school and tried to work on her poor grades. She tried not to pressure Ray about his lack of concern for her feelings during the holiday, wondering why he never called or talked to her about the photo shoot.

Instead, Brenda pretended it didn't bother her and decided not to mention Christmas. Again she loaded up her car and went back home to Charleston. If he wanted his space, she would give it to him.

This time, however, her momma was not waiting outside for her. There was no smell of chicken coming from the house. Everything seemed strange and surreal. Usually the house was decorated inside and out with Christmas music playing on the stereo to put Momma Greene in the holiday spirit; not this time.

HER WIDOW'S PEAK

Brenda sensed something wasn't right. As she opened the door she called out to her mother, she didn't get an answer. She could hear the television in her mother's bedroom.

"Momma, I'm home!" She shouted. There was no answer.

Brenda, trying not to panic, ran to her momma's room. Elnora Greene lay face down and unconscious on the floor. Immediately Brenda turned her over, trying to wake her, but with no success. She checked her pulse and heart to see if she was still alive, then desperately dialed 911.

Holding her mother in her arms, the tears flowing, she began to speak.

"Momma, everything is gonna to be alright...the ambulance is on the way... just please hang in there. Don't die Momma...please don't die!"

Just then the ambulance arrived to take Momma Greene to Medical University Hospital. Brenda followed along in her car, frantically dialing her mother's prayer circle and the pastor.

When she arrived at the hospital, she checked her mother in while the nurses and attending physicians took her into the emergency room. As she sat waiting, she began to pray, distracted by the sound of ambulances and clerks asking patients and families for information. "Doctor Johnson you're wanted in ICU, STAT!" The voice bellowed over the intercom. Immediately Brenda's heart raced, *Lord please don't let that be my momma*, she prayed.

"Hello...are you Mrs. Greene's daughter?" The voice came out of nowhere. Still deep in thought, Brenda tried to process a rational response.

"Yes, I'm her daughter...Is she alright? Can I see her? Please tell me she isn't dead..." she blurted it all out in one breath.

"I'm Dr. Powers, the attending physician assigned to your mother's case. Your mother is stable...we are going to admit her for more test," he said.

"Do you have any idea what caused her to pass out?"

Brenda couldn't think clearly; she could think of nothing but Momma Greene. "My mother is a strong woman...she has never been sick a day in her life that I can recall, except for an occasional headache."

"You should go home, get some rest. If there's any change I will give you a call, Brenda..."

At the sound of her name coming from this stranger, she snapped to attention, "How do you know my name... have we met?" He looked vaguely familiar but her mind was to fuzzy with concern to be sure.

"Yes, we met over the Thanksgiving holiday. My name is James, James Powers. We met at church during Bible study..." Ding, the light popped in her head...

"Yes, of course, I remember now. I'm sorry I didn't recognize you. If it's at all possible, I would like to stay with her tonight." Brenda gave him her most imploring look; he smiled. What a nice smile.

"I'm sure we can work something out for you," he said. He called for a nurse, admitting Momma Greene to a private room with a bed for Brenda.

≈

While waiting for her mother to be placed in a room, Brenda began pacing back and forth thinking about what she needed to do next. The strong aroma of antiseptic and urine in the hospital made her nauseous. Every ten minutes she would ask the nurse at the desk what was taking so long.

"We will let you know when she has been placed in a room, Ms. Greene. Why don't you go to the cafeteria and get a cup of coffee or a bite to eat. I will page you as soon as I know something." The nurse was trying to calm her.

"Okay, I could use some fresh air...I'm just going to step outside...I'll only be a few minutes. Please send someone to get me if anything happens."

Standing there wondering how she would ever be able to make it without her mother, she looked at the patients with tubes in their noses, IVs attached to long poles and casts on their legs, and the tears began to fall.

After about an hour, exhausted from lack of sleep and food, Brenda closed her eyes for a mini power nap when suddenly a hand gently tapped her shoulder.

"Brenda..." this deep but gentle and caring voice woke her. "I didn't mean to interrupt... I just wanted to let you know we've placed your mother in her room." It was Dr. Powers. "The nurse told me you were out here, so I told her I would let you know personally what was going on." He had such a kind smile on his face.

"Thank you," she said.

"It will be a while before we get the room situated for you...uhm...I was just about to head down to the cafeteria to get a bite...would you care to join me?"

Hesitant and a bit flattered he would ask, she said yes. While heading to the elevator, Brenda questioned him.

"Do you know what's wrong with my momma?"

"Well," he said, with a look of concern, trying not to alarm her, "We still have a great deal of tests to run and the tests we've done so far haven't come back from our labs yet, so I don't want to speculate on a diagnosis without any facts to back it up..."

Hours passed as they sat talking about everything. James seemed to be very interested in Brenda and her life. They talked about the church, their educations and training until he pretty much told her almost everything about his life. Brenda was feeling comfortable with him and somehow knew he'd do his best to help her mother.

Too soon a page came across the intercom calling for Dr. Powers. "Well, I guess that's for me" he said, gathering his things.

"I guess so..." she looked away for a moment, slightly embarrassed.

James noticed, "Listen...I'm going to handle this and make my rounds, but after I 'm done, I'll check in on you and your mother before I leave for the evening."

"Thank you again for everything," she said with a huge smile on her face as she finally chanced to look into his eyes.

Suddenly, out of nowhere, he hugged her. Brenda, so shocked, just stood there like a cardboard cutout.

As he walked away, she mused, *What just happened? Was he coming on to me? Nah, what am I saying...he was just being nice. Why, it's the man's job to make people feel comfortable so don't start jumping to conclusions...that's how you get yourself in trouble. He is Momma's doctor, for heaven's sake!*

The next morning Brenda woke up to the sound of Momma Greene on the phone praying with one of her prayer partners. After they finished, she began to give God the glory and praise for giving her another chance. As Brenda lifted herself off the small couch, she found herself getting caught up in the praise and worship.

"Thank you Lord!" she screamed out without thinking. Momma Greene looked in Brenda's direction, reaching out for her. Crying and shaking, Brenda climbed into the small hospital bed, laying her head on her mother's chest as Momma Greene stroked her.

"Everything is going to be alright baby...I'm fine, see? God is not through with me yet...Brenda...I need you to hear me child and listen good..."

As Momma Greene began to speak, Brenda knew this was going to be one of her deep, insightful revelations that would be pressed in her heart and mind for the rest of her life, as she laid there, eyes glued to her mother's.

"I'm not always going to be around...we all have an appointment to keep. I want you to remember everything I've tried to teach you and never lose your identity to another person. Be who God created you to be and enjoy your life child. I've made bad choices and good ones, but the best decision I ever made was raising you...

"I love you and I want you to love yourself. I also want you know what real love feels like from a man. Don't give up on your hopes and dreams."

Why is she talking like this? Brenda thought. *Why is she talking like she's ready to walk into the light?*

As she started to rebuke her mother for talking negatively, there was a tap at the door.

"Come in," Momma Greene said.

"Good morning ladies." It was Dr. Powers. "Hello," they spoke in unison.

"Good to see you up and about, Mrs. Greene. I'm Dr. James Powers, your attending physician. I have the results from the test we took last night..."

"Alright doc, give it to me straight, no beating around the bush," she replied. Brenda was nervous and looked at Dr. Powers' lips as they moved in slow motion. "I'm sorry to tell you that you have CANCER on your liver and it looks like it is pretty aggressive..."

Brenda blacked out. Dr. Powers yelled out into the hallway for a nurse, as he dropped the chart, catching Brenda before she could hit the floor and easing her back onto the chair she had just fallen from. He continuously tapped her face to wake her. Slowly, opening her eyes, she felt as though she was in a nightmare; *this just couldn't be happening,* her brain relayed. Dr. Powers' voice broke through the fog collected in Brenda's brain, sounding faraway but urgent.

"Brenda! Brenda, can you hear me? Nurse, please get me a glass of water..."

Her mouth felt dry and there was a sudden throbbing in her temples "...Yes...uhm...what just happened?" she questioned.

He handed her the glass of water while still holding onto her, in case she passed out again. "You fainted."

The word 'cancer' slammed into her head as she sat up frantically looking around the room.

"Momma!" Brenda cried out.

"Yes baby, I'm here..."

"...I had a bad dream that you had cancer..."

Momma Greene looked at Brenda, taking her hand and squeezing it lightly for reassurance "...It was no dream baby...that's what they tell me, but it's not what my Heavenly

Father says. He has the last and only word over my life." She stated this in her usual matter of fact way.

Still troubled by her mother's diagnosis, Brenda left the hospital in a daze. So much so, she found herself driving to her church not even remembering getting into her car. She saw several cars parked in the lot and wondered, *what's going on?*

As she got out, she met up with one of the older members of the church, Mrs. Jenkins.

"What's going on today Mrs. Jenkins?"

She smiled her response, "Noonday prayer service, dear..."

Brenda knew it had been God leading her to church. She had never been to noonday prayer before, didn't even know it existed but this was the very place she needed to be.

When she entered the sanctuary, she sat in a pew in the back of the church listening as prayer after prayer went up; all she could think about was her momma and if she should mention anything about her being in the hospital with cancer.

As if on cue, Deacon Capers stood up asking if anyone had another prayer request before they closed. Shaking and holding back the tears, Brenda sat glued to her seat, wanting to stand up, but fighting against the Spirit. "This is the time and the place where we can stand in the gap for one another and bombard heaven on one another's behalf. The word of God tells us we have not because we ask not..." he chided.

Why would God answer me? I know I haven't been doing what He asked me to do and I know I have sinned against Him. Maybe I am being punished for backsliding.

Deacon Capers continued, "...The word of God also tells us that when two or three are gathered together touching and agreeing on one accord, there He is in the midst..."

Brenda stood. Before she knew it, she felt her lips separate and the words began to spill from her mouth. After she laid her petition before the congregation, everyone surrounded her and began to pray for her and her mother.

She felt hands on her head, shoulders, and back, and the burdens she had been carrying seemed to lift off her. Her knees buckled as she collapsed onto the floor. There was a sense of peace that overwhelmed her as she lay there; it was as though she could hear Jesus telling her everything was going to be alright.

Getting up a little shaken up by her awesome experience, she thanked everyone and headed to her car. She heard a familiar voice calling her name...

"Brenda, how are you doing?" Turning, she saw Dr. Powers.

"I'm ah…fine...what are you doing here?"

"I come to noonday prayer as often as I can..." he said. Brenda felt a little embarrassed for her thoughts but though them nonetheless. *Is this man stalking me? Or my momma must be worse off than I thought if her doctor came to church in the middle of the day!*

"...It's really good to have that extra support from other saints when you are dealing with some tough situations in your life..."

What could possibly be tough about his *life... he's a doctor, he's rich and young and fine as all get out...*

"I have the rest of the afternoon off...would you care to join me for a bite to eat?" he asked.

"Well, I have to get home and pack some things to take to the hospital...I need to take some time off from school...I have some things to figure out..." She was rambling.

"You still need to eat; we could discuss your mother's treatment options or just enjoy the time away from the hospital before you need to go back..."

He took her to a nice quiet bistro where they sat in a corner booth for hours talking. Brenda found she forgot about her mother's illness for just a while; he was so funny. He was charming and he reassured her he would keep her informed of everything regarding her mother.

Excusing herself to head for the ladies room, she realized it was dark outside; lunch became dinner as the waiter changed along with the menu, and she knew she had to get back to her mother. She really didn't want to leave. With every word he spoke, he drew her in.

Her cell phone rang; she jumped to answer, thinking it may be the hospital. "Excuse me...hello?" she said.

"Hey baby, what's up?" It was Ray.

"Hello nothing..." She was hesitant to let on to James that it was another man.

"When are you coming back, I really miss you. I know you're upset with me and I'm sorry. I want to make it up to you..." He said.

"Can I call you back? I'm in the middle of something right now..." She hung up.

"Is everything alright? Do you need to leave?"

"Everything is fine" she said. "Have you noticed you've been asking me that question since we first met?" she asked him.

"Have I? Well, I guess it comes with the job."

The phone rang again; it was Ray, but this time Brenda didn't bother to answer. She didn't want to feel pressured or stressed. She enjoyed being with this man. There was no guessing or pressing for information; he was open. He didn't seem complicated and she needed to hear a man's voice communicating back to her right now without the guilt.

As they stood to leave the restaurant, Dr. Powers asked if he could see her again, and he told her to call him James. Playing dumb, she replied "You're my mother's doctor...of course you will see me again."

"No, I mean away from the hospital. I don't mean to sound out of line, and believe me when I say I have never done anything like this before," he said in a cute little nervous voice.

Brenda didn't know what to say. She was attracted to him, but Ray's face popped into her head.

"I'm sorry, I didn't mean to put you on the spot like that, I know you have a lot going on...I'm just the kind of man that goes for what he wants, and I want to get to know you a little better..." He smiled in her direction but his eyes were piercing. "...You don't have to answer me now; I will see you at the hospital tomorrow."

On her way home she thought about everything that had happened. She remembered Ray's call and tried calling him back. There was no answer, so she called it a day.

Weeks went by and Brenda had a big decision to make. Would she return to school for the next semester or stay home and take care of her mother? She knew if she told Momma Greene she was thinking of staying out for a while to take care of her, she wouldn't allow it. It was her dream to see Brenda graduate, and she planned on being there no matter what. With the help of her church and the social workers at the hospital, Momma Greene had all the support she needed emotionally and financially.

Most of Momma Greene's money was depleted after the death of her husband, due to his struggle with cancer and bailing Karen out of all her troubles; however, she managed to save what she could for Brenda's college education. She had been putting money away ever since Brenda was born and swore she'd never touch it; she never did.

It was time for Momma Greene to come home from the hospital, and Brenda was very excited. She had responded well to treatments and had been placed on a very strict diet. She also was given medication for any discomfort.

Brenda packed her bag as they waited for Momma Greene to be discharged. She finally mustered up the guts to tell her mother she didn't think she should return to school for the semester—she wanted to remain home to take care of her until she could get a nurse in to help on a regular basis.

"Brenda, you will do no such thing! You are going to carry your behind right back to school and get your education. Don't worry about me...I have the Lord on my side and He will supply all my needs. I didn't work hard all those years to get you to this point for you to let it go to waste now!" she said.

"But Momma—" Brenda tried to interrupt. Momma

wasn't having it.

"Don't you 'but Momma' me child...you heard what I said!" she exclaimed with great demand in her voice.

Brenda knew better than to say anything else; she knew what her mother said, she meant, and there was no debating or compromising. Like clockwork, Dr. Powers entered the room to Brenda's great relief.

"I have some good news!" he said, heading toward his patient with a smile and her chart. "Your second set of test came back this morning and it appears the cancer has gone into remission..." Brenda ran to her Mother, grabbing her and giving her a big hug and kiss. Without much thought, she walked over to James and gave him a big kiss on his lips.

After lasting a bit longer than a 'thank you' kiss should last, Brenda backed away, shocked and embarrassed by what she'd just done. "I'm…oh so sorry...I don't know what got into me..."

He was beaming! "Don't apologize...it was a nice thank you; I need to bring good news to you more often."

Momma Greene, watching this love fest unfold before her eyes, said "Thank you Dr. Powers. Won't you please join us for dinner tomorrow? I'd like to thank you properly with a nice home-cooked meal. I know you must be tired of all this hospital food...and please bring your wife." Nothing got pass Momma Greene.

"I am not married," he answered the veiled question with a smile, but she wasn't finished.

"Well, if you don't have plans with your girlfriend...please do come by." Now she was being just plain obvious.

"I don't have a girlfriend either...haven't really taken the time..." If it was information about his personal life she needed, he was more than happy to oblige her.

Brenda, feeling even more embarrassed by her mother's obvious attempt at match-making, quickly stood. "Momma, this man is very busy with other patients, so I'm sure he has better things to do tomorrow. Besides, you don't need to be up cooking, you should be resting..." she said, trying to persuade her mother to change her mind.

"Girl, what are you talking about? I am just fine. I am ready to get back to my normal routine. Does six o'clock sound good, Doctor?"

The beam was now a full ray of sunshine. "Yes ma'am. Should I bring anything?" he asked politely.

"No baby, just bring your appetite and that cute smile," she said, looking at Brenda.

Dr. Powers laughed "I can certainly do that. Well ladies, I need to make my rounds and I will see you both tomorrow."

The next day Momma Greene had Brenda cleaning and shopping for dinner like she was expecting the President. She was constantly commenting on how handsome Dr. Powers was and how she noticed him in church. She was saying stuff like "he sure is smart" and "he certainly did take good care of me in the hospital," but the icing on the cake was "he sure would be a great catch for somebody!" She even went as far as to comment on how much they had in common—with Brenda wanting to be a scientist and James being a doctor—

and how cute their children would be.

Brenda wondered what she was going to do... should she tell her mother about Ray or just let her have her moment? After all, she was on her way back to school and that would give her more time to talk Ray into going to church and maybe even coming clean with his personal life.

As they worked together in the kitchen, there was a knock at the door. “I’ll get it...you go get dress and put on something nice and pretty...”

Momma Greene went to answer the door; it was Dr. Power. “Good evening, young man,” Momma Greene said as she opened the door.

“Good evening Ma’am” he smiled, offering her a beautiful bouquet of fresh cut flowers.

“Brenda!” Momma Greene yelled, “Dr. Powers is here so come on downstairs.”

When Brenda came down, the two were in the living room seated on the couch; as she entered the room, you could hear a pin drop. They just sat there staring at her. Dr. Powers stood up with his mouth wide open; he began stuttering as if he'd forgotten how to talk.

Outfitted in a midnight blue dress that showed off her shapely curves, nice legs, and great bust, not to mention her toned buttocks, Brenda was a knockout. Her face was beautifully made up, and her hair was styled to accentuate her heavenly features. Her own mother didn't recognize her. Momma Greene figured Brenda's looks had a little something to do with the good Dr. being suddenly tongue-tied.

As they ate dinner, Brenda tried with very little success not to stare in James' direction. She could feel his eyes watching her all night. Her mother constantly dropped hints as she continued her intense matchmaking.

After desert, Momma Greene quickly dismissed herself from the table so the two of them could be alone. "Why don't you two go sit in the living room while I take care of the dishes and—"

Brenda interrupted her "Momma...why don't ***you*** go sit down and I'll do the dishes; you've been on your feet all day."

James was in total agreement with her. "Yes, Mrs. Greene, I think you should get some rest; I'll help Brenda with the dishes..."

Mission accomplished! "Okay, I'll let you two handle it." She gave them a huge smile.

"The dinner was excellent; I haven't eaten a meal like that in a very long time—thank you for inviting me..." His smile was even bigger.

"You are more than welcome young man—goodnight."

****

With each dish they washed and dried, the conversation got more interesting; the time passed quickly. It was 10:30 before they realized it was time for James to leave. As she walked him to the door, he caught her hand.

"I really had a nice time..." she smiled up at him.

"... So did I." In that instant, he looked into her eyes, lifted her chin and gave her a long kiss goodnight. "Have a safe trip back to school," he said as he walked out the front door.

Chapter 4

DOUBLE CROSS

The next day Brenda made sure her mother's needs were met before she headed back to Atlanta. She drove for hours thinking about James and the kiss he'd planted on her. She recognized just how much they really did have in common and how good looking he was. It wasn't until she drove up to the campus that she realized she hadn't heard from Ray since he called her at the restaurant.

Alright girl, you had better snap out of it before you see Ray, she smiled to herself; she was feeling giddy. She registered for her classes, paid for her books, then headed straight for Ray's apartment.

When she drove up, she saw his car parked in the driveway, and the excitement about seeing him started to flutter like butterflies in the pit of her stomach; she rang the doorbell. There was no answer. She tried again...nothing.

She put her ear to the door to see if she could hear any movement inside. Pulling out her phone, she dialed his number, still no answer.

"Maybe he went out of town on a shoot," she said. Just as she walked away, she heard Ray's voice, so she went back to pounding on the door and ringing the bell. *Why won't he answer his door*? She went to each window to see if she could get a clearer view of inside the apartment, and she couldn't believe what she saw.

Ray was with another woman, and that woman was none other than Debbie her roommate. She was shocked and hurt to say the least.

Standing there angry and upset, she went to her car and sat for at least an hour waiting for them to come out. The longer she waited, the more upset she became, and the more upset she became, the more she cried; the more she cried, the angrier she became. Brenda wasn't about to let them make a fool out of her. She was going to confront the both of them, and she was going to end her relationship with Ray once and for all.

Finally the apartment door opened; Debbie came out first with Ray following. As they approached his car, Brenda got out of her vehicle, walked up to Ray and hit him dead center in the chest. Shocked and stunned, he grabbed her hand trying to stop her blows.

"How could the two of you do this to me?" she screamed.

"You played yourself; you don't own him—he is a free agent," Debbie said.

"Shut up and get in the car girl!" Ray said as he held Brenda back from going after Debbie.

"Look Brenda, nothing happened. We were just talking..."

Brenda wasn't down for the lies. "Talking...talking! What kind of a fool do you take me for? I saw the two of you; I've been here for hours..." She was through with the entire situation. "You know what, she can have you—it is over!"

Following her to her car, Ray continued to try and explain. Brenda jumped in, not paying him any attention, as he hung onto the door trying to convince her to stay and talk. She backed out of the driveway and sped off with him hanging on for dear life until he finally let go.

Crying all the way back to campus, she called Shannon to meet her at the apartment. She filled her in on what went on between Ray and Debbie. With her eyes filled with tears and her nose running, Brenda laid across Shannon's lap as Shannon stroked her hair. She was very quiet and didn't respond to anything Brenda was saying. When she finally spoke, her words chilled Brenda to the bone.

"Hon, I wanted to call you while you were away to let you know what was going on behind your back, but I knew you were dealing with so much...what with your mother being sick and all...I just didn't want to upset you. I told Debbie she was scandalous and she should be a woman and find a man of her own.

"She has been pushing up on Ray ever since you left for Thanksgiving holiday. He came by here looking for you one day to see if you had come back after Christmas break. The next thing I knew, Debbie was lending him a listening ear and a whole lot more. I guess maybe they thought you weren't coming back."

"I don't think I can stay in the same apartment with her," Brenda sniffed. "I'm going to see if I can get another room somewhere else on campus."

Just as she opened the door, there stood Debbie with a smug look on her face. Brenda walked right pass her, making no eye contact and proceeded to her car. As soon as she got to the car, there was Ray, trying to look sad and sorry for what he had done. She didn't respond to any of his attempts to explain or apologize. She left him looking stupid and drove off to the housing office.

The housing office was packed with new students. The line was out the door. Phones were ringing off the hook. The staff was juggling two, sometimes three things at a time. Everyone needed the same thing Brenda wanted. *Why should I be the one to leave my nice room? Debbie is the back-stabbing whore that should leave,* she thought to herself.

At that precise moment, the Spirit spoke to her: "***Forgive those who despitefully use and persecute you***..."

"What!" She yelled out loud as she stood in the line waiting, startling the girls in front of her. An hour and half passed before Brenda finally reached the front of the line.

"Hello, how may I help you?" the woman at the desk asked.

"I would like to change my room please."

Looking a bit confused, the woman asked, "Why do you want to change rooms?"

"My roommate and I had a disagreement..."

"Is that it?" she asked, really not interested. "You need to give me something a little better than that. Shoot, if I had a room for every student who came in here every time they fell out with their roommate, this school would own this city. We barely have a room for the students who are enrolled this semester."

On the brink of tears again, Brenda got back in her car, just driving around until it was dark. She was so deep in thought that the ringing of her cell phone startled her. She picked up. Of course it was Ray. She slammed the phone down on the seat and began to cry again. She cried so much she couldn't see, so she pulled her car over and put her head down on the steering wheel.

She suddenly heard singing. It was an old gospel song she remembered singing at church when she was a little girl: "I Will Trust In the Lord." She looked up, realizing she had pulled into the parking lot of what appeared to be some type of church service.

Brenda was curious; she wanted to know what was going on inside. She needed some spiritual guidance right about now. After all, she knew if she had to go back to her room and see Debbie, she would do something very un-Christ like.

She got out of her car. She opened the door and went inside. The building was beautifully decorated with fresh flowers, marble floors, a high ceiling sporting a crystal chandelier and a mahogany receptionist desk in the lobby. Brenda followed the voices until she found the room from whence the singing radiated; there were about fifteen people in this room.

She turned to leave but heard a man's voice say, "Come in...Welcome to Holy Rock Temple of God. Please come in and join us for prayer service and bible study." After all she'd been through today she needed prayer so she sat down.

As the service came to a close, Brenda began to feel a little better. God had led her to this church.

"How are you this evening young lady? We are so happy you joined us. My name is Pastor Walter Benjamin and your name is?"

Brenda smiled at his friendly manner. "I'm Brenda, Brenda Greene..." she said.

"It's a pleasure to meet you Brenda Greene." He held out his hand in welcome. Just then, an attractive woman walked up with a smile on her face. "This is my wife, Mrs. Benjamin." Her smile seemed to be very genuine.

"Nice to meet you...is this your first time at Holy Rock?" she asked.

"Yes ma'am."

"How did you hear about us?" he asked.

"I was just driving by and I heard the singing. It reminded me of back home in Charleston. I was a little upset but now I feel a lot better."

"Well, I hope you come back and visit us again. We would love to see you on Sunday at one of our services."

"Okay, I will see you on Sunday."

When she returned to her apartment, she went straight to her room. She looked at her cell only to see that there were ten messages on the phone from Ray. Brenda knew that the events of the day were a sign from God to get her attention. She knew that she had strayed from the path for her life. The Lord brought her mother through a difficult bout with cancer, and now this mess with Ray and her roommate was the icing on the cake.

It was time for her to focus on getting her soul right with God and her future. Brenda began to search for her Bible. It had been a while since she read it, but she knew that all her problems started when she stopped reading it, and it was time to hear what God had to say about what she needed to do with the rest of her life.

≈

Sunday was finally here. Brenda woke up early just to get ready. She had been looking forward to visiting Holy Rock's early morning service. She picked out her most conservative outfit, styled her hair, and applied her makeup. Brenda opened the refrigerator door to get a yogurt.

As soon as she entered in to the hallway, Debbie exited her room to go to the refrigerator, rubbing her eyes as she pulled out the carton of milk. Debbie stood watching to see if Brenda would say anything to her, standing at the table pouring cereal into a bowl. Brenda took a spoon from the kitchen drawer, grabbed her Bible and purse, then proceeded to the door.

Lord Jesus, help me to be able to stick it out in this apartment with that girl. I don't think I can take seeing her everyday knowing what she did to me. She proceeded to the church. It was a beautiful day. The sun was shining and the birds were chirping. *This is the day that the Lord has made; I will rejoice and be glad in it,* Brenda said to herself.

When she got to the church, she saw cars for miles. She found a parking spot close to an old abandoned store about a block away from the church. People were going inside and the ushers were directing them to a seat. Brenda was impressed with how friendly and professional they looked. One usher asked her if she was a visitor and gave her a packet welcoming her to the church as they ushered her to a seat right in the third row from the pulpit. As she sat through the service, Brenda clapped her hands and sang songs along with the choir. A warm sensation filled her heart as she sat there thinking about how much she missed worshiping and praising God.

How had she found herself in this condition all for a man, a low down trifling man who used her and cheated on her?

Pastor Benjamin's message was "Serving the Lord with Your Whole Heart." *Momma Greene was right about everything*, she said to herself. Forget Ray and Debbie; they deserve each other.

≈

Weeks, then months, went by. Things were still a little strained between Debbie and Brenda. Debbie would try to hold conversations with Brenda and Shannon, but they would just answer whatever was apartment related and end the conversation. From time to time, Debbie would make sarcastic remarks about Brenda being a Christian and how she should forgive and forget, but Brenda would just walk away, go in her room, and pray for strength not to slap the black off of her. Shannon attempted to keep the peace by telling Debbie to back off.

Ray continued to call two or three times a day to no avail;

he would drive by the library or coffee shop where he knew she would be studying just to talk to her. One day he actually caught Brenda on her way to church. She'd been attending regularly and was thinking about becoming a member under watch care.

As she left the coffee shop to go to prayer service, Ray walked up to her.

"Why don't you just leave me alone? Can't you take a hint?" she said vehemently.

Ray was border-line desperate. "Brenda what do I have to do to show you how sorry I am? What can I say to make things right between us again?

"Debbie didn't mean anything to me...it was a big mistake! I tried to get you to talk to me, but you left without saying a word and I didn't know what was up. I'm a man and I have needs...Baby you know I love you..."

He lowered his voice to a soft caress while touching Brenda's arm, trying to get her all hot and bothered. "Can we get pass this and get back what we had? I miss holding you and making love…"

"Hold up!" Brenda interrupted sharply. "I know you are not trying to blame me for what you did! I don't have time for this farce. You must have lost your mind if you think I am going to fall for your lies. I have better things to do with my time than to play fool for you! There will be no more rubbing or touching or anything with me. Any man who wants me has to go through God to get me. What's between my legs is attached to my heart and my heart belongs to the Lord!" With that Brenda got in her car and went to church.

Ray was stunned. He didn't recognize this person. *What happened to that sweet, innocent southern girl who was so naive?* He was curious to find out.

The next morning Brenda woke to the sound of her phone ringing. She was still half asleep, but she turned over in bed to pick it up.

"Hello," she answered with a dragging voice.

"Good morning, Brenda, how are you?"

"Look Ray I told you…"

There was a moment's pause before the voice replied. "Ray...who's Ray?" he said, interrupting her.

"This is James...you remember, Dr. Powers." Brenda jumped up, straightening herself as if he could see her through the phone.

Clearing her voice to sound a little sexier, she said, "Hi, how are you?"

She could almost hear his smile. "How have you been? I apologize for waking you up. I sometimes forget everyone is not on my schedule."

"Oh no, it's quite alright. I'm up..." That little white lie would have her repenting later. "Is everything alright with my mother? Is she back in the hospital? Do I need to come home?" However, now she was fully awake.

"No, no," he interrupted her, trying to calm her down, "nothing is wrong with your mother. Actually, she's coming along quite nicely."

"That *is* good to hear because we just spoke yesterday, and she told me she was going to a church banquet." She headed into the bathroom.

"Yes I know; I saw her there. In fact, I told her I had a conference in Atlanta this weekend, and she suggested I give you a call to see if we could get together and do lunch or hang out while I was in town."

Brenda's heart raced with excitement. *Lord, this man wants to spend time with me...what should I do?*

"Brenda, are you still there?" he asked.

"Yes I'm still here...it sounds like fun," she said, not waiting for a reply from the Lord.

"Great, I'll be in town about noon. I have a rental and I'll be staying at the Atlanta Marriott Marquis on Peachtree on Peachtree Center Avenue. I'll call you once I check in and get settled...I can come by your apartment to pick you up. Does that sound good to you?" He asked.

"Yes that sounds just fine....I'll talk to you soon."

Butterflies fluttering—that's how her stomach felt all morning as she tried to find the right outfit to wear for her lunch date with James. Flashbacks of the first time she met him ran through her mind while she got ready. *What am I going to do with this man for an entire weekend?*

Brenda thought about the times they had spent together back home. He made the most difficult time in her life seem more bearable. Now here he comes again during another rough patch in her life. Could he be her guardian angel? *Lord, I hope not because the thoughts I've been having about him are so graphic even God would blush...I wonder where he's taking me for lunch. I don't know what to put on...*

Shannon's head popped in her door. "What's up chick? Do you wanna go get some lunch or something?"

Articles of clothing were piled on her bed. "I can't...I have a date," Brenda said.

"A date," Shannon looked confused. "A date with who? I know you are not going out with Ray! Have you lost your cotton-picking mind?" Shannon asked with an angry look on her face.

"No, it's not with Ray," Brenda laughed.

"Oh, then who is it then?" Shannon persisted.

"If you must know...it's with a guy from back home..."

This whole business was just a little too sudden for Shannon; she wanted the full story.

"What guy from back home?" She was eager for Brenda to get to the point.

"Alright, if you must know, it's my mother's doctor," Brenda replied still shuffling through her wardrobe.

"Is your mom okay?"

"She's fine...he's in town for some type of convention or something this weekend and wanted to hang out with me—"

She was rudely interrupted by Shannon's outburst. "You mean to tell me you are going out on a date with some old geezer! Girl, if I knew you were *that* desperate, I would have fixed you up with one of my boyfriend's frat brothers..."

Brenda didn't have time nor did she take time to explain everything to Shannon. James was due any minute and she wasn't finished dressing, but Shannon kept pushing the issue. When her cell rang, it was James calling to let her know he was on campus and needed to know which building she lived in. She gave him the address, instructing Shannon to let him in while she finished getting dressed. Debbie came bopping out of her room and sat in the living room area. She'd overheard some of their conversation and decided to see what was going on.

Within a few minutes, there was a knock at the door. Shannon headed to the door while Debbie stood up to see who it was. Shannon's jaw dropped to the floor when she saw him standing there.

"Hello, is this where Brenda Greene lives?" *OMG! He has a voice to die for...*she thought.

"Yes it is. Come on in and have a seat...she'll be out in just a minute." James sat down on the sofa. "I'm Shannon, Brenda's roommate." She held out her hand, not bothering to introduce Debbie.

"Hi...I'm James Powers. It's a pleasure to meet you..." His handshake was firm yet gentle and his palms were nice and dry; Shannon hated a wet, flimsy handshake.

"Brenda tells me you are her mother's doctor," Shannon

continued, trying to make small talk while looking him up and down.

"I am," he responded, perfectly aware of the inspection and the other young lady in the room.

"I'll go see what's keeping Brenda..."

Just as Shannon rose, Brenda walked into the room.

"Hi James...I'm sorry to keep you waiting." He smiled as his eyes took in the sight; she was drop dead gorgeous!

"Oh that's okay...your roommates have been keeping me company..." he moved in closer giving Brenda a kiss on the cheek. "You look beautiful..." He let the words linger just a moment before continuing. "Are you ready?" Reaching for her hand bag, she answered that she was.

As they headed for the door, Brenda looked back at Shannon; she grinned as Shannon mouthed the words "Girl, he's soooo fine!" Debbie, on the other hand, didn't say a thing, upset she hadn't been introduced to James.

James walked Brenda to the black Mercedes convertible he was driving and opened the door for her. They drove to a nice restaurant that played a lot of old songs. They talked about what had been going on back home and how her mother's treatments and visits were going. Brenda laughed at his poor attempts to sing all the songs that came on, realizing it was first time she'd laughed in months. James took her hand, placing it between his, gazing into her eyes as he spoke, "Brenda, I'm so glad you agreed to have lunch with me. I've been looking forward to seeing you ever since the night I had dinner at your mother's house... I couldn't stop thinking about you..."

Brenda didn't know what to say. She was flattered and completely attracted to James, but in the back of her mind all she could think about was Ray and how much she still loved him.

"I've enjoyed spending time with you, too," she responded quietly, slowly pulling her hand away.

He mistook her action for nervousness and continued, "I have a meeting with some people all morning, but I will be out about 12 and I would love to spend the rest of my day with you. We can do lunch, take a drive, go to the museum or something, and later go to dinner and maybe a movie afterwards."

Ray would just have to wait; she was having too much fun to concern herself with him right now.

"Sure that sounds really nice...I would love to," she said with a big smile on her face.

After lunch they drove to a park to walk off their meal. As they watched children frolicking on the playground, James asked her if she wanted to have children and if so, how many? A little shocked by the question, she said yes—three, two boys and a girl.

James looked at her and smiled, "I love kids...I want at least two." Brenda couldn't resist asking why he wasn't married and had a family. After all, he was thirty-two, handsome, saved, and had a great career. He said he just hadn't found that special someone he could relate to on a spiritual, emotional and intellectual level. "Most women see that I'm a doctor and they see dollar signs..."

They see more than that! You must not know how fine you *are, brother,* Brenda thought to herself.

They walked, talking for more than two hours about his family and where he grew up, how they were raised, and their likes and dislikes. They both were surprised at how much they had in common: he, a Morehouse man and a doctor, and she, a Spelman woman and a future chemist. They watched the sun set before grabbing a bite to eat and driving around the city listening to music until well past midnight.

When they got back to Brenda's place, James walked her to the door.

"I really enjoyed myself today," he said. "I'll see you tomorrow..."

"Sure thing," she said as she turned to open the door. He lightly touched her shoulder, slowly turned her around and leaned in, caressing her cheek before bending to kiss her goodnight.

Waiting in the hallway for Brenda to come in was Shannon, eager to find out how her date went. Brenda wasn't in the door all the way before Shannon jumped up behind her asking her a lot of questions.

"Girl how was your date? He is too fine... Why haven't you told me about him before...?"

Shannon kept rambling; Brenda tried to answer but was constantly interrupted.

"I didn't get a chance because of all the stuff with Ray and Debbie...it just slipped my mind."

"Well tell me now!" Shannon was bursting with excitement.

Brenda filled her in on everything. Shannon was breathless and in awe.

"Wow girl, that man is really into you, and he is a gorgeous hunk of flesh and blood, not to mention a doctor...wow!"

"Do you really think he's into me?" Brenda asked.

Shannon just shook her head, "Girl, are you really *that* slow when it comes to men? Of course he's into to you. That man didn't come all the way up here just for a conference.

Can't you see the way he looks at you...? Does he know about Ray?"

"No, there's no reason to tell him because it is over between me and Ray...besides James and I are just friends—it's not like we are in a relationship..."

"I didn't know friends kiss like that..." Shannon said very sarcastically.

"What are you doing now, spying on me?"

With that she went into her room to get ready for her next date with James.

Chapter 5

FORGIVE AND FORGET?

Beep__Beep___Beep.

The alarm clock sounded, waking Brenda up to her second date with James. Sliding her leg off the bed onto the floor and into her slippers, and grabbing her robe, she headed to the kitchen to get a cup of tea. As she prepared the kettle, Debbie walked into the kitchen.

"Good morning Brenda," she said with a half-cocked smile.

"Good morning," she responded, trying to be Christ-like.

"You sure are up early for a Saturday. You must have another hot date with that fine doctor you went out with yesterday." She was simply prying. "That is none of your business." Brenda replied, trying not to lose her temper as she headed back to her bedroom. Debbie just stood there with her mouth gaped wide and her eyes bulging.

With her back against the bedroom door, Brenda couldn't believe she said that to Debbie. Her flesh wanted to cuss her out and tell her to get out of her face, but she knew it had to be the Lord who intervened. Besides, she had enough things to repent about, so she decided to just forget about it and began getting ready for her date.

James arrived at the apartment right on schedule. He was dressed casually in a pair of neatly pressed dress jeans and a light blue button down dress shirt with the sleeves rolled up just below his elbows. His cologne danced through Brenda's nostrils, intoxicating her, making her dizzy with delight. Laughing at all his corny jokes, they stopped at a restaurant near the campus for lunch.

"What do you want to do after lunch?" he asked.

"Do you bowl?" she asked.

"Do I bowl? Girl, I invented bowling," he said with his chest sticking out.

"Is that so? Well, an expert like yourself should be able to get a strike every time?"

He gave her a cocky smile and a thumbs up. "A strike, no problem at all."

Just as they were finishing their lunch, Ray walked in. Brenda had forgotten that this was his usual hangout after working out at the gym. She tried to hide her face behind the menu.

"Is there something else you wanted to order?" James asked.

"No, I was just checking to see if they added anything new to the menu." Slowly, she slid the menu down below her eyes, but still covering the rest of her face.

"Are you ready to leave?" he asked.

Brenda, looking around to see if Ray was still in view, said, "Yes."

James got up to pay the bill while Brenda hurried to the door. Before she could grab it, she heard Ray call out to her.

"Brenda!"

She pretended not to hear him as she touched the door

handle. He tapped her shoulder. Brenda turned around.

"Leave me alone!" she said as she jerked away from him.

"Please baby can we just sit down and talk?"

"No."

James, turning to see what the commotion was, walked over.

"Is everything alright Brenda?" he asked.

"Yes, everything is fine—can we go?" she asked.

"Who is this?" Ray asked.

"My date," she said in a hostile tone.

"Your what?" he yelled, staring James in the face.

James extended his hand to shake Ray's. "I'm Dr. James Powers. And you are...?"

"Ray...her man!" He looked James up and down, not responding to his attempt to shake hands.

James, turning to look at Brenda. "Is this true Brenda?"

"No, not anymore it's not!"

Glaring up at Ray, she grabbed James' arm and they walked out the door, leaving him standing there watching them through the glass as they walked to the car.

When they got inside, Brenda was visibly shaken and on the brink of tears.

"What was that all about...who is that guy?" he asked with a serious look on his face.

Brenda didn't know where to begin. She didn't want to tell James about Ray this soon and not this way.

"He is my ex-boyfriend, Ray." She tapped her hands nervously on her lap.

"Does he know he's your ex?" James asked.

"It doesn't matter whether or not he knows it as long as I know..."

James needed to know more.

"Why haven't you mentioned him before?" He asked.

"It just never came up I guess..."

"Never came up! Brenda, I've known you for more than two months now, and you never said anything about this man. Do you love him?"

Brenda began to cry. "I am so sorry, James! I didn't mean

to lead you on...I don't know what I feel anymore. I am so ashamed."

James, as hurt as he was, tried to console her. "Is he your first love?" he asked, praying she would say no.

"Yes." She wiped the tears from her eyes.

Sitting back in the car with his hands on his head, James became very quiet. He was falling in love with Brenda. *She is so young. What in hell was I thinking!* he asked himself. Looking into her eyes he could see that she wasn't over Ray, and he didn't want to be her rebound guy.

"I understand if you don't want to finish our date." she said.

"It's obvious you two have some unfinished business you need to work out...I'm falling for you, Brenda, but I can't be your second choice. I need someone whose heart belongs to me completely..." he said. "I think it's best we call it a day."

Brenda didn't know what to say. James was right though. It wouldn't be fair to him knowing she still loved Ray.

Cranking up the engine, he headed back to Brenda's

apartment. On the way, they didn't say a word to one another. There was no music coming from the radio, no singing, no corny jokes— nothing but dead silence.

Brenda glanced over at James. He looked so hurt. She could even see tears welling up in his eyes, but he held them back. Brenda knew this was the end. *What the hell is wrong with me?* she chided herself. *This man is really into me. He's nice, handsome, rich, smart and funny...any woman would be lucky to have him. What's the matter with me?*

She could feel James glancing at her out the corner of his eyes. She could tell he wanted to change his mind—that he had something more he wanted to say. Again she looked at him, but when their eyes met, he just turned away.

Finally they arrived at the apartment. They sat in the car for a few minutes in complete silence. Neither wanted to get out nor wanted to say goodbye. They somehow knew that if they did, it would be the end. Their almost relationship would end before it began.

James got out of the car and walked over to let Brenda out.

Making no eye contact, they walked up to her apartment door. Looking into her eyes, still holding back the tears, he said goodbye. Brenda got a burning sensation in her chest. *I can't believe I just screwed up...*

"Brenda, I want you to know I enjoyed spending time with you." He said softly, his broken heart bleeding into each word.

"I enjoyed spending time with you as well." Turning to walk away, James stopped, turned back again, walked up to Brenda and planted a long, passionate kiss on her lips. It felt as though they were standing outside her door for hours kissing—saying goodbye. With the end of the kiss, he got in his rental, driving away and out of her life...

As she entered the apartment, Brenda had never felt so alone. She didn't see Shannon or Debbie, and that was a good thing. She didn't want anyone to know how stupid she felt. She knew that they weren't the ones she needed to be worrying about; it was her momma. She knew her mother was hoping for a connection with James—that she really liked him and wanted them to get together. She knew Momma Greene would call asking a lot of questions and want details…that when she saw James she would ask him questions, and she didn't want him to tell her about Ray, so she decided she had better beat him to the punch.

Brenda went into her bedroom, got on her knees and began praying,

"*Father, in the name of your son, Jesus, please help me. Help me to do your will. Keep me from myself and help me to live for you. I don't know what I am doing. Please tell me what to say to my mother. Strengthen me, Father. In Jesus name I pray, thank you...Amen.*"

The telephone rang; it was Momma Greene.

"Hello, Bre-Bre...how's things going out there? I felt in my spirit that something wasn't right with you so I had to make this call."

Lord, I didn't expect you to answer me this way. I wasn't ready to deal with her right this minute...

She knew she didn't have the words to say as she just sat

there looking blankly at her cell.

"Brenda!" Momma Greene yelled. "Are you still there?" she asked.

"Yes ma'am, I'm here."

"Then answer me, what's going on?"

Brenda decided to tell her momma about Ray and what happened with James—leaving out the kissing, her grades, and sex, knowing that her mother could fill in the blanks. When she finished talking, she noticed there was complete silence on the other end.

"Momma, are you still there?" she asked.

"Yes baby I'm still here."

"Okay, let me have it!" Brenda said, waiting for her to preach.

"Let you have what?" Momma Greene asked. Surprised by her cavalier attitude, Brenda wondered if her momma was feeling alright. It wasn't like her not to make a comment. She always had some type of advice. "Alright baby, I got to go. You take care of yourself: I love you." With those words,

Momma Greene hung up.

Brenda looked at the phone in amazement; she couldn't believe what had just happened. In a flashback, she remembered what her mother told her in the hospital.

"I'm not always going to be around; we all have an appointment to keep. I want you to remember everything I've tried to teach you and never lose your identity to another person. Be who God created you to be and enjoy your life child. I've made bad choices and good ones, but the best decision I've ever made was raising you. I love you and I want you to love yourself. I also want you to know what real love feels like from a man and don't ever give up on your hopes and dreams..."

With another year behind her, Brenda was now a senior; all the drama of last semester was past, so she brought up her grades and focused on her education. She often thought of Ray and how much she missed being with him and how much she still loved him. Sometimes, they'd run into each other off campus. He would wave but keep his distance. After about three months, she stopped running into him.

Brenda became more involved in church. She became a member of Holy Rock and started working diligently. Pastor Benjamin noticed Brenda's degree of dedication in the ministry and often asked her to work with the youth, helping them with essays, homework, and scholarship applications. She attended special seminars pertaining to health issues, oftentimes serving as the spokesperson for the church.

On several occasions, Brenda caught Mrs. Benjamin staring at her whenever they were in bible study or during prayer service. She brushed it off, turning her attention elsewhere. Several times, she examined her clothing, checking to see if maybe she was dressed inappropriately...she wasn't.

First Sunday in February was Men's Day. The Spirit was high—the guest minister had just preached a powerful sermon on respecting women and taking care of your family. When he finished, he gave the altar call. One by one the line got longer as people came up for prayer.

Just as the preacher gave one last plea, Brenda noticed a man walking up in a nicely pressed dark blue, pin-striped suit; she couldn't get a good look at him until he turned around. It was Ray.

Brenda couldn't believe her eyes. *Could this really be happening?* she thought. Before she realized, she had walked up and hugged him to congratulate him.

"Please stand here with me," he asked. Brenda agreed and stood by his side as the guest minister prayed with him.

After the service, Ray followed Brenda to her car.

"Brenda, can we go out for something to eat and talk?" he asked.

Hesitant yet curious to find out how he was feeling about giving his life to the Lord, Brenda muttered, "I don't know, I really have…"

"Please don't say no," Ray rushed in, stopping Brenda before she could finish. "I have so many questions about

Christianity, and I need someone who can explain it all to me." Brenda agreed and they went for a bite to eat.

During lunch, Brenda tried to answer Ray's many questions about church. Suddenly, Ray reached for her hand.

Looking deep into her eyes, he said. "Brenda, I still love you, you know. I know you probably will never forgive me for what I've done. I don't blame you...I'm sorry for hurting you, but I just want you to know that I will spend the rest of my life trying to make it up to you if you give me another chance. I may not be rich like that guy I saw you with. I don't have anything to offer you except my heart...Please forgive me."

Brenda was speechless for a moment. She thought about all Ray put her through....she thought about Debbie and the fact that she was still her roommate. How did she know they weren't still creeping around with each other? She didn't know if she could trust him with her heart anymore.

"Ray I really can't discuss this right now..." she said. "I really need to pray about us." With that she got up, walked out the door, and headed to her car.

Weeks went by. Every Sunday Brenda would see Ray in church with his Bible praising the Lord. He started attending Bible study and would often sit next to her. He also became very active in the men's ministry. More and more, Ray became the man she had hoped he would be. She observed him on several occasions reading his Bible.

My goodness he still looks good she would think, but she kept those thoughts to herself. He asked her to dinner numerous times, but she turned him down. Until one night after a youth meeting, she decided to take him up on his offer.

She told him to pick her up at the apartment when she knew Debbie would be there just to see how they would interact with one another.

"What time should I pick you up?" he asked.

"How about six o'clock."

He smiled, "I will be there with bells on..."

When Brenda arrived back at the apartment, she wanted to give Shannon a heads up that she was going to dinner with Ray; Shannon wasn't too keen on the idea.

"Are you crazy?! Don't you remember what that man did to you? How can you be so naive? Why are you putting yourself through that mess all over again?"

Shannon was trying to make Brenda open her eyes but she wasn't hearing it.

"You don't understand girl...he's changed. He's not that same man..." Brenda spoke with passion, trying to convince Shannon.

"Girl you can't be that stupid... Don't you know a leopard can't change its spots?" Shannon persisted.

"God said we must forgive those that spitefully use and persecute us," Brenda said, but Shannon wasn't buying what she was selling.

"You can forgive him without dating him! I can't believe you let that fine doctor go to be with that dog Ray...

"Look, you know I care about you, girl, and I don't mean to be so hard on you, but I got to be straight with you. I don't care how mad you get with me..." Shannon continued. Doesn't the Bible say 'the truth shall make you free?"

Brenda couldn't say anything. She knew Shannon was right, but she couldn't help herself. She thought about everything Shannon said, but she just couldn't help how she felt.

Please let Ray be for real, Lord, she prayed. To get ready for her date, she wanted to borrow something from Shannon, but knew Shannon was upset, so she just wore something of her own.

When the door bell rang, Debbie rushed to answer. She opened the door and there stood Ray with flowers in his hand.

Debbie squealed with delight, "Ray! What are you doing here? This is a nice surprise. Come on in...thanks for the flowers..."

She reached for the flowers just as Brenda entered the room. Ray didn't know what to do.

"Hello Ray," she said.

"These are for you Brenda...are you ready to go?" he asked while taking the flowers right out of Debbie's eager fingers.

"Yes, just let me get my purse and wrap," she said, looking at Debbie with a huge smile on her face.

Debbie stood there in shock, not believing what just happened, watching them as they walked out the door.

"Are you still sleeping with Debbie?" she asked, stopping Ray outside the door.

"No! Not since that day." His voice was barely above a whisper, yet his tone was urgent as he looked deeply into her eyes, trying to reassure her. Brenda was relieved to hear him say those words.

Ray took her to a very upscale restaurant with live music and dancing. Brenda was impressed. *He's never taken me anywhere this nice before,* she mused. The tables were decorated beautifully with white crisp linen table cloths and lit candles. The waiters were dress professionally in their tuxedo shirts, black bow ties, and black slacks.

"Are you ready to order?" the waiter asked, taking a pad from the neatly pressed apron around his waist.

"Yes, I would like a bottle of your best champagne..." Ray

beamed, taking her hand and lifting it to his mouth. "...We have something to celebrate."

"Oh, what?" she said.

"You and me getting back together," he responded happily, poring champagne into her glass. Brenda sat silently watching the liquid fill her glass. On one hand, she wanted to get back with Ray; on the other, she just didn't know if she could trust him.

As they sat there listening to the band play, Brenda watched Ray dance in his seat. *He still looks good to me...I really did miss him, but is he the right man for me, Lord? So many questions!*

The evening went better than Brenda could ever have dreamed. They danced, they laughed, and they enjoyed a wonderful meal. Now all that was left was to say goodnight. This was the most difficult part. Before, when they spent a great day or night together, it would end at Ray's apartment with romantic music playing and her naked in Ray's arms. She knew this time had to be different. *She* had to be smarter this time. Her body wasn't going to be his playground any more. Brenda knew she had to take it slow and lay down her rules before they went any further.

As they left the restaurant, sitting in the car nervous and a bit tipsy from the champagne, Brenda knew she had to keep her wits about her. *Look at him— he sure has buffed up these last few months. His butt sure looks firm in that suit, and that cologne is driving me crazy,* she thought to herself.

STOP IT and get yourself together girl...

It had been a long time since she had been with Ray, and she knew that if she showed any weakness, the moon wouldn't be the only thing in the sky. She needed to be strong and stick to her principals if she wanted Ray to take her seriously.

As he drove her home, it seemed to be taking forever to get there; Ray wasn't going his normal 70 miles an hour. She noticed every light they approached stopped on red. The night air was a nice 73 degrees and the stars were twinkling in the sky as smooth Jazz radiated from the radio. The evening was perfect for romance; it couldn't have been more romantic if

Ray had planned it himself.

"Have I told you how beautiful you look tonight, Brenda?" Ray purred, glancing over at her, looking her up and down as if he was undressing her with his eyes.

"Thank you," she said looking straight ahead.

"I really missed you baby...why don't we go back to my place and talk things over, have a glass of wine, and listen to some music and catch up on the time we've lost," he said.

Brenda knew that was her cue to let *him* know where she stood. "Ray I think it's time you take me home," her voice was firm as she looked him dead in his face.

"Did I do something wrong?" he asked.

"No, you did and said all the right things... I don't want to do the wrong thing. I'm not having sex again until I'm married, so if you don't think you can handle that we can call this off right now." Pulling up to her building Ray stopped the car and turned his body all the way around to look directly at Brenda. "Brenda, look at me...did you sleep with that guy?"

That got Brenda just a little heated.

"No, you **did not** just ask me that question; that's none of your business! You gave up any right to ask anything a long time ago!" she said.

"Calm down, I'm sorry; I didn't mean to upset you...I know I don't have any right to ask you anything; don't be mad at me, please." He leaned over to hug her and give her a kiss. "I will respect whatever you want." Like a gentleman should, he got out of the car to walk her to the door.

"Goodnight, Ray. I had a nice time," she said, putting the key in the lock.

"Can I get a kiss goodnight?" he asked. Brenda, on her tiptoes, pecked him on the cheek and quickly opened the door. She could see the disappointment on his face, but was determined to stand her ground; she knew if she kissed him, it wouldn't stop there. It had been a long time since they'd been intimate, and if he touched her in the right places, she would melt with desire.

"Will I see you tomorrow?" he asked, with a hungry look in his eyes.

"I have to study for my exams...I'll call you when I'm done."

She closed and locked the door.

LEVEL

II

Chapter 6

YIELD NOT TO TEMPTATION

Tree buds began to bloom as the pollen fell, covering everything in its path. The days were now longer and summer break was quickly approaching; exams were almost completed with another school year quickly coming to a close.

Brenda was anxious to go home and be with her momma. She hadn't been home in a while for fear of running into James. She knew she'd broken his heart, but it was time for her to face him and hope he had forgiven her. They hadn't been sharing information on her mother's health like they once had; deep inside, she missed talking to him. Now, Brenda had to rely on her mother to tell her the truth about her condition.

She and Ray had been getting along beautifully and spending quite a bit of time together. He was becoming more involved in church activities, working closely with Pastor Benjamin arranging photo shoots for conventions and other major church events.

They were becoming the star couple in the church with everyone constantly asking when they were planning to marry. Ray would hint jokingly and say, "soon." *If only he meant it*, she would whisper inside her thoughts. She knew better than to take him seriously, but couldn't help but hope he meant every word.

In the past, she'd tried asking him questions pertaining to marriage and family, but Ray would change the subject or he'd say he needed to get his career off the ground first before he could think about having a family. *Who knows...maybe now he's changing his mind,* she contemplated, watching him as he talked with a group of young boys outside the church.

When they arrived at Brenda's apartment, she prepared a nice dinner; they spent most of the evening watching old movies.

"Will you be heading home next week?" Ray asked.

"Yes, it's time I got home to check on my mother and make sure everything is going well with her." She was curious as to why he was asking. "In fact, I need to start packing right now; Monday will be here before you know it." Getting up from the couch and heading to her bedroom, she went to the closet to pull out her suitcase.

"I was thinking about taking that ride down to Charleston with you if that's okay?" He said suddenly. Brenda was shocked! Ray never mentioned, let alone showed, any interested in traveling to Charleston with her before. What brought on this sudden change of heart? Could it be he knew James was her mother's doctor and attended the same church or the likelihood that they would probably run into each other?

Early on in their relationship, this was all Brenda had wanted. Ray was saved, going to church, their situation was stable, and he wanted to meet her mother. Why wasn't she more excited? Could it be she knew her mother wanted her to be with James, or perhaps she knew she would run into James and he would see her with Ray and that would be awkward?

She knew she had strong feelings for James, no matter how much she loved Ray, and in the back of her mind she knew he was more compatible for her.

"Okay, just let me call my momma and tell her you will be coming with me. She is old-fashioned about bringing company to her house without calling first." She was already dreading the call.

"Sounds good—I'll go move my schedule around and make my hotel reservations," he responded, picking up his keys. "I think I can stay for at least a week before I need to go on my next shoot, so I'll bring my church clothes and maybe we can hit the beach." He kissed her before walking out the door.

Brenda picked up the phone to call her mother. As she told her about Ray, she waited to hear what Momma Greene would say.

"Bring him on, I would like to meet this young man," her mother said. Brenda couldn't believe how nice and calm her momma appeared to be.

"Don't worry, Momma. He's staying in a hotel nearby," she quickly added, trying to convince her that there wasn't any hanky-panky going on.

Shannon had been silent about Ray and Brenda's relationship for quite some time. She and Brenda had come to an understanding that the conversation was off limits. Although Shannon knew he was not sincere, she also knew Brenda wasn't going to listen and it would be a waste of time talking to her, no matter how much she begged her to cut him loose.

Debbie had moved on to another person's man, so Ray was no longer on her radar. So when Brenda mentioned that Ray was going to meet her mother, Shannon just smiled and listened. Brenda knew Shannon didn't approve.

"Spill it!" she prompted, standing with her hands on her hip.

"Spill what?" Shannon asked, shaking her head

nonchalantly.

"I know you have something to say about Ray coming home with me..."

"Girl you are grown and I have my own business to mind—besides you don't want my opinion." Shannon turned, heading to her room to gather her things together.

"Shannon, you are my best friend, and I do value your opinion and your friendship."

Shannon sighed before continuing, "It's because I value *our* friendship that I will always tell you the truth—he is a D-O-G and he is using you."

Pulling out her suitcase and putting it on the bed Brenda replied, "You haven't seen him in a while...he has really changed. It was his idea to come home with me." She seemed almost desperate to plead Ray's case.

"I wonder why--could it be because he knows that fine hunk of a doctor is there waiting to swoop down and take you away from him? Ray is no fool...he knows he has major competition and that doctor has your momma wrapped around his fingers..." Shannon's growing agitation was showing in the way she was grabbing clothes from her drawers. "...He knows exactly what he's doing." She said as she went back to packing her things. Brenda didn't have a rebuttal because she knew Shannon was probably right.

Things were finally going the way Brenda had hoped since she met Ray, and she wasn't going to let Shannon or her mother or anyone discourage her. She believed deep in her heart that God answered her prayers when Ray joined the church. She knew she had to follow her heart. He was the love of her life. Besides, it was time to forgive and forget—time for a new beginning. *Ray just needs to impress Momma and that's all I need to be concerned about right now.*

Although Shannon was a good friend, she wasn't going to change her mind about Ray. She would have to accept that Brenda loved this man if they were going to remain friends and roommates; she would just have to keep their relationship to herself.

Whenever Ray came to the apartment, Shannon went into

her room or she would leave. Brenda wanted the two most important people in her life, other than her mother, to get along.

Shannon was planning her end of the year party. She wanted it to be something they would enjoy and remember for years to come. They knew it was their last year at Spelman, and they wanted to have a big send off before they started their internships in their various fields. Shannon wanted to become a psychologist, and she was well on her way with all the practice she was getting dealing with Brenda and her personal issues. Debbie, however, moved out of the apartment a month prior because she failed all her classes due to partying. The last they heard, she was pregnant by some drug dealer and living somewhere nearby. Brenda felt this party would be a great opportunity to get Shannon and Ray in the same room to talk before they left for the summer.

“The guest will be arriving shortly Brenda...do we have everything we need? Is there enough ice, napkins, drinks…?” Shannon asked nervously.

“Would you calm down...” she chuckled at Shannon’s nervousness. “All we need is the ice, and I’ve already called Ray and told him to stop by the store on his way,” Brenda said as she stacked the cups on the table.

“Brenda, I know you want Ray and me to get along, and I will try my best to be cordial to him while he’s here,” Shannon said.

“Thanks girl, that really means a lot to me,” she said, giving Shannon a hug.

“Does he know about your internship at MUSC?” Shannon asked.

“No, I haven’t had a chance to mention it to him,” she said.

“Is it because you don’t want him to know that James is a doctor there, and you might run into him on occasion?” She was looking closely at Brenda, hoping to pry the truth out of her.

Brenda knew Shannon had a way of seeing right through her, but she continued to decorate and clean, never responding to Shannon's questions.

"Isn't he coming to Charleston with you for a week? Didn't you tell me James attends the same church as your mother? How are you going to avoid seeing James there?" Shannon continued with the questions.

"Okay, okay, I get it—I need to talk to Ray. Can we change the subject, please?" Brenda said, grabbing the broom from the closet.

Suddenly the doorbell rang. It was Ray with the ice.

"Hi baby, I brought four bags...I hope that's enough?" he said as he hurried in the door to get the cold bags out of his hands and into the sink.

"It should be more than enough, thanks." She gave him a kiss as she wiped the sweat off of his brow.

"Hi Shannon, is there anything else you ladies need?" Ray asked, looking directly at Shannon.

"No, that should do it, thanks." Shannon said, as she continued to clean, not looking at him.

"Why don't you go freshen up in my bathroom and I'll put the ice into the freezer?" Brenda said.

"Okay, I think I have a clean shirt in my car." He headed back to his car. *How am I going to tell him about the internship?* Brenda thought to herself. *Will I be able to trust him for an entire summer when he goes back to Atlanta?*

*Okay girl, you need to get a grip—he is a new creature in Christ Jesus—besides he has enough things to keep him busy, between work and the church, so he shouldn't have time for anything else...*she corrected herself as she looked through Shannon's CD collection.

The guests began to arrive and everything was going well. Everyone was eating, drinking, and laughing, just having a good time. Shannon was in a new relationship with one of the TA's in her Psych class, Ben. She never stayed in a relationship more than three months; she said her attention span was too short and no man ever held her interest longer than that.

Brenda secretly admired Shannon. She was impressed with how confident Shannon was in her sexuality; when it came to men, Shannon called all the shots and the men seem to go along with it. Although Shannon wasn't the most attractive female, she had a certain quality that men seem to be drawn to. She was tall and had a nice shape. She wore her hair in dreads that came down to her shoulders; her eyes were almond shaped and her legs were long and toned.

The word around campus was that a married professor propositioned her for sex in exchange for a better grade in her freshman year. Shannon, being the type person she was, set him up by telling him she would meet him at a motel outside the city. When he arrived, Shannon met him at the motel room door with a see through negligee on. She threw him on the bed and told him to get undressed while she went in the bathroom to freshen up. While the professor lay there naked, she called out to ask him if he was ready. When the bathroom door opened, out came the professor's wife with a gun; not only did she get an A, but a car as well. The professor, however, lost his job and his wife.

As the party wound down, Brenda decided she would pull Ray aside to talk about her internship at MUSC. They went into her room, closing the door to drown out the music.

"Ray, I am not going to be coming back to Atlanta with you," she said, waiting for his reaction.

"What do you mean you're not coming back with me?" he said with a shocked look on his face. "Is there something wrong with your mother?"

"No, she is doing fine, thank God! Since this is my last year, it's time for me to do my clinical work." Brenda was edgy, pushing back on the bed trying to get more comfortable.

"Okay, I get that, but why aren't you coming back to Atlanta if you're mother is doing okay?" He said with a confused look.

"I was accepted at Medical University in Charleston to do my clinical work..." she said, hoping he would not bring up the fact that James is a doctor there. "This way, I will be close to home and I will be able to take care of my momma and work at one of the best medical schools in the country..."

Ray just nodded without a response. He leaned in to give Brenda a kiss. Brenda responded; the next thing she, knew they were making out like two teenagers in heat. It had been a long time since they had been this close, and her body had craved his touch ever since they got back together.

As Ray's kisses moved closer to her chest and his hands moved down her legs, she knew she had to put a stop to where this was going. She heard the Spirit say in her head "***There is no temptation such as common to man that God will not make a way for you to escape!***"

What am I doing?! I can't do this, not after I've rededicated myself to the Lord. I promised God I would wait and I meant what I said, she reasoned, pushing Ray off her.

"What's the matter?" He asked in lustful confusion.

"Ray, we need to stop before we go too far." Buttoning up her blouse and getting up off the bed, she turned her back to him.

"Did I do something wrong?" he asked disappointed, holding on to her hand while trying to get her to come back to the bed.

"No, that's the problem—you are doing everything right. That's why we need to stop and go back to the party." Pulling her hand away, she headed for the door.

"I can't go out there like this..." he said looking. down at his lap. "...Brenda, I know you still don't trust me, but I do love you—"

She quickly interrupted him. "No, it's not that. It's just that I made a vow to God to remain celibate until marriage and I want to keep that promise this time." She inched closer to the bedroom door, hoping he would understand and get the hint. With that, he got up and they went back to the party.

Everyone had already left, with the exception of Ben, who was sitting on the couch listening to music while Shannon cleaned up.

"I wondered what happened to you two; I thought I'd have to do this all by myself. That one over there is no help whatsoever," she smirked, handing a dish tower to Brenda and a broom to Ray.

After they cleaned the apartment, Brenda and Ray said goodnight. Ben fell asleep on the sofa, so Shannon turned off the music and left him there as she and Brenda went in her room to talk.

"Well what was going on in there? Ray looked a little upset when the two of you came out of the room... did you tell him about the internship?" she rambled on.

"Yes, just some heavy petting and total disappointment all the way around. I don't think he is going to remain faithful while I'm in Charleston." She said, going deep into thought.

"Well if you know that, why are you going to put yourself through all that mess all over again girl? Shit...shoot Old Yella and put him and yourself out of each other's miseries," Shannon said, covering her mouth as she realized what she'd just said. "I didn't mean to curse girl, but that celibacy act can get old after a while. We all have itches we need someone else to scratch for us from time to time." Shannon switched her hips as she headed out to the living you to wake up Ben.

Tossing and turning in her bed, Brenda thought about everything she went through with Ray. More and more her dreams were about them being intimate. Suddenly, it was no longer Ray's face she was seeing but James'. She even began to smell James' cologne and hear his voice telling her how much he loved her and wanted to make her his wife.

Brenda jumped up in a cold sweat, disturbed and confused.

"What the…" she murmured, reaching for the clock to see what time it was. It was five o'clock in the morning. The birds in the tree outside of her bedroom window had not yet awakened. She stumbled into the bathroom to wipe the sweat off her face, but decided she needed to shower instead.

As she stood under the streaming water, she began to pray.

"Lord forgive me...please help me... why am I dreaming about James? What are you trying to tell me..." Brenda prayed in that shower for almost an hour, until the sun came

up. When she got out, she decided to get dressed and take a walk in the park nearby to clear her head.

Afterwards, she got into her car and headed for a local coffee spot. Sitting there reading a magazine, she heard a quiet voice behind her say hello. As she looked up, she saw that it was Mrs. Benjamin.

"Good morning, Brenda," she smiled, taking a sip of her coffee.

"Good morning," Brenda said.

"You are up early for a Saturday," Mrs. Benjamin said.

"Yes ma'am, I was having a little trouble sleeping," Brenda offered, closing the magazine.

"Oh, I'm sorry to hear that...is there something bothering you? Do want to talk about it?" Mrs. Benjamin appeared concerned, putting her hand on Brenda's shoulder.

"No ma'am, I've already prayed about it, but thanks for your concern," she said, embarrassed to tell the woman about her dream.

"Well, just know that if you want to talk, I'm here to

listen, okay?" Smiling as she removed her hand, she turned to walk away.

"Thank you, I will."

Brenda was surprised that Mrs. Benjamin spoke to her, let alone offered her a listening ear. She had been a member of the church for a year, and she had barely said two words to her since she joined. Just the same, it was good to know that she did reach out and show some concern for her well being.

Brenda decided to stop by Ray's apartment to apologize for how things ended between them the night before. When she got there, his car was gone. Flashbacks of the last time she'd driven up to his apartment floated through her mind.

Suddenly, feelings of hurt and jealousy flooded Brenda's emotional memory bank. Feelings of anxiety and distrust tiptoed through her consciousness as her thoughts went haywire. She imagined Ray in bed with Debbie and even women she didn't even know.

Stopping her car at the red light, she tried to get herself together, only snapping out of her trance when a man in the car behind her frantically honked his horn to let her know the light had turned green.

With shaking hands, she attempted to hold on to the steering wheel. "I can't go on like this...I need to get myself together or I'm going to lose it... I have to believe that Ray will never hurt me again... I have to learn to trust him..." With a single tear streaming down her face, she headed back home to finish packing.

Chapter 7

HAPPY MOTHERS' DAY

The next day Brenda and Ray took their time and drove down to South Carolina. They did a little shopping at the local outlets and flea markets along the way and got a bite to eat. Although the drive was pleasant, Brenda couldn't help but wonder what would happen when her mother met Ray for the first time. She knew her mother would not embarrass him or her, yet she also knew she would size him up and ask a lot of questions about his family, job, and faith.

If Momma Greene had met Ray earlier in their relationship, this would have been a serious problem, but now that Ray had joined the church with his womanizing ways in the past, Brenda felt more comfortable about them meeting.

Knowing that Mother's Day was coming up, Ray picked out a nice gift for her in one of the shops. He had the store clerk gift wrap it with a nicely placed fuchsia ribbon, her mother's favorite color. It was a nice crystal vase that she could place her freshly cut flowers in. Brenda was impressed he took the time to even ask what her mother would like.

As they got closer to her street, Brenda's heart began to pound in her chest. *Why am I so nervous? You would think my mother was God Himself judging Ray.* With every turn, the sound of her heart became louder. *Look at him, he's just as cool and confident as ever, not a sweat on his forehead, looking and smelling all good* Brenda mused, watching Ray as he drove the car into the driveway.

"Is that your mother on the porch?" He asked.

"Yes, that's her," she smiled, ready to jump out of the car and into Momma Greene's arms. Brenda introduced Ray and they went inside.

The smell of smoked neck bones signaled to Brenda that a pot of greens was on the stove, followed by a pan of Barbecue spare ribs, baked macaroni and cheese, white rice, cornbread with a large pitcher of sweet iced tea, and for dessert, her famous sweet potato pie.

Ray was intoxicated by the aroma.

"Something sure smells delicious. I can't wait to taste it," he said, rubbing his belly.

"Well, I hope you brought a big appetite because I cooked more than enough," Momma Greene said as she walked into the kitchen.

Brenda and Ray sat down in the dining room while Momma Greene brought out the food.

"Momma, why don't you sit down and get off your feet and let Ray and I bring out the rest of the food?" Brenda said as she motioned for Ray to come into the kitchen with her.

"Sounds good to me; I've been on my feet since five o'clock this morning—Ray why don't you sit down and keep an old lady company?"

"Yes, Ma'am," he smiled, taking a seat in the chair beside her.

Brenda, nervous about leaving Ray alone with her mother, went into the kitchen while Ray and Momma Greene sat in the dining room. Momma Greene continued to ask Ray question after question about his life. She wanted to know about his parents, childhood, and career, answers Brenda had been trying to get out of him for a year with little or no response.

Sweat dripped from Brenda's forehead as she listened at the corner of the kitchen door while her mother continued drilling him. Ray, on the other hand, was cool, calm and collected. With every question he didn't want to answer, he would simply say it wasn't a good time in his life, or he didn't have much of a childhood, or he would change the subject altogether. Knowing her mother wasn't going to settle for his vague answers, Brenda brought the food to the table, looking at the expression on her mother's face. She knew her mother wasn't pleased with the responses she was getting from Ray, so when they sat down to eat, she proceeded to tell of all Ray's accomplishments and the work he was doing in the church.

After the meal, Momma Greene was tired, so she decided to turn in early. Brenda and Ray cleaned up after dinner then sat in the living room to relax while looking through her family albums.

"Your mother is a really good cook; I never had a meal that good in my life," he said, patting his stomach.

"I'm glad you enjoyed it; she really pulled out all the stops." Brenda said.

"Well, what would you like to do now?" he asked.

"Why don't we get you settled in at the hotel, and then we can drive downtown on King Street and maybe to the Battery—it is a good night to take a walk—just let me let Momma know that we're leaving; then we can go." She was already heading up the stairs.

"Sounds good; I will go start the car," he said.

After Ray checked into his hotel room, they headed downtown to see the sights. It was a clear night; the moon was full and there were thousands of stars in the sky. They walked down King Street looking into the windows of the shops as they walked, talking about nothing in particular until they turned on the street where the old slave market was located. There they watched tourists go into the restaurants and ride in the carriages pulled by horses with sacks on their rear ends to catch the horse dung.

They watched as the basket weavers created their masterpieces. Brenda, playing tour guide, spoke of how much she hated coming downtown as a child because of what she was told about the market—how slaves were sold there and what little history she knew.

Momma Greene told her of how she once sold fruits and vegetables there and how other vendors would sell dolls that were offensive to blacks. As much as she hated certain things about Charleston, there were more things that she loved…the weather, the people, the beaches, the culture, and the food.

Afterward, they drove down to the Battery and watched the boats sailing under the stars.

"This has really been a nice day, I'm glad I came," he said, holding her close as they looked into the night sky.

"I'm glad you came, too. Maybe I can come with you to meet your family?" she asked, waiting for a response.

"You know...it's getting late and we need to get up early

for church. I want to be fresh when I meet all your friends."

How smooth he thought he was at changing the subject. Brenda, now frustrated, took the keys from Ray, got in the car and drove Ray back to the hotel. On her way back home, her mind wouldn't rest. *What is he hiding...why does he do that...why won't he let me in...?*

It was Mother's Day and Brenda was excited to be spending the day with her momma and Ray. After she got dressed, she removed the silk red rose from the clear plastic container. She had planned a special day for Momma Greene. She and Ray were eager to give her all the gifts they'd bought on the way to Charleston, and she was eager to introduce *him* to all her friends.

Brenda waited until her mother got dressed for church. *What is Momma doing up there? It's not like her to take this long to get dressed,* Brenda thought to herself. When Momma Greene came down the stairs, she looked a little flushed and

Brenda became concerned.

"Momma, are you feeling up to church this morning? Maybe we should stay home today." She went into the kitchen to get her a drink of water.

"No, I'm just fine. This is the day that the Lord has made, and I will rejoice and be glad in it!" she shouted.

Brenda helped her out to the car and they drove to pick up Ray. He was standing outside the hotel waiting, dressed in a nice tan suit with a straw hat.

"Good morning, Mrs. Greene. How are you feeling this fine day?" He was bright and chipper, getting in the back seat.

Momma Greene looked him up and down.

"Blessed," she said with a faded tone.

Brenda started the car, still keeping her eyes on her mother, while Ray sat in the back seat singing along with the gospel music on the radio.

As they turned the corner, they could hear the loud music and voices praising the Lord from inside the church. The sky began to look a little overcast, except the spot where the church stood. Brenda began to think how odd it was that the sun was shining only in one spot. The beams were directly over the steeple. She dismissed the sight and parked the car while Ray escorted her mother inside the church.

As soon as they walked in the door, she noticed the female ushers and other women standing in the lobby eyeballing her and checking out Ray from head to toe. They were taken to the front row, which was unusual for a second Sunday, not to mention Mother's Day. After the choir sang, it was time for visitors to be recognized. Brenda was quite taken by surprised when Ray stood and addressed the congregation. She noticed the ladies staring at him and whispering. As the service continued, she glanced around the church, hoping to see where James might be sitting; he wasn't in his usual seat behind the deacons.

As she continued to peruse the church, her mother nudged her.

"He still comes to service every Sunday, honey," Momma Greene said.

"Who?" Brenda asked.

"James, that's who." Supposedly, they were whispering so Ray wouldn't hear them but not doing a very good job of it.

She finally noticed James sitting across the aisle about three rows back next to a strikingly beautiful woman she had never seen before. This woman was tall, almost reaching his curly jet black hair. She was slim with long brown hair down to her shoulders, with pouty lips and firm perky breasts that she made sure everyone saw in a low cut dress that clung to her toned, shapely body.

Brenda tried not to stare; she couldn't help but feel a bit jealous and envious each time the woman touched James in that intimate sort of way and spoke to him. She saw James looking in her direction as their eyes connected. She tried looking away; she couldn't. *She looks like one of those slutty nurses that enjoy pushing up on doctors* Brenda thought, allowing her jealousy to creep into her mind. *He couldn't possibly be serious about her...why...she has gold digger written all over her!* Trying to look away and focus on the service, Brenda was having very little success.

"Brenda...Brenda!" Her mother said, trying to get her attention.

"Huh…what?" she was startled from her staring.

"What's the matter with you child? Stop being disrespectful to God and pay attention! Besides, you made your choice," Momma Greene said, turning back to the service.

Finally, Pastor Hamilton got up to preach, his words grabbing Brenda's attention unlike any time before. He spoke about the power of a mother's love and sacrifice and how Mary, the mother of Jesus, knew she would have to let her son go for the sake of the world. He also spoke on a mother's wisdom and discernment, how they know and want what is best for their children and how a mother is loaned to us only for a season.

Her eyes filled with tears as she turned to Momma Greene. *Lord I can't bear to lose her; I don't know what I would do without her in my life,* she thought, holding her mother's hand.

After the pastor finished preaching and giving the alter call, the benediction was given and Sunday school began.

"Did you want to stay for Sunday School, Momma?" Brenda asked.

"Yes," Momma Greene said.

"Are you sure you're up to sitting in church that long, Mrs. Greene? I thought I would take you beautiful ladies to brunch," Ray said.

"I'm just fine...besides, I give God glory all day and that includes Sunday school."

Brenda walked her mother to her class while she and Ray went to the class Brenda usually attended when she would come home.

Upon entering the room, a couple of her church sisters' eyes seemed to have popped out of their heads. Samantha approached them, pretending to have a greeting for her but she couldn't take her eyes off Ray.

"Brenda, girl, how you been doin? It sure has been a while since we've seen you…who is this?" Samantha was acting as if she was about to jump out of her underwear just from looking at him.

"This is my boyfriend Ray...Ray this is Samantha," Brenda said with a "you better watch your step" tone in her voice.

"Nice to meet you," he said, with his deep, romantic voice, extending his hand to shake hers. "Well, I guess it's time for Sunday school to start... let's take a seat."

Choosing two seats way in the back by the window, Brenda tried to concentrate on the lesson but found it quite difficult with the distractions coming from the women in her class. Every time the teacher asked someone to read, a different woman would get up, turn in Ray's direction to flirt. One even dropped her pen just so she could bend over to put her rear end in his face. Another conveniently forgot her Bible so she would have an excuse to walk across the room to show her many feminine curves. Brenda watched Ray as he smiled, turning to her to reassure her as these woman continued with their total display of disrespect and desperation.

Fifteen minutes of this foolishness went by before James suddenly walked in with his mysterious guest. Brenda felt a burning sensation in her chest. Ray looked at Brenda to see the expression on her face, then looked over at James to see his reaction. When James glanced in their direction, Ray reached for Brenda's hand.

The two of them took the only two seats left in the back of the class, right across from Brenda and Ray. For Brenda, the day just became even more awkward as time seemed to drag on. She sat there feeling anxious, praying for class to end so they could leave. She didn't retain anything from the lesson; all she could think about was getting out of the door as quickly as possible with Ray *without* having to say anything to James and his companion.

Unfortunately, Ray had different plans; he remembered James and he wanted James to remember him. With every tug and pull towards the door Brenda tried, Ray would stall by asking her to introduce him to her church friends in the class until James and his lady friend came by.

"Hello, Brenda. How have you been?" James asked, holding hands with the woman.

"I'm..." she cleared her throat. "I'm fine…and yourself?" she said, trying not to look him in the eye.

"I'm Ray..." He said this as he wrapped his hands around Brenda's waist.

"I'm Simone, James' fiance," she boasted, flashing her ring in Brenda's face.

"Fiance…you're engaged?" Brenda was feeling quite hurt, attempting to swallow the big lump now stuck her throat.

"Congratulations!" Ray said with a relieved tone in his voice, happy to know James would no longer be a threat to him.

"Yes…about a month now." James' smile didn't quite reach his eyes—eyes that looked at Brenda for the slightest sign of hope so he could call it off.

"Momma never mentioned anything to me...I'm happy for the two of you. You have a wonderful man here, Simone, and I wish you to the best." She spoke these words while hoping in her heart she would get hit by a bus.

"Ray, we better go get Momma...we don't want to keep her waiting too long," she said, heading for the open doorway.

At that moment, one of the ushers yelled out for a doctor or a nurse. James ran out the door with Simone, Brenda, and Ray hot on his heels. When they reached the vestibule, Momma Greene was on the floor passed out. James attempted to wake her up with no success.

He yelled for someone to dial 911 as he checked her pulse; she wasn't breathing, so he continued to administer CPR until the paramedics arrived. Brenda was beside herself, crying and screaming, trying to get her mother to wake up.

"Momma, don't leave me! Lord, please don't take her yet! I can't make it without her! She's supposed to see me get married and give me advice about raising my kids..."

Ray, trying to calm her, took her outside while James worked. The members that were still in the church went into prayer mode with the pastor. They formed a circle around James as he continued CPR on Momma Greene.

Prayers from the congregation became more and more intense as the remaining members stood outside waiting for the ambulance. Two of Momma Greene's friends brought a chair and some water outside for Brenda to drink while they prayed with and for her.

Sirens interrupted the prayers as the twirling lights broke through the grey sky; rain pounded hard atop the awning of the church. Paramedics rushed frantically to assist Dr. Powers as he continued to administer CPR. Brenda watched the paramedics as they placed her mother into the ambulance.

"I want to ride with her to the hospital!" she insisted, pulling James by the arm as he spoke to one of the paramedics.

"Brenda, it will be better if you followed along...that way they can focus on your mother. I'll tell you what...I'll ride with her and make sure she's getting the proper care, okay?" he said.

"Thank you, James. I appreciate that," she whispered, giving him a hug. James gave Simone the keys to his car, telling her to drive herself home.

Harder and harder the rain fell as the lightning and thunder became sharper and louder. Brenda felt in her spirit that this was the end, that her momma was making her dramatic exit out of this world and her grand entrance into the presence of the Lord.

"Momma just hold on so I can say goodbye," she silently mouthed as she rested her head on the passenger side window, tears falling profusely from her now reddened eyes.

When they arrived at the hospital, James was waiting for Brenda with a somber look on his face.

"Where is my momma?" Brenda asked.

"Brenda, there was nothing we could do for her...her heart just gave out. The paramedics worked on her on the way here, but she passed away just as we pulled up to the hospital...I am so sorry." He said, putting his arms around her to comfort her.

Ray walked through the emergency room doors, soaked after parking the car, and saw James hugging Brenda. He stood there for a while, realizing her mother had passed away, yet feeling a little jealous.

Walking towards them, he touched her.

“Baby, I’m sorry. I wish there was something I could do to take the pain away.” Brenda broke down in Ray’s arms.

As James watched them, he realized there was no longer any reason for Brenda to communicate with him. The one person who believed in the two of them getting together was no longer alive to help Brenda see that he was the right man for her.

After things settled down a bit, James took them to the morgue to see Momma Greene. Brenda just stared at her mother’s corpse and for the first time, she began to understand what her mother had always told her.

“Don’t cry over me child...when I die that won’t be the end of me. If you live for Christ you will live again...I am just trading one house for another. When you see me lying in that coffin just remember it is just a shell...I will no longer be in there but with my Master, giving Him all the glory, honor, and praise.”

Suddenly a peace fell over her, and she simply asked Ray to take her home.

When they arrived back at the house, Brenda was very quiet.

"Would you like something to eat or drink?" Ray asked, as they walked on the porch. "I could fix you a sandwich...you haven't eaten anything all day." He was genuinely concerned about her.

"No thanks," she said, reaching in her purse for her house key.

When Brenda walked in with Ray holding her hand, she looked around at the empty rooms. Evidence of her mother was everywhere: her favorite rocking chair by the television with her blue and white blanket neatly folded across the back and the aroma of her famous turkey wings she had prepared the night before still sitting on the stove for them to eat later on that day.

As she continued into the living room, it suddenly dawned on her that she would never see her mother walking through the house or hear her praying in her room or see her reading her Bible until she fell asleep sitting up in the chair with her glasses sliding down her nose but just hitting the tip before they fell into her lap.

"Why don't you go lie down Brenda...I'll be right here when you wake up." Ray gently wrapped his arms around her shoulders, leading her to the staircase and then to her bedroom.

"I want to go in here," she said, directing Ray to her mother's room.

"I can't sleep...I have so much I need to do. I have to find Momma's papers, call the funeral parlor, and order the flowers…" she said, not taking a breath, pulling open drawers and lifting doilies on her mother's dresser.

"Baby, it's Sunday...everything is closed. We can do what needs taking care of tomorrow. Right now I want you to rest and let me take care of you for a change."

Brenda knew Ray was right. There wasn't much she could get accomplished today so she did as Ray suggested.

HER WIDOW'S PEAK

She went to her mother's bed, grabbed her pillow in her arms, and took a big whiff of her mother's scent falling asleep.

Chapter 8

WITH THIS RING

When Brenda woke the next morning, she thought what happened to her mother was a bad dream, until she realized she was in her mother's bed, and it all came crashing back to her. She looked around the bedroom.

"Lord, give me strength; help me to do what I need to do," she prayed. When she opened her eyes, Ray was standing at the door with a tray of breakfast.

"Good morning...how did you sleep? I hope you're hungry...I made toast, scrambled eggs, bacon, and I have a glass of orange juice and a cup of hot tea," he smiled as he placed the tray on Brenda's lap.

"Thanks, babe, but I'm really not that hungry. I need to go through Momma's paperwork and make a few calls about her funeral arrangements..."

He interrupted her, gently restraining her as she tried to get up.

"I know you have a lot to do, but you still need to eat to keep up your strength. I won't take no for an answer. I'll help you do everything you need to do. I canceled my return flight back to Atlanta for Saturday and I'm going to stay here for as long as you need me..." he said, putting jam on her toast.

"What about work? Don't you have a big shoot coming up in California?" Suddenly she was very hungry, taking a bite of the toast from his hand.

"I gave it to another photographer. We've been talking about partnering up and opening a studio together; all I need to do is come up with about twenty-five grand and he will match me. We could probably get a loan for the rest."

"Wow that sounds great! How come you never mentioned this before?" she asked, appetite gone once more as she played with the food.

"I don't know...I guess I just didn't want to jinx it. Besides, it's too far off to even imagine in this economy," he said wiping the jam from the corner of her mouth.

After breakfast, Brenda began the process of getting her mother's paperwork organized and making the necessary telephone calls for her funeral arrangements.

She sifted through every piece of paper her mother had, finding telephone numbers from people Brenda had never heard of, let alone met. There were numbers from as far away as Seattle, Washington, and Wyoming.

Who in the world could Momma have been talking to in Wyoming? she wondered. She found old birthday and Mother's day cards she had made for her back when she was in kindergarten. She also found old drawings, certificates, and report cards her mother had placed in a box marked 'Brenda's Accomplishments.'

"I can't believe she kept all this stuff all these years," she said, her eyes welling with tears.

As she pulled out the last box marked 'KAREN,' Brenda was shocked.

"These are my mother's things!" she squealed out loud as

she began to open it, hoping to find a photo or something that could help her get in touch with her biological mother.

One by one she pulled out toys, report cards, drawings, awards, and certificates won by Karen but no sign of a photograph or a telephone number where she could be reached.

"Why wouldn't Momma have a picture somewhere of her own daughter? I know she had to love her." Brenda became more and more baffled.

None of this made any sense to her. There was no real evidence that Brenda had a mother, or for that matter, a father. Not until that very moment had she ever felt so alone. She began to cry, so loud Ray could hear her downstairs, waking from his nap on the sofa. He ran upstairs to see what was wrong.

"What's the matter, baby?" he asked, kneeling down on the floor with her.

Huffing and puffing as she sniffed up the snot streaming down her nose.

"I'm an orphan now... I don't have anyone. I don't have a mother or a father. I'm alone in this world," she sobbed, placing her head on his shoulders.

"You're not alone baby... you got me." Ray said has he lifted her up off the floor and placed her on the bed.

Is he being sincere? Is he really going to be here for me? Brenda thought. She wanted to believe Ray. Right at that moment, he was there for her and she needed him now more than ever. The kiss became more and more passionate. Brenda found herself lifting up Ray's T-shirt trying to undress him.

"I thought you wanted to wait," he said, knowing that she might regret it later if they made love.

"I need you to hold me and make me feel better," she said, pulling him closer.

"As much as I want you right now, I know you don't want to do this. You're not thinking clearly," he said as he tried to pull away from her.

"Please Ray, don't reject me…I don't think I can handle that right now," she whimpered, starting to cry again.

Ray didn't know what to do. His body was responding to every touch and kiss, his manhood about to explode. It had been a while since he and Brenda had been intimate, and he wanted her more than she could possibly know. He knew Brenda wasn't thinking clearly and he didn't want her to hate him later, but on the other hand, he couldn't stand to see her so distraught. She began kissing his neck then his ear. Ray couldn't hold out any longer; he began to undress her.

Suddenly the doorbell rang. They didn't hear it, continuing to undress one another. Again the door bell rang, then the telephone. Brenda was startled back to the reality of the situation.

What am I doing? she reasoned, sliding out of Ray's warm embrace. The telephone continued to ring while the doorbell still chimed.

"I need to get that...it might be the pastor or the insurance company calling." It was her perfect escape as she reached for the phone. "Could you get the door while I answer this please?"

She felt relieved, knowing that God had to have intervened and kept her from breaking her vow to Him.

Ray ran downstairs to answer the door still fixing his clothes. When he opened it, there stood James, surprised to see Ray standing there half dressed. He'd been hoping Brenda would be alone so they could talk.

Ray couldn't resist rubbing the fact that he was there for Brenda during her hour of need in James' face. He stood there refusing to invite James in, all the while buckling his belt and zipping his pants.

"I came by to see how Brenda is doing and to see if there was anything I can do to help her?" James said, feeling crushed that he'd basically walked in on them making love.

"She's upstairs resting but I will tell her you stopped by…Doc," Ray said hastily, starting to close the door.

"That won't be necessary," James murmured, turning to leave.

"Ray, who is it?" Brenda was coming up behind him to see who was at the door.

"Your mother's doctor," he said.

"James…what a surprise...come in," she offered, very glad to see him, but realizing how things must look.

"No…I need to get back to the hospital. I just came by to let you know that the funeral parlor came by this morning to pick up your mother's body and...to once again offer my condolences." He looked hurt and disappointed.

Brenda, seeing the expression on his face, wanted to crawl into the biggest hole she could find. She wanted to tell him Ray had slept there but in a separate room, that nothing happened…thanks to him and God; but it didn't matter.

Why is he upset? He has a fiance. He doesn't have the right. It shouldn't matter what went on between Ray and I. Brenda's anger was tripped as she watched him walk away.

"Who was on the phone?" Ray asked, interrupting her angry thoughts.

"What? Oh...it was the pastor. He said he will be by in about an hour to help me go over the funeral arrangements..."

Ray noticed her sudden hostility but mistook it as nerves and tiredness.

All the arrangements had been made and it was the day of Momma Greene's funeral. The church was decorated with all kinds of flowers. Brenda hoped the announcement in the paper and all the telephone calls she'd made to all the numbers she'd found, in her mother's phone book, would bring her biological mother or father out of hiding.

What child wouldn't come to her own mother's funeral? she thought, as they lined up to walk into the church.

Normally, the funeral procession would be a long line of family members walking two by two. Man on the right...woman on the left. However, this would not be the case in Brenda's family. There would be no long line: no aunts, no uncles, no sisters, no brothers, no grandchildren, not even her own biological mother—just her, Ray, and her mother's friends marching into the church. Brenda felt very empty.

She won't see me graduate from college. She won't be there to give me advice or to help me get ready for my wedding or see my children. She won't be there when I become a scientist. All these thoughts rushed through her mind as she tried holding back the tears but failed.

The funeral was over and everyone went back to her mother's house for the repast. A very professionally dressed older gentleman in his sixties with grey hair approached her.

"Hello Brenda...my name is Mathew Banks and I am your mother's attorney. I want you to know how sorry I am that we had to meet under these circumstances. I was out of town when I heard about your mother's passing and I just got back in yesterday. Your mother had a will prepared about ten years ago, and there has been a trust fund set up for you ever since you were about six months old. I would like to see you in my office tomorrow about twelve o'clock to go over your mother's estate," he spoke in a hushed yet urgent tone.

"Sure..." She was attempting to be cool to cover her shock at his words. *A trust fund? Really?* "...I can meet with you then."

Ray, who stood next to the table, overheard their conversation, asking Brenda if it would be okay if he came along for moral support. Brenda agreed. After all she was going through, she felt that she could use some support.

They rose early the next morning, ate breakfast, and headed downtown to Broad Street. The traffic was a bit congested due to the horse carriage tours, but Brenda felt confident they would make it there in time to find a parking space.

Waiting for a car to move from the front of the office, they pulled into the space. Brenda was anxious to find out what her mother's final wishes were. She stepped out of the car searching through her small Coach handbag for loose change to put in the meter.

"I have it." said Ray, handing her four quarters.

The office was decorated with green and purple striped

wing back chairs and a purple couch with green pillows accented with purple flowers. The highlights were fresh cut carnations everywhere with a beautiful floral arrangement on the office coffee table.

The phone was ringing off the hook. An elderly man sat waiting, reading a sports magazine with a collar around his neck and a cast on his left arm. A young woman sat behind the receptionist desk taking one call after call while juggling paperwork as she greeted each client approaching her.

"Good afternoon, may I help you?" she asked, placing the next call on hold.

"Yes, I have an appointment with Mr. Banks at twelve o'clock. I'm a little early," Brenda said.

"Yes, I'll let him know you're here...please have a seat." She smiled warmly, pressing the button to his private line. They took a seat on the couch.

Brenda watched as each person walked through the door, wondering how many of these strangers came in the office for the same reason as she.

The clocked ticked by slowly. One by one, the waiting room emptied, leaving just Ray and Brenda .

"I wonder what's taking so long. We came early, and he still hasn't come out his office. I can't stand these lawyer types..." Ray said, feeling restless and agitated.

"It's only twelve-thirty...maybe he's running a little behind schedule." Brenda lightly rubbed his forearm, trying to sooth him.

Eventually, Mr. Banks came out of the office. "Sorry to have kept you waiting so long...it's been one of those mornings. Please come in and do have a seat."

He ushered them into the office, taking a seat behind his polished mahogany desk. Brenda was impressed by all the degrees and certificates neatly placed on the wall behind his head. She glanced at the pictures of his family placed in frames around the office. Pictures of artwork that might have been drawn by his grandchildren were matted and framed like masterpieces on a wall all to themselves.

"Ms. Greene, I want you to know how truly sorry I am for

your loss. I've been your mother's lawyer for over fifteen years. She was a very special woman and she really spoke highly of you," he said as he opened the will to read it.

"Is this it, just me, no one else?" Brenda asked, hoping her birth mother would walk through the door.

"Yes, this is everyone. I won't delay you any longer…shall we begin...?"

"Your mother left you the house, of course, and everything in it as well as her car. She also had a trust fund set up for you when you were a baby and she invested a portion in stocks and bonds totaling $200,000. She also left you property on John's Island appraised at about $50,000 in today's market..." Brenda was overwhelmed by everything her mother had left to her.

"What about my biological mother, Karen—did she say anything about her?" She was hoping her mother left information about her whereabouts or hoping she would have left some clue.

"Yes, your mother *did* request that I try to locate her in

case of her death; however, we were unsuccessful." He opened his mouth to continue but Brenda halted him with another question.

"Was there a last known address or telephone number you could give me?" She was sounding desperate.

"No, but what you can do is place an ad in several newspapers regarding your mother's passing, and hopefully she will answer one of them. Perhaps you might want to consider hiring a private investigator to track her down." That was all the information he could give, so he closed his file on Brenda, Karen, and Mrs. Greene.

On the way back home, Brenda thought about the Mother's Day gifts she would never give to her mother, yet again, her mother continued giving to her even after she was gone. The attorney's suggestions continued to permeate over and over in her head.

"What do you think I should do?" she asked Ray.

"About what?" Ray asked.

"About looking for my birth mother."

"It's up to you," he said, reaching for her hand.

"I know but I really want to hear what you have to say," she said, hoping he would say what she wanted to hear.

"Well, since you asked...I think you need to leave well enough alone. If your biological mother wanted to be in your life, she would have been there. Why dig up the past? It may not turn out the way you want it to..." he said as though he was speaking from experience.

Brenda knew Ray had a point, but she knew deep down in her heart she wouldn't be able to rest until she knew more about her biological mother and why she'd left her with her grandmother. She wanted to know what she looked like. Did she have her eyes, her nose, her mouth? Did they have the same laugh or smile and habits? Brenda knew she couldn't let it go. She needed answers.

Ray needed to get some items before he went back to Atlanta so they drove to the Mall. They walked around for a while then got a bite to eat. Brenda was getting tired so she decided to sit while Ray went to Radio Shack to look at camera equipment and other supplies he needed. He was gone for about forty-five minutes, and she became concerned. She noticed when he came back with nothing in his hands, but was too exhausted to question him about his items. She was ready to leave.

When they arrived back at the house, Brenda felt a heavy weight come over her. Again, the memories of her mother and the times they'd shared in the house flooded her thoughts.

I will never see her again. Loneliness fell upon her like a ton of cinder-blocks and she began to cry.

"What am I going to do without her? I don't have anyone...no one. My own mother didn't want me." She was flooding Ray's abs with her tears and bawling like a baby. Lifting up her head with his hands on her chin, he bent down to kiss her.

The kiss became more and more passionate until neither one of them could control themselves. He picked her up and carried her upstairs to her room where they made love. As he looked in her eyes, she began to cry again.

"Brenda please don't cry...you didn't do anything wrong. Girl, don't you know how much I love you?" he said has she laid her head on his chest.

Ray sat up and turned to pick his slacks up off of the floor. He reached into his pocket and pulled out a small white box. When he turned around, he reached for her left hand.

"I don't ever want you to feel alone another day in your life...will you marry me?" he whispered, sliding a diamond, white gold engagement ring on to her finger. Excited, she grabbed Ray by the neck and hugged him.

"Yes…yes...I'll marry you!" she screamed, kissing him over and over again.

Brenda wanted to hear Ray ask her those four words from the first day they met. *Lord thank you!* came silently from her lips as she pulled Ray closer and closer until they consumed one another again and again.

The next morning Brenda helped Ray pack his clothes and took him to the airport.

"I hate to leave you alone baby, but I have to get back to

work," he said, pulling his suitcase out of the trunk.

"Thanks for staying with me...I don't think I could get through all of this without you, but I'll manage. Besides, I start my internship on Monday," she said.

"I'll call you when I get back to the apartment," he promised, giving her a kiss goodbye. As she watched Ray walk into the airport, she looked down at her ring.

"Momma, I'm going to be okay now..."

Orientation began promptly at 7:30 a.m. The hospital was buzzing with employees and doctors heading to the cafeteria for breakfast; orderlies transported patients down hallways on gurneys and in wheelchairs. The corridors echoed with the sounds of calls over the intercoms for one thing or another.

As Brenda searched down each tiled hall for the room where the lab technicians were to assemble, she thought about the day her mother was admitted into this very hospital and diagnosed with liver cancer—the day she met James. Her mind flashed back to her mother's last words and how much she wanted her and James to get together. Sadness began to overwhelm her spirit. One tear fell from her eyes.

Turning down the fourth hallway, she saw the glass door marked laboratory. Swallowing the lump in her throat and wiping her eye, she entered the class. It was filled with students eager to get to work. Her excitement building, she pulled out pad and pen hanging on every word the instructor said. The lab door opened; she noticed a pair of leather burgundy, laced shoes, neatly pressed black slacks and a partially opened white lab coat. When she looked, up there he was—James; as confident and gorgeous as ever.

"Class, this is Dr. Powers. He will be taking you all through our hospital today," the instructor said. Brenda got all nervous and fidgety; she knew his last image of her wasn't a pretty one and she was a bit embarrassed to say the least.

After a tour of the laboratory and the hospital, the

students were asked to pick their specialty of research. Brenda knew this summer program was an opportunity of a lifetime and she wasn't going to let her past relationship with James keep her from choosing Cancer Biology Research. She also knew he was the lead specialist in his field and his knowledge and insight could help her achieve her future goals. After turning in her information, everyone was assigned their teams and the day came to a close.

As Brenda headed to the door to leave, she heard James call out to her.

"How have you been, Brenda?" he asked.

"I'm coming along," she said shyly.

"I see you chose Cancer Biology Research for your area of study. I look forward to working with you this summer. Say, I'm about to go get a bite to eat, would you like to join me?" James was hoping against hope she would say yes.

"Well, I…" Brenda was hesitant.

"Do you have other plans? Are you meeting your boyfriend?" He was prying to find out if Ray was still in town.

"No, he had to get back to Atlanta," she said.

"Well then, we can go get a bite to eat and we can talk about the program," he said, sounding relieved.

James drove to a nearby deli and they sat on the nicely shaded patio as the cars passed and people walked by. Brenda couldn't help but notice the way James' mouth curled as he chewed his food. She thought about how those lips felt when he kissed her.

Girl you need to snap out of it!

"How have you been? I've been meaning to call or stop by, but I didn't want to intrude." James was being subtle but quite thorough.

"I've been doing okay. I wanted to thank you again for all you did to help my mother. She really thought highly of you," she said, keeping her left hand out of sight as she spoke.

"Your mother was a strong woman. I've never met anyone quite like her. She had such strong faith. I will surely miss our dinners on Sundays," James said as he took a sip of his soft drink. Brenda was stunned. She never knew her mother was having Sunday dinners with James. She hadn't assumed they were that close.

Her curiosity got the better of her. She wanted to know more about what was going on while she was at school and what about his fiance...was she eating dinner with them as well? Brenda felt out of the loop.

"Momma never mentioned that the two of you had dinner together every Sunday. When did the two of you start doing that?" She wanted to know if it was really just the two of them.

"Well let me see…I think after I first came to your home for dinner. She always told me she wanted a son, and I was the closest she ever came to having one. Ever since then, when I got off my shift or if I was off duty, I would call her up or she would call me for dinner." He was smiling like the cat that ate the canary.

"What about your fiance, Sandy?" Brenda blurted out.

"What about Simone?" he asked.

"Has she ever joined the two of you for dinner?" The

jealous feelings were simmering again. "No, I didn't get a chance to introduce her to Simone...we should be getting back to the hospital..."

What is it with men and changing the subject?

The day had come to an end. As she walked out of the building to her car, Brenda reflected on her lunch with James. It had been a long time since they spent any time together and she didn't realize until that moment how much she missed him. She knew she should have mentioned that she was engaged, but somehow it just didn't seem as though it was the right time to bring it up.

As she backed out of the parking space and proceeded to drive out of the garage, she noticed James walking to his reserved parking space. Brenda started to honk her horn to say goodbye until she notice a woman jumping out of the car from the driver's side and directly into James' arms. She planted a long passionate kiss on his lips as she gave him the car keys.

It was Simone. Feeling a sharp pain in her chest, Brenda just drove off.

Chapter 9

BURDEN BEARER

The next morning was more intense than Brenda could ever have imagined. There was so much she needed to learn and so little time to get it all down. She knew she couldn't afford to get discouraged. She had already picked her four areas of study, and now all she needed was to find a mentor to help her through her research.

She thought about choosing James, but she knew it would be awkward working closely with him every day. She couldn't bear seeing him, smelling him, and hearing his deep, soft spoken voice.

What is the matter with me? I am a grown woman. I can handle being around him for ten weeks...I can't let my emotions stop me from doing what I have to do. Besides, there could never be anything between us—he has Simone and I have Ray. I can do this she thought, trying to convince herself as she worked up the nerve to go to his office.

As she approached the door, her hand froze on the knob. She was about to turn it when the door swung open. James was on the way out.

"Hello, Brenda. This is a nice surprise. Were you coming to see me?"

"Ya...yes, ah, but if you have some place you need to be, I can come back another time."

"No, I was just about to get a cup of coffee from the lounge...would you care to join me?" he said with a big smile on his face.

"Sure, why not?" she said as she followed him to the lounge.

James poured her a cup and they sat down. "What can I do for you?" he asked.

"I wanted to know if you would be my mentor this summer. You are number one in your field and I think I can learn a great deal from you. I will understand if you say no...considering our history," she said, hoping he wouldn't.

"I would be honored to mentor you, but what would your boyfriend think about us working so closely together?" he asked. Brenda didn't quite know how to answer since she hadn't discussed her plans with Ray...besides he was miles away and this was her future.

She knew Ray wasn't going to be too happy with the idea of them seeing each other or working so closely together all the time.

"He knows how much my career means to me," she said, blowing on the hot coffee then placing it to her lips...

Weeks went by with Brenda and James becoming the dynamic duo of the program. He allowed her to sit in on his meetings with top physicians and staff at the hospital regarding breakthrough treatments. They worked endless hours together in the lab as James worked on case after case, trying to find treatments for each of his patients. She also helped him with his workshops and lectures.

One night after leaving the hospital, they decided to call it a day.

"Why don't we get a bite to eat?" James asked.

"I should be heading home...it's been a long day and I promised Ray I'd call at ten o'clock. Don't you need to be spending some quality time with your fiance?"

"Actually, we called it quits."

Brenda was curious and quite relieved. "Oh…I'm sorry to hear that. What happened?"

"Well, we wanted different things out of life. To tell you the truth, I wasn't in love with her the way I love…" He stopped before he said the wrong thing.

Brenda knew how James felt about her, and she still had strong feelings for him, but her heart belonged to Ray. *How am I going to tell James about the engagement?* she wondered.

They said goodnight, and Brenda drove home to call Ray.

After taking her shower and propping herself up in bed, she dialed his number. The phone rang three times then she got his voice-mail. Where could he be? This was the third time she'd called and he wasn't there.

Brenda was trying not to get paranoid; after all, she knew he still worked at the club a couple of nights a week, so she tried calling him there. The bartender picked up the phone.

"Hi, Jack, this is Brenda...is Ray working tonight?" She asked.

"Naaa, I haven't seen Ray in about two weeks... not since that big fight he had with Mr. Gadsden."

Mr. Gadsden was the owner of the night club and bar where Ray worked as a bouncer.

"Fight... what fight?"

"I don't know all the details...all I know is Ray just went ballistic about his hours and pay, and the next thing he hauls off and punches Mr. Gadsden and the cops were called. The cops took Ray away in handcuffs. That was the last I saw him."

In shock, she became very worried. *Lord I hope Ray is alright. Where can he be? Why hasn't he called me? Why didn't he call and let me know what happened?* She could hear the panic in her own thoughts.

She got on her knees and began to pray out loud. "*Father, this is Brenda. I know we haven't talked in a while and I know I have made a lot of mistakes lately. Please forgive me. You know Ray is all I've got left in this world...please let him be okay... please let him call me and tell me he's alright. Thank you, Father...Amen,*" she concluded as she got up off of the floor.

All night Brenda tossed and turned thinking about everything the bartender had told her. She kept seeing Ray handcuffed and being pushed into the back of a patrol car, having his fingers printed, and sitting in a jail cell. It wasn't until about 3:30 a.m. that she decided to try calling him again to see if he would answer. Again, she got nothing.

Too upset to attempt sleep, she decided to get ready to go to the hospital. She picked up her Bible to search the scriptures for answers but became frustrated and decided to get into her car and drive to the Colonial Lake to clear her head.

She remembered the days when she and her mother would walk around it and watch the sun go down. She thought about all the conversations they used to have as she sat in her car watching the sun slowly rise and the fish jump.

Tears began to fill her eyes. Brenda placed her head back against the seat to rest for just a moment, but as she was about to drift off to sleep, she heard a tap on the window. Startled, she jumped up, hitting her hand on the horn and looked out the window; it was James.

"I didn't mean to frighten you. I recognized your car and saw you lying back like that; I thought something was wrong. Are you alright?" he asked, soaking wet from jogging. Noticing the sweat beaming off his shirtless light brown chest, she said, "I'm fine...just a little shaken up, that's all.

"I didn't know you came out here in the mornings," he said as he wiped his face. "Actually, I don't. I couldn't sleep so I decided to come kill some time until I had to be at the hospital."

"Would you like some company?"

"I don't want to keep you from your work out...besides, I don't think I would be very good company right now. I've got a lot on my mind."

"Maybe I can lend a friendly ear; we are still friends, aren't we?" he asked as he flashed his pearly whites at Brenda.

"Of course we're still friends. I just don't want to keep dumping my problems on you."

"Doesn't the Bible say we ought to bear one another's burdens?" he asked, opening the door for her to get out. "I don't want to funk up your nice clean car so come walk with me...talk to me." He took her by the hand, leading her to a nearby bench.

They sat talking for what seemed to be hours about everything that was troubling her. She remembered how easy it was to talk to James. Before she knew it, they were laughing and cracking jokes until she forgot all about Ray.

James is uncomplicated and a good listener. He truly cares about my feelings and he knows just what I need, she thought to herself. Glancing down at her watch, she realized it was time to get to the hospital. James walked her back to her car.

"Thank you so much James...you really are a great guy. You'll make some woman a wonderful husband..."

"I was hoping that woman would be you," he blurted, staring into her eyes as he closed the car door behind her. Brenda pondered James' last words as she watched him jog off into the morning sun.

The entire day, her thoughts drifted back to that morning with James by the lake. She thought about how he'd once again come to her rescue like a knight in shining armor and how he showed up out of the blue to rescue her from her doubts and insecurities. It was as if her mother and God sent him there just in the nick of time, before she went off the deep end.

The talk with James gave her the confidence and extra boost to continue the day, and for that she would always be grateful to him. She suddenly realized that she might be making a big mistake if she married Ray.

Maybe he isn't who I need to be with after all. He hasn't called me in almost two weeks. Maybe he went back into the world and stopped going to church...maybe he's cheating on me again. She spoke all these things to her inner woman as second-guessing her decision to marry took on new life...

The program was coming to a close. Brenda became anxious towards the end, but managed to complete all her research projects and papers with flying colors, thanks to James. Her hard work paid off when she received word that she'd ranked highest among her fellow interns. Excitedly, she pulled out her cell phone to dial her house. After the phone rang several times, she realized what she had done.

What am I doing...she's not there. Swallowing the lump in

her throat, she closed her phone.

Her professor congratulated her, telling her there was to be a small ceremony and formal party for the students who completed the program, so with an overwhelming sense of accomplishment yet saddened by her mother's absence, she packed up her things.

She wondered if Ray could possibly make it to the ceremony on Friday night as she dialed his number for the umpteenth time; again, there was no answer. Hurt, she headed out of the building. Just as she began to walk into the garage, she heard James call her name.

"Congrats, future colleague...I just heard the good news," he said, flashing his deep dimples.

Giving him a big hug, she beamed, "I owe it all to you James...I don't think I could have done it without your help. How can I ever repay you for everything you've done for me?"

"I would be honored if you'd be my date for the party on Friday...that is, if you don't already have one." He prayed she would say she didn't.

"No, I mean yes, I would love to go with you..."

"Are you sure you don't want to share this special time in your life with the man in your life?" he asked, feeling her out about Ray.

"I haven't heard from Ray in a few days. He must be on a shoot. Besides, it is only right that you and I share this milestone in my life. You are the key to my doing as well as I did..."

"Yes, I am …" His smile could light up the darkest night."...I'm just kidding. It was my pleasure working with you. You've reminded me why I chose this field of study in the first place... sometimes it gets to me when I lose a patient because of cancer. When I see the intensity and excitement in your eyes every time you get into the lab or try to research a case, it encourages me and I just want to keep pushing."

"Well, I need to find something nice to wear for the party. I'll see you around six thirty," she said, walking to the elevator.

While getting ready for the event, the phone rang. With her hair half curled and pantyhose partially placed just above her knees, she answered.

"Hello."

"What's up, girlfriend...how are things going down in Redneckville?" the person asked with a laugh.

"Shannon, it can only be you. I'm doing great. How have you been?" Brenda asked, as she pulled up her hose.

"Life is fantastic. What is this I hear about you and Ray getting engaged?" Shannon asked.

"How did you find out about our engagement so fast? I haven't even told my pastor," Brenda asked, surprised.

"Girl, you must have forgotten who you are talking to...I have my sources. Stop beating around the bush and answer the damn question. Is it true?" Shannon asked in her usual pushy tone.

"If you must know, yes—it's true," she said, knowing Shannon wasn't going to let it rest. "Brenda, you know I love you, girl, and I only want the best for you, but have you lost your mind? Why are you rushing into things? You have your whole life ahead of you. What about finishing school and getting your career off the ground?" Shannon said as her voice got higher and higher.

Brenda didn't want to get into an argument with Shannon. She knew she meant well, but it was getting late and she had to finish getting dressed.

"Shannon, I can't get into this with you right now...I'm on the way out." She put her cell phone on speaker so she could finish curling her hair.

"Where are you off to?"

"If you must know, the program is throwing a party and an award ceremony tonight for all the interns who completed the program."

"Will that fine Dr. Powers be there? I know you had to have seen him a few times since you've been at that hospital," Shannon said, laughing.

"He is my escort for the evening…Rona Barrett."

"Escort! Girl why didn't you lead with that story? Fill a

sister in on the 411 and don't leave anything out," Shannon insisted.

Brenda knew Shannon wasn't going to give her any peace, so she filled her in on the entire summer. As she told her about all the things she and James did and said, Shannon made all her "I told you he was the right man for you" sounds and comments.

It was almost six o'clock. Brenda knew James was a timely person and she wasn't anywhere near ready for their date.

"Girl, I need to get off this phone...James will be here any minute," she said, pulling out her makeup case.

"Brenda, I am glad the two of you are reconnecting. You need to seriously reconsider your relationship with Ray and jump on that fine hunk of a man Dr. Powers. He is really showing and telling you how he feels, and you are just too stubborn to take advantage of the real thing staring you in your face. You need to dump the trash," Shannon said sternly, trying to get her point across.

Brenda realized Shannon was repeating herself a little more than usual. She sounded more determined than ever to make Brenda leave Ray.

Knowing that they may get into a fight and probably never speak again, Brenda decided to bring the conversation to a close.

"Okay, you know you are crossing the line so you must know something you aren't telling me...Spill it." Brenda was getting annoyed with Shannon.

For a while the phone went silent. Brenda called out to Shannon to see if she was still on the line.

"I heard that he got in a fight at the bar some weeks ago and got arrested," she said.

"I know all about it," Brenda said sarcastically.

"You did? Well, did you know this isn't the first time he's been in jail? He did time about five or six years ago for assault and battery. They say he almost killed a man," Shannon continued.

Shocked and devastated, there wasn't anything Brenda

could say. She told Shannon she needed to finish getting dressed and she'd call her later. Just then the door bell rang. Brenda turned to look at the clock. Six thirty on the dot.

"Oh no...it's James and I'm not finished getting ready!" She ran downstairs still a little shaken by the news Shannon had just dropped on her.

Touching up her makeup in the mirror on the wall, she opened the door.

"Hello James...come on in...I'm almost ready. Have a seat. Would you like something to drink?" she said, a bit discombobulated.

"No, thank you, I'm fine." He was staring her up and down, like he wanted to throw her to the floor and consume her. She ran back up the steps while he waited in the living room. After about fifteen minutes, she came down again, ready and eager to go.

Taking her hand to kiss it, he spoke softly, "You look beautiful."

Feeling a bit awkward, she murmured, "Thank you. I'm

sorry I kept you waiting."

"No problem...you are worth the wait. Shall we go?" James asked as they walked arm in arm out the door.

Brenda watched James as he opened the door to the car to let her in and walked over to the driver's side. As he drove, her mind began to wander. She couldn't shake everything Shannon had told her about Ray.

What do I really know about him? she thought as she watched James maneuver the powerful car.

When they arrived at the party, the place was filled with specialists and doctors capable of helping Brenda with her future goals. James introduced her to everyone. He worked the room like a public relations professional. It was easy to see he had the respect and admiration of his peers, and she found that very appealing.

Brenda decided she wasn't going to let the information about Ray ruin her night. She was going to enjoy herself; she had earned it. Plus, she was with someone who wanted to be with her and had helped her get where she was, and that meant the world to her. As they danced and laughed, Brenda forgot everything that has transpired earlier that evening.

It was soon time for the awards to be presented. The head of the department presented Brenda with her award for Outstanding Performance. She thanked God and her mother for getting her to this point and gave a special thanks to James for all his support and training as her mentor.

The night was more than Brenda could ever have imagined. It was perfect, James was perfect, and she didn't want it to end. It was the first time she'd enjoyed herself in a long time, and it was all because of James.

He really is a wonderful man and we have so much in common. He's saved, he loves the Lord, and my mother really loved him like he was her own. She reflected on all this as she watched him from across the room talking to his colleagues.

Shannon is right...maybe I do need to cut Ray loose... Other than him being saved now, the two of them attending the same church, and great sex, what did they really have in common?

I really don't know anything about his past and now he's not even calling me! She was trying to weigh the pros and cons of their entire relationship in a matter of minutes.

At that moment, James came over.

"Are you ready to blow this joint and take advantage of this wonderful night? There's a full moon, and I would like to spend a little alone time with my men-tee," he said has he rubbed her shoulders.

"The party isn't over," she said, a bit hesitant, "...wouldn't it be rude of us to leave?"

"Look, if they had someone who looked as fine as you do tonight with them, they wouldn't want to share her with anyone either. Anyway, we've spent enough time with them all summer... tonight I want you all to myself before you have to leave and go back to school," James said, being very direct with her.

Brenda collected her purse as they said their good-nights to a couple of people and then left.

"Where are we going?" she asked.

"I thought we could go back to my place and listen to some real music and unwind," he said, looking straight ahead as he drove.

Speechless, she sat silently wondering if she should take James up on his offer. After all, this was the first time he had ever invited her to his place. She felt she could trust him and she was a bit curious. He'd never made her feel pressured or uncomfortable before. Her mind quickly went on Ray and all he had put her through—not calling, getting arrested, and this blow about his past.

Glancing over at James, she began to rationalize the situation. *James is uncomplicated and gorgeous...I must have been crazy not to have given him a chance.*

They drove across the bridge to the Isle of Palms where they pulled up to this huge, three-story house on the beach; they got out of the car and went inside.

Brenda was impressed. The house was beautifully decorated as if it had been professionally done. African American art accentuated the walls with hard wood floors and high ceilings as well as a balcony with a full view of the ocean.

James turned on some smooth Jazz and poured her a glass of red wine.

"You have a really lovely place here; I love the view."

Taking a sip of his wine, James responded in kind.

"Thank you. I find the ocean really calms me after a hard day at the hospital." They went out on the balcony to sit, enjoying the night.

"It is really a beautiful night and there are so many stars out," she said, rubbing her arms.

James, noticing, put his arms around her.

"I only see one beautiful star out tonight and that's you..."

Looking deep into her eyes, he kissed her like never before. Before she knew it, she found herself surrendering in his arms.

"Brenda, I know you are with Ray and I do respect that, but I can't help how I feel about you and I know I am not alone."

Dazed, she finally told James how she felt about him. "I can't deny it any longer...I do have strong feelings for you as well," she said, kissing him again.

"I don't think you understand Brenda...I'm in love with you and I want us to be together for the rest of our lives," he expounded, lifting her chin until their eyes connected. As the music played and the ocean waves crashed, she got caught up in the moment.

"I think I am falling in love with you too..."

Before she could stop herself, they were making out on the patio furniture under the stars.

"I want you…but I know we shouldn't." he said holding her closer. Her heart was beating a mile a minute.

"No, we shouldn't."

"Can I just hold you in my arms like this all night? I don't think I can let you go."

With all her defenses completely down, Brenda agreed and they lay under the stars in each other's arms until the sun came up.

Chapter 10

ALL IS FAIR IN LOVE AND WAR

Sounds of the waves crashing and seagulls squeaking released Brenda from her calm sleep. It had been a long time since she felt this relaxed.

James was gone. She stretched out her arms and looked up at the sky. The sun was cascading over the ocean as the reflection of the bright orange ball of fire danced across the waves.

"It is so peaceful out here...I see why James loves it." She spoke aloud since she was alone.

When she walked into the house, the smell of turkey bacon glided up her nostrils. Following the delicious aroma into the enormous kitchen, she saw an elaborate display of food neatly placed on the table with a note against the fruit bowl.

I thought you might be hungry. Eat up. I left some things

in the bathroom for you if you would like to take a shower or a bubble bath. I'll be back soon. Make yourself at home,

James.

Brenda enjoyed the fresh fruits, bagel, and coffee, and then she took James up on his offer and went into the bathroom. Neatly placed on the side of his sink were a new toothbrush, towel, and washcloth for her to use. There were also bath oils, body wash, and underwear in her size. After she took her shower, she found a beautiful robe hanging on the back of the bathroom door.

A girl could get use to this... she thought, feeling a bit perplexed. *Is this his M.O.? Does he make this a habit? Maybe he brings all of his female interns and nurses back to his place to seduce them. Why else would he have all this stuff?*

She decided to do some investigating. Going from room to room, she became more and more impressed with his home. She searched for evidence of any female presence throughout the house as she entered the master bedroom. On the bed she found a cute sun dress and a pair of slide on sandals in her size.

"This man knows what a woman likes," she said, holding the dress up to her as she looked into the mirror.

Feeling very comfortable in her new surroundings, she decided to lie down on his plush mattress to watch television. Just then, she heard the door open. Brenda jumped up and went into the living room.

"Good morning, sleepy head. I see you found the things I laid out for you. How are you feeling this fine day?" he asked, giving her a bouquet of flowers and a kiss on the cheek.

"Yes, I did, and I must say I was surprised to see all the items you had for me in your bachelor pad," she replied, eager to hear his response.

"I know how this must look, but it is not what you think."

"Oh, it's not?" she said sarcastically.

"No, it's not. I thought you might need a few things so I called up a friend of mine who owns a boutique; she brought some items over as a favor to me. You were sleeping so peacefully I didn't want to wake you so I decided to get a run in before breakfast."

Again Brenda was impressed that he went to all that trouble for her. There was nothing left to say.

"Don't you have to go to the hospital today?" she asked.

"I had Dr. Baker take my shift so we can spend the entire day together. I thought we could enjoy our breakfast on the patio before we go for a walk on the beach, after I take a shower and you get dressed. The rest of the day we can do whatever."

After breakfast, Brenda went in the bedroom to put on her outfit while James took a shower. It was a perfect fit; she really liked it. Thoughts of their evening together made her tingle inside.

"Last night was so perfect; he is such a romantic."

They took a stroll along the beach holding hands and laughing. They drove downtown to the Farmers Market and bought fruits and a bite to eat as they enjoyed a picnic lunch on Marion Square. Brenda was having so much fun Ray didn't cross her mind. James was making him seem more and more like a distant memory.

It was getting late. Brenda knew she had to prepare to head back to school. The day with James was a perfect end to her summer.

She still had some loose ends to tie up before she headed back to Atlanta. Her mother's belongings needed to be taken to the Goodwill and to some of her prayer partners. James offered to help her box up the items and take them where they needed to go.

When they arrived at the house, she noticed a strange car in the drive way with Florida license plates. As they approached the stairs, she saw Ray standing on the porch with a strange look on his face. Shocked to see him, Brenda stood paralyzed.

"Where have you been?" he asked, looking very upset. With his eyes fastened on James he continued, "I've been waiting outside this house since last night. I tried calling you, but your cell went to voice mail."

With James standing behind her, Brenda was lost for words as she looked at Ray.

"I was at a function for the interns last night," she said.

"All night? And what is he doing here?" he said, as his voice elevated in anger.

"There is no need to raise your voice..."James said, trying to calm him down.

"Man, why are you even talking to me right now? This is between me and my fiance," Ray said.

Stunned, James turned in to look at Brenda. His entire demeanor changed. What started out as a magical night and wonderful day was about to turn into a nightmare.

"Is this true? Are you two engaged?" James asked, looking at Brenda as if his heart was just ripped from his chest.

"Yes, it's true. Didn't you see the ring on her finger?" Ray said, lifting Brenda's left hand. When Ray noticed that she wasn't wearing the ring, he became even more upset.

"Is there something going on that I need to know about?

Were you with him last night?" he asked.

Brenda walked Ray to the door and let him in the house. They started to argue for a few minutes before she remembered she left James outside. Realizing what she had done, she left Ray inside fuming and went back outside to talk to James, but he was gone.

Once again, she knew she'd hurt James. She felt like the worse human being alive. She wanted to call him to explain, but she knew she had to defuse the situation at hand.

"What are you doing here?" she asked.

"What do you mean what am I doing here? I came to see my woman and I find out that she's been running around on me!" Ray yelled.

"For your information, I didn't sleep with him, and how dare you get angry with me! I've been trying to contact you for weeks, and all of a sudden you show up at my door step calling me your fiance! You have some nerve! Besides, I know everything. It's bad enough I had to hear about it from someone else."

They argued for hours. Ray noticed that she wasn't buying his jealous routine. He hoped Brenda wouldn't dump him, so he finally apologized and told her what took place. He also told her about what he had done to land in jail years ago. Now it was her turn to explain where she was and what she was doing with James.

Brenda wanted to be honest with Ray and tell him everything. She told him that she had deep feelings for James and that she didn't know if she still wanted to marry him. Ray couldn't believe what he was hearing.

He got on one knee and begged Brenda not to call off the engagement. He told her the reason he wasn't calling her was because he was trying to start up his business in Atlanta and he'd wanted to surprise her with the good news. He and his partner were working together trying to get their business off the ground. They had gotten a small business loan and found a building in the heart of downtown Atlanta. He even spoke to the pastor about them coming to counseling at the church when she came back to Atlanta.

All this caught Brenda off guard. Confused about her feelings for Ray and James, all she could do was turn and walk away.

"I really don't want to discuss this right now," she said, heading up the stairs.

Ray noticed how distant Brenda was becoming. He attempted to follow her.

"I need to be alone right now; I will call you. Where are you staying?" she asked.

"Well I thought I would be staying here," he said, surprised.

"You thought wrong. I have some things to sort out and I can't do that with you here," she said, leaving the staircase and walking towards the door to show Ray out. He realized how serious Brenda was, so he backed out the door. He knew that when she was angry, there was no reasoning with her.

As Brenda watched him drive off she began to cry.

What am I doing? How can I love someone so inconsiderate of my feelings and so self-centered? Again thoughts of James entered her mind. She decided to give him a call. There was no answer so she left him a message. Not sure if she said enough, she called again hoping he would answer.

He must really be upset with me.

She called every hour on the hour until she fell asleep.

All night, she tossed and turned, thinking about the two men in her life. She played the entire scenario out in her head of how her life would be with both of these men. *Maybe I will give James time to cool off.*

Days went by and James didn't return any of her calls. Feeling that enough time had passed, she left the house early to go to the hospital to find James.

I have to talk to him and explain.

When she arrived, she asked several nurses and staff members if they'd seen Dr. Powers. They told her he'd come in late the previous night to make rounds and another told her he called an important meeting with the department heads and the hospital administrator first thing that morning; then he left about thirty minutes before she arrived.

Brenda decided to go to his house. Not knowing exactly what she was going to say, she rehearsed word for word what she could possibly say. Brenda knew James wasn't the type of man who played games. He wanted her and she had to go to him with what he wanted to hear. Still unprepared to make a commitment to him, there was no turning back. Before she knew it she was in front of his house.

His car was in the driveway; the door was partially opened. Brenda knocked. There was no answer. She rang the doorbell; still no response.

She could hear Teddy Pendergrass' "It Don't Hurt Now" playing on the stereo. She peered inside. It was coming from the bedroom. Slowly she entered the house and walked down the hall to his room. She tapped on the cracked door then went inside.

There was a practically packed suit case on the bed with his suits and shirts lying alongside still on hangers. She picked up his shirt to get a whiff of his scent. *Where is he going?*

Before she knew it, she was lying on his king-size bed

fantasizing about her and James living in his house with two children and a Cocker-Spaniel name Trixie. It finally hit Brenda: he was the one she wanted to be with, and as soon as she saw him she was going to tell him so.

Excitedly, she sat up with James' shirt draped around her shoulder. Before she could put her foot on the floor James came padding out of the bathroom. He was naked, soaked from head to toe.

"What are you doing here? How did you get in?" he asked, surprised to see her but not covering himself with the towel.

My Lord! she said to herself as her eyes slowly cascaded from head to toe down his masculine frame.

Not being able to concentrate with James standing there like that, she stuttered, "I'm….ah.. sorry for barging in like this but I rang the bell and knocked…the door was open so I came in." Finally wrapping a towel around his waist, he walked over to the stereo to turn off the music.

James continued to question Brenda.

"You still haven't told me what you are doing here," he

said, sounding cold.

"I came by to say I'm sorry and I wanted to explain."

"Explain? There is really nothing to explain. It seems very clear to me that you are engaged to Ray and again I was the chump that filled in for him while he was off playing you. Does that sound about right?" he said, packing his suitcase.

Once again she was at a loss for words. James was never this bitter and harsh with her. She tried reaching out to him to tell him what he meant to her and that she was going to call off the engagement with Ray, but before she could say anything, James walked into the bathroom to get dressed.

When he finally came out, he was completely dressed.

"Where are you going?" she asked.

"I'm leaving Charleston. I'm putting my house on the market and I'm moving to Colorado. I got an offer to work at The University of Colorado Cancer Center a few weeks ago and I decided to take the job," he said, not making eye contact with her.

"This is the first I heard you mention any job offer," she

said, getting emotional.

"Well, I just made up my mind a couple of days ago," he said, taking his frustration out on his clothes as he placed the last of them in the suitcase.

Grabbing his hand, Brenda pleaded, "James can you stop and look at me please?"

This was it. She had to put it all out there if she wanted to keep James in her life. Before she could get the words out, the doorbell rang. Pulling away from her, he went to open the door. Brenda followed. It was Simone.

"Hello sexy, are you ready?" she said.

Brenda was totally flabbergasted. *What was this heifer doing here?* she thought.

"Hello…Brenda, right?" Simone said as she hugged James.

"Could you wait in the car? I'll be right down." he said, closing the door as he turned to look at Brenda. Neither said a word for a few seconds.

"I guess I'm the fool in this story," she said.

"Not that I owe you any explanation, but Simone is just giving me a ride to the airport. If I were seeing her again, so what? You have Ray and you know what they say… all is fair in love and war."

He went in the room to get the rest of his luggage. As tears welled up in her eyes, Brenda decided to leave. There was nothing left for her to say.

Walking down the stairs and into her car, she felt sick to her stomach. She knew she had made the biggest mistake of her life and there was absolutely nothing she could say or do about it. She watched James come down the step and put his luggage into the trunk of the car. He turned in her direction, but looked right at her with no expression on his face before proceeding to the car.

"Momma, what have I done? I don't think he'll ever forgive me. I am such a fool," she said as she watched them drive off, trying to stop the tears from flowing.

Attempting to compose herself, she proceeded to drive home. Not quite sure how she made it with her eyes red and practically swollen shut, she went into the house, locked the door, drew the curtains, went upstairs, and fell asleep.

Awakened by the sound of the phone ringing off the hook, she turned over in bed and covered her head with the sheet until it stopped. Again it rang. This time she threw it on the floor.

On the other end was a male voice hollering for her to pick up. Brenda knew it was Ray and she wasn't ready to talk to him. This was her pity party and he wasn't invited; after all, he was the reason she was mixed up in the first place.

Finally, she decided to get out of bed to prepare for her return to school. Hoping that a shower would energize her, she stood under the hot water for thirty minutes to wash away the pain and stress.

Again, loneliness overwhelmed her. Everywhere she went in the house reminded her of her mother. There were memories everywhere: on the coffee table, on the mantle, and on the wall.

"Momma, I need your strength," she whispered,

collapsing on the couch in tears.

Just then, there was a knock on the door. Exhausted, she went to open it. It was Ray.

"I came to check on you to see if you were okay. I tried calling you then I heard the telephone drop. When you didn't say anything, I got scared and ran over here," he said.

"I'm fine... you didn't need to drive all the way here," she said, walking back into the living room to lie down on the couch.

"Brenda, I want us to work things out. How long are you going to stay angry with me? I know I've made a lot of mistakes and I want to make it up to you.

"You're all I have in this world, baby, and I don't think I can survive without you in my life. Please forgive me." He bent down on one knee.

Brenda looked at Ray. She knew that she had heard all of this before. He would always do something to lose her trust then make promises to get her back under his spell.

As she watched the tears roll down his cheeks from his

dark brown eyes, her heart beginning to soften, she thought about how empty her life would be if she lost him, too. Her mother was gone. James was gone. There was no one else but Ray, and he wanted her. After all, she was really in no position to judge, since she'd just broken the heart of the only man who ever treated her with respect.

"Alright, I forgive you and I am willing to move past this as long as you put forth a better effort at respecting my feelings," she said, giving him a kiss.

They sat and talked about their future together. He shared his vision for his photography studio with her for the first time. This gave Brenda a new hope for their relationship. *Maybe things can work out after all,* she thought.

They stayed up until about 3 a.m. talking about how their lives were going to be, how many children they were going to have, where they were going to live, and what they were going to do when they got back to Atlanta. It all sounded like the dream life Brenda was praying for.

Since it was so late, she allowed Ray to stay the night in

her old room. She knew she wasn't quite ready to trust herself lying next to him, feeling the way she was feeling.

After a good night sleep, they packed everything. Brenda contacted a Realtor to put the house on the market. Everything was ready to be picked up and put in storage. It was time to put her old life behind her and start anew.

She knew that she could no longer call Charleston her home. It was no longer anything or anyone keeping her here. There were too many memories that caused her pain. She wanted to forget. She wanted to start over and create new memories with Ray and have a family of her own one day.

As she locked the door, Ray packed up the U-Haul, and they headed back to Atlanta.

LEVEL

III

Chapter 11

I WILL NEVER LEAVE YOU

The day had finally arrived. Waves of black caps encompassed the university grounds. Families came from all across the United States to witness their investments walk across the stage to receive their future rolled up and handed to them.

The day, however, was not as special as Brenda had hoped. She was happy all her hard work had paid off, but it had been a rough journey. She knew no one but the Lord had brought her this far, but with all the excitement, all she could do was feel sad.

She had always hoped Momma Greene would be sitting in the front row smiling and praising the Lord as she walked across the stage to receive her degree.

As she zipped up her gown, tears uncontrollably began to fall from her eyes. Looking for a tissue on her dresser, she saw her mother's Bible holding up her jewelry box. She removed the box, sat down on the bed and began to look through it. She turned to her mother's favorite scripture.

"***I will never leave you nor forsake you.***"

As she lifted the book to put it back on the dresser, an envelope fell to the floor. Brenda bent over to pick it up. It was addressed to her. Slowly she opened it. It read:

My dearest baby girl,

If you are reading this, you have done what I have asked you to do and finished school. I want you to know how proud I am of you. Know that I am always with you. I thank God everyday he brought you into my life.

Look after yourself. Follow your dreams. Don't let anything or anyone stop you from reaching them. When things get difficult, look to the hills from whence cometh your help. It comes from the Lord.

I know you have questions about your mother, Karen. Well, I tried to spare you the hurt that I've been feeling all these years. The truth is your mother was very young when she had you. She was only sixteen. She was a smart, beautiful girl with a promising future. Just like you. I tried my best to raise her right but somehow she fell with the wrong crowd, and the next thing I knew, she was telling me she was pregnant. She tried to get an abortion, but I found out from a friend of hers. I went into that clinic and dragged her out of there. I told her I would adopt you and raise you as my own.

After she gave birth, she packed her things one night and took off. She never told me who your father was. I only heard from her once a year. She kept moving from state to state. I always sent pictures of you to different P.O. Boxes. The last was in Atlanta, GA. This is the last address I have.

I love you, Bre-Bre.

Momma Greene.

Shocked and speechless, Brenda sat on the bed holding the picture of Karen in one hand and the letter in the other. So many emotions started rushing over her all at once: feelings of joy, confusion, excitement and anger. Tears came flowing down her face uncontrollably like a waterfall. *Why, why?* she asked herself. Just then Shannon burst into the room to her.

"What's wrong—what's the matter? Why are you crying? What's wrong?"

Barely able to speak, she handed Shannon the letter, then the picture of her mother. After reading the letter, Shannon just stood there with a blank expression on her face. She wasn't much for being spooked by supernatural things but even this was a bit much for her. She put her arms around Brenda and handed her a tissue to wipe her face.

"You know I'm not much for this spiritual stuff, girl, but even I think this is a sign from God."

"What do you mean?" Brenda asked.

"Brenda, don't you see? Your mother is with you and she is trying to tell you that it is time you go on with your life and walk across that stage, get your diploma, and follow your dreams," Shannon explained, lifting Brenda up off the bed.

"But what about my mother?" Brenda asked.

"What about your mother?" Shannon asked, handing

the picture back to Brenda.

"Don't you think I should try to find her? Isn't that what you think Momma Greene wants me to do?"

Looking at the old picture of her mother as a teenager, she could see her own eyes staring back at her.

"I think you should leave well enough alone! It is apparent that your "bio" momma knew where you were. If she wanted to see you she would have found you. As far as I am concerned, I would let that go and do what your "REAL" momma said and move on with your life. Now come on…we have a graduation to attend ….ours."

Brenda knew everything Shannon said was true, but deep down inside she was curious. She wanted to know more about her biological mother, who her father was, and why she had left her with Momma Greene. Did she still live in Atlanta?

But those questions weren't going to be answered today. Today was hers and Momma Greene's. Even though she wasn't there sitting on the front row, she knew she would be with her in spirit walking across the stage when she received her degree.

It wasn't easy but she did it. She waited patiently until they called her name, looking around at the hundreds of families and friends supporting her fellow classmates. Brenda couldn't help but feel sad, fighting back the tears.

Help me get through this, Momma, she whispered in her heart.

Finally her name was called. As she approached the stage, she heard her mother's voice cheering her on. She looked out into the audience and saw Momma Greene's smiling face; she was wearing her special blue dress with the gold and blue satin buttons she bought over two years ago just for this occasion.

They had taken a trip to New York for a friend's wedding and decided to do some shopping while in town. As they visited several stores, Momma Greene saw the dress hanging on a mannequin and immediately fell in love with it.

Brenda remembered how she'd looked trying it on in the store while she painted this beautiful picture of herself sitting on the front row at the graduation, cheering as Brenda received her degree.

Along side her, wearing a big smile and blowing kisses was James. He was looking as fine as ever in a handmade, Italian navy blue suit that fit him like a glove, with a bow tie. It was exactly how Brenda hoped it would be.

As she descended from the platform, she ran over to where she'd imagined they were sitting with her arms stretched out to hug them. With a tight grip she embraced a lady dressed in blue. As she lifted her head from the woman's chest, she continued in her fantasy. Shocked and a bit alarmed, the woman tried to push Brenda away. The young man standing with her tried to help loosen Brenda's grip.

"Momma, we did it. Thank you for being here. I know you couldn't stay away. I love you, Momma; this is for you." She said handing her the degree and kissing her, she then turned to the young man.

"James I am so glad you made it. I am so sorry for what happened. Please forgive me." Brenda reached out to give him a hug.

Watching from their seats in total disbelief and horror, Shannon and Ray ran over to stop Brenda from causing an even bigger scene. The audience was staring and whispering as the faculty attempted to proceed with the ceremony. They finally freed the terrified woman and escorted Brenda away from the activities. A good shake from Shannon finally brought her out of the trance-like state she was in.

Realizing what just transpired, she looked at Ray and Shannon and broke down.

"What did I just do?! Oh my God...everyone must think I'm crazy."

"Who cares what they think?" Ray said as he tried to comfort her.

"That's right! This has really been a trying year for you and today just brought it to a climax. Let's get you home so you can relax for a while. We still have some celebrating to do!" Shannon said.

After lying down for about two hours, Brenda woke to

voices coming through the walls of her apartment. Slowly sitting up, she could hear Shannon's voice getting louder.

"She needs you right now."

"I won't be gone that long. She'll be fine," Ray said.

"Can't you see that this year has taken its toll on her, that she might be on the verge of a nervous breakdown?" Shannon insisted.

"Keep your voice down...you'll wake her up," he said.

"Maybe she needs to wake up and see what kind of selfish bastard you really are. She needs to know how much you value your work more than her well-being." Shannon replied.

"I'm working hard for the both of us—for our future. This job can land me some really big clientele and the money can help me open my business sooner than expected. Vincent is riding me about coming up with my half of the money or we are going to lose the building...Look, I know you don't like me, but this isn't helping Brenda right now," he said, heading out the door.

"For once I agree with you. I don't like you, and us arguing isn't helping her. Just this once I'd like to see you put her needs and feelings before your own. This is one of the most important days in her life and all you can think about is your business...I swear on a stack of Bibles, if you aren't back here in three hours, Ray, you had better watch your back!" Shannon exclaimed, walking up to him pointing her finger in his face.

Brenda got up and walked out of the room to catch Ray before he left. She had hoped to spend a quiet evening with him. She knew Shannon wanted to throw a small gathering at the apartment with a few of their fellow graduates for dinner and partying at a local spot they frequented. After her fiasco at the ceremony, she knew she'd feel self conscious around them and she didn't want folk asking her if she was alright all evening.

"Where did Ray go?" Brenda asked.

"He had some business he had to attend to...he said he'd be back in about three hours, which leaves us plenty of time to celebrate with our fellow classmates one last time."

"Would you mind if I passed, Shannon? I'm really not feeling up to it. Not after I made a complete fool of myself at the graduation. I don't want anyone feeling sorry for me," she said, flopping down on the sofa.

"You need to stop worrying about everyone else, including Ray. For once think about you. Now I'm going to get dressed and head over to the restaurant. Call me if you change your mind, okay?" Shannon said as she headed to her room to change.

Hours passed and Brenda was getting a bit concerned. It was 10:30 p.m. and not a word from Ray. She tried watching television and reading a magazine just to pass the time and relax, but it wasn't working. She tried not to get upset.

What in the world could he be doing? This is supposed to be my day and here I am waiting on him.

Thoughts of James flashed through her mind as she remembered their evening together after she completed her internship from the Cancer Biology Program. She remembered how much fun they had together, how romantic and magical the evening was, and how he looked at her.

Visions of the night they'd spent together, how he held her under the moonlight, the smell of his cologne, the music, the entire atmosphere consumed her every thought. Reflecting on how he looked when he dropped his towel, took her imagination further than she dared to go in reality. She became all tingly inside as she envisioned him lifting her up and carrying her off into his bedroom.

The doorbell rang, shaking her out of her x-rated thoughts. Heading to the sink to splash some cold water on her face to cool herself down, she went to answer the door. It was a delivery man holding a beautiful bouquet of flowers.

"Ms. Greene…Brenda Greene?"

"Yes, I'm Brenda Greene."

"Sign here please."

Taking a big whiff she signed and gave him a tip.

They're so beautiful. Why didn't Ray bring them in

person? I guess this means he isn't going to make it back in time, she said to herself as she pulled the card from the clip. It read:

Congratulations on your graduation!

James.

She almost collapsed from shock. *I thought he hated me and never wanted to see or hear from me again!*

Her mind started to wander back to the afternoon they spent together in Charleston. She reminisced on how much fun they had on their picnic on Marion Square and how romantic James was as he fed her fresh strawberries and blueberries they'd purchased from the local vendors at the Farmer's Market. Tears began to slowly drop from Brenda's exhausted eyes.

This time it was the ringing of the phone that snapped her out of her what seemed to be an ongoing pity party.

"Hello"

"Hi, girl. How you feeling? Has Ray come back yet?" Shannon asked.

"No, I haven't heard from him."

"Well, me and the guys are over at the club; why don't you come on over and join us for a while? It might take your mind off some things," Shannon said, screaming over the loud noises in the background.

"Thanks, but I don't know if I would be good company," she murmured, sniffing the flowers and wiping away the last of the tears from her eyes.

"Well, if you won't come here, I will come back home and we can have our own celebration… just the two of us," Shannon said as she turned down a dance request.

"No, don't do that. Don't ruin your night on account of me," she said begging her. Before Brenda could talk her out of it, Shannon hung up the phone.

Knowing Shannon was going to get her way, she sat back down on the couch to finish watching television, hoping to distract the thoughts from her mind with not much success. Suddenly James' face appeared in place of every black man on the television screen. Shaking her head like a wet dog trying to snap herself out her day dream, she began to pace the floor. In what seemed like mere minutes, Shannon entered the apartment holding a big paper bag.

"Girl, what are you doing home so early?" Brenda asked.

"I got tired of the loud music and all the smoke. Besides, I couldn't really enjoy myself knowing that you were sitting here all by your lonesome. So I stopped by the grocery store and picked up your favorite ice cream, banana fudge, and a pack of Oreos," she said as she opened the container. Grabbing two spoons from the drawer, she handed one to Brenda.

"Girl, you are a great friend...I don't know what I would do without you." Brenda smiled, taking a scoop of ice cream out of the container.

Eleven o'clock... twelve o'clock...one o'clock—they sat talking and laughing about the past four years in college and all the people they'd had the opportunity to encounter along their journey at Spelman. They even discussed the first time they met one another.

Meanwhile, in the midst of all the recollections and reminiscing, the thought of Ray constantly scattered across Brenda's mind as the time passed. Shannon, noticing Brenda drifting off from time to time in the middle of the conversation, decided to talk a bit of nonsense to see if she was paying attention to her.

Realizing that it wasn't working, she kicked her. "OUCH! Why did you do that?" Brenda exclaimed rubbing her ankle.

"Because you're not paying me any attention."

Trying to think of the last thing Shannon said before she drifted off into la-la land, she came up with nothing.

"Yes I am I heard every word you said."

"Honey, you know your mind is on Ray," Shannon said in her *I-told-you-so* voice.

"Don't start," Brenda said, holding her hand up to her face as to block whatever Shannon was about to say.

"Don't dis me sweetie...cause you know that ain't

gonna stop me from saying what I got to say."

Bracing herself for what she knew was going to be the brutal honest truth in a way only Shannon could bring, she placed her elbow on the armrest of the sofa as to soften the blows of truth about to come blasting through her eardrums.

"Go ahead let me hear it since you are the expert on men and how I should handle mine. Even though you don't seem to keep one long enough to know how I'm feeling," Brenda said, knowing that she might live to regret those words.

"I know you think I've always been able to handle men, that I haven't been in a serious relationship a day in my life, and that I couldn't possibly know how you're feeling, but that isn't true," she said, looking deep into Brenda's eyes as if she was trying to pierce some deep revelation into her brain.

Bracing her back on the couch in anticipation, Shannon had her full attention.

What deep dark secret was she about to reveal? After all, Shannon was a rock and nothing seemed to faze her as far as men were concern. When she gets bored, she kicks them to the curb. If they do or say something she doesn't like, she sets them straight. She never lets anyone take advantage of her nor does she settle for the average Joe off the street. What could she possibly tell me that's so deep it's causing her to look so serious and on the brink of tears?

Waiting for Shannon to form the words after what was an extremely nerve racking five minute pause, Brenda realized something different about Shannon. She couldn't quite explain it, but she seemed a bit more humbled. Finally Shannon began to speak.

"I know you think I was always this strong black woman you see before you who never takes shit from these trifling-ass men, but I wasn't always this way. I used to be just like you, only a lot more naive and a lot younger...

"I met this guy when I was sixteen working at Wendy's in high school. Girl, he was fine and a lot older than I was, maybe about thirty two. Anyway, he would come in every night about ten just to get a frosty and an order of fries.

He did this for about a month until one day he and I started talking. He then began to flirt with me constantly, asking me for my telephone number until one day, I finally broke down and gave it to him. He called a few times and we talked, mostly about me..."

"Whenever I would ask him something about himself, he would avoid answering and turn the conversation back to me. During this time, I was living with some messed up foster parents who were hardly ever home, so I could stay out late and pretty much do whatever I wanted. He and I would go out after I got off work and go to dinner or a movie or to night clubs.

"I started drinking, smoking, and he bought me nice, expensive clothes, shoes...you name it; I got it. Before I knew it, I was falling head over heels in love with this man. If he told me the sky was made of $100 bills, I would have believed him...

"Brenda, he was my first. I would have done anything for him…and I did." Tears began to flow down her face.

This was the first time Brenda had ever seen Shannon cry. In her mind, Shannon had only one emotion and that was no-nonsense.

As Shannon continued, Brenda braced up on the couch, trying not to show any emotion other than compassion for her friend. She reached for a tissue and gave it to Shannon, which for once was a big change, considering it was usually the other way around. She clung to every word that came out of her mouth.

"After about two weeks of endless sex and partying, he asked me to meet some friends of his at an apartment not far from where I worked. They were going to have a big celebration for him because he had closed some big deal for his company and he wanted to show me off to his coworkers...I agreed, of course..."

"There were about three big dudes and one other girl about my age or a little older dressed in a skimpy bathing suit dancing on a coffee table where there were all types of drugs. I told Stan (that was his name) I didn't feel comfortable around all that stuff, and he turned into someone I didn't recognize. He said if I wanted to continue to be with him I had to be more grown up and do grown up things, so..."

Here Shannon took a long pause before continuing, "...so that night I started doing drugs and the next thing I knew, I was having sex with all of his so-called friends while he sat there and watched!" Brenda sat stiff as a statue and just as speechless.

"After it was all over, I felt so sick to my stomach and so sore I could hardly move. He didn't say a word to me all the way home. He just looked at me and told me to **GET OUT**!

"Weeks went by and I didn't hear from him, so I asked some of the girls who worked with me if they had seen him or knew where he worked. They didn't know, so I tried looking him up in the phone book and called the company to ask if he worked there...no one knew who he was. To make a long story short, the man worked at a strip club on the South side of town as a bouncer, he was married, and had two small kids in diapers..." Shannon swiped at the one tear clinging to her lashes.

"You see I never asked him a lot of personal information. I just assumed that he was on the up-and-up. After I found all this stuff out, it was too late. I was three months pregnant with that fool's baby, and I was smoking weed and popping pills to numb the pain. When I finally did see him again, I told him about the baby and he just laughed in my face, telling me to get rid of it..." There was another long pause and a deep intake of breath.

"I had no money and my foster parents kicked me out, so I stayed with another family who helped me get an abortion and put me in rehab for about four months until I got clean. After I got out, they were kind enough to let me stay with them until I got a job and finished school...

"I was determined after all of that that I was never going to let another man hurt me or use me or even get that close to me ever again," she said, composing herself as she returned to her normal no-nonsense self.

Brenda began to realize she had misjudged Shannon all these years. She also realized she wasn't as good a friend to Shannon as Shannon was to her. Not once had she asked Shannon ***why*** she was the way she was towards men. Now she understood why Shannon disliked Ray so much. It all started to make perfect sense.

"Girl, why didn't you share all of this with me sooner? After all it's a wonder you still like men," Brenda said, giving her a big hug.

"Girl, back up off of me... I don't swing that way," Shannon said, pushing Brenda away from her as she burst out laughing.

"I had something bad happen to me, I've learned from it, and I'm over it. You know the saying…that which does not kill us only makes us strong….or some crap like that."

The hours continued to pass as Brenda and Shannon talked. Before they knew it, it was daylight. Exhausted, they fell asleep on the couch.

Suddenly, there was a knock on the door. Half-asleep,

Brenda dragged herself to the door, tip-toeing around the coffee table and kicking aside the empty ice cream container in order to not wake up Shannon.

"Who is it?" she whispered.

"It's me, baby… Ray."

Excited and upset, she reluctantly opened the door.

"Good morning, babe. I know you are angry with me and I know I deserve it, but please let me explain," he said, bending down to give her a kiss on the cheek while attempting to hug her.

"Keep your voice down...Shannon is asleep on the couch," she said, whispering while shutting the door behind him.

"My bad. Can we go in your room so we can talk in private so we don't disturb her?" he said, hoping to avoid waking Shannon up and getting into another altercation with her.

Brenda, secretly hoping that Shannon would wake up so she could tear into Ray and say all the things she wanted to say, agreed, and they went into her room.

"Before you go off on me, I just want to say how sorry I am for not coming back last night. I didn't mean to be gone that long, but once you hear what I have to say, I hope you will forgive me," Ray said as he took Brenda's hand, looking deeply into her eyes.

What could possibly be more important than spending time with me on one of the most important and yet most difficult days of my life? she thought, gathering the strength to call off the engagement.

Pulling two pieces of paper from his pocket, he smiled broadly. "This and this." He handed the papers and a set of keys and two set of wedding bands to Brenda.

She opened the papers. It was the deed to a building in downtown Atlanta. Totally flabbergasted, she sat on the bed to catch her breath and collect her thoughts.

"Look, I know this is sudden, but I don't want to wait another second to start our life together. I love you and now that things are finally going the way I want them to, this is the only logical thing to do—make you my wife today," he explained on bended knee as he kissed her left hand. Brenda had never been more perplexed in her life.

Why did he pick out the wedding bands without me? What is the big rush all of a sudden? What will Shannon say? What about James?

All these thoughts came rushing to her mind, but before she could say anything, Ray pulled out his cell phone and called Pastor Benjamin, making the arrangements. Still in shock, he handed her the phone. *What does he expect me to say to this man? I don't know if I'm ready to get married right now,* she reasoned within herself.

"Babe, I can't wait for us to start our life together. I know you've been feeling a little depressed, and I know I haven't been emotionally available the way you needed me too, but all that is going to change when you and I make it legal. I promise you, babe, I'm going to be the best husband and father to our children..."

Brenda only heard white noise until he got to the part

about children. She'd always wanted to have a big family because of her being an only child. The fact Ray mentioned children was surprising to her because the only time they had ever discussed it was when they first met. Even then, he didn't say he wanted to have any.

After hours of convincing, Brenda finally gave in. This was something she had been hoping for since she first laid eyes on him, and today it was finally becoming a reality.

The day ended with them getting their marriage license and her standing in their church before her Pastor and first lady. Shannon reluctantly agreed to be her maid of honor, all the while trying to talk her out of rushing into something she felt Brenda would eventually regret.

Chapter 12

"WELL TO DO?"

"So this is what marriage is all about," Brenda said, looking at her ring and wondering what it really represented.

For the past eight years she had tried to make it work. Finally, Brenda had the life she thought she wanted with the man of her dreams and the job of a lifetime in the cancer research department at Emory University as one of their top researchers.

Ray's photography studio was doing well and his clientele was growing. They were both very active in their church and were approached by Pastor Benjamin to help one of the more seasoned married couples in the church with the married couples' ministry.

Things seemed to be going well for a while until after about the fifth year. Ray became more distant. He had been taking on more freelance work with local and out of state modeling agencies, which often took him out of the country on assignments. He began to find fault with everything Brenda said and did. He was no longer giving her the attention and time she so desperately wanted and needed as a woman. With each passing day, they were becoming more like roommates instead of husband and wife.

She tried everything she could possibly think of to get Ray to open up to her. Reaching for her computer to search for cruises and mountain retreats, she thought, *Maybe things aren't going well at the studio. We've both have been working too hard these past few years perhaps we need to get away for a while and reconnect....after all we've never really had a honeymoon.*

After months of trying to talk to Ray about his Dr. Jekyll and Mr. Hide personality with no success, Brenda decided to reach out to Pastor Benjamin for advice. They scheduled several appointments but Ray never showed. He always had to go out of town on a photo shoot, so most of the sessions were canceled or she went alone.

"I don't know if I want to stay in this marriage anymore. Ray isn't affectionate, he's distant, and he's always preoccupied with work. This isn't what I signed up for," she said, grabbing the handkerchief from her purse.

"Perhaps the two of you should schedule a date night and talk things over," her pastor said.

"I've tried that, and I've tried scheduling a romantic getaway and giving him his space, and nothing seems to work. I don't know what else to do. Pastor, can you try talking to him?"

"Maybe he and I can get together away from church and talk man to man," he said as he escorted her to the door.

"Thanks for everything."

"I just want you two to work things out. Marriage is hard work and a lot of people your age just want to have a wedding and a honeymoon. They don't really know how hard it is."

After the counseling session, she decided to reward herself to a stress free afternoon at the day spa. *I can sure use this*, she thought as she undressed. While lying on the table, the soft eclectic music and the sweet smell of lavender began to lull her into a deep trance.

"Hello. My name is Charles and I will be your masseuse this afternoon. Is there a particular area you would like me to focus on?"

She was nervous; being rubbed down in hot oil in a dark room by this good-looking black man with a deep sultry voice was not what she had bargained for, although taking care of herself was something she had been neglecting for quite a while.

"Hum…huh…I've been having problems with my neck," she said, staring at his chest as she pointed to the specific location.

"Well, let's get the kink out, shall we? Why don't you lie down, and I will work my magic," he said as he rubbed the warm lotion in his large hands.

Brenda began to feel calm as his soft hands caressed her neck. They were strong but gentle as they manipulated every part of her until she felt like wet noodles hanging out to drain. All the tension and stress from her marriage seemed to melt away until she fell asleep.

She could hear the sounds of the ocean crashing as she found herself back on the balcony of James' beach house with smooth jazz playing from his stereo.

"Here's your drink, baby. Why don't you sit back while I massage your feet?" James said, pulling off her sandals.

This was a dream Brenda did not want to wake up from.

"Come with me," he said, leading her into the bathroom where there were lit candles around his massive tub that four people could fit into.

Slowly he undressed her and lifted her into the tub. "Tonight I am your servant and you are my master. Tell me what you want me to do," he said, removing his clothing as he stepped into the tub.

"Ma'am…..ma'am, our secession is over for today," a

deep voice said, snapping her out of her fantasy.

"Wow, that truly was nice and I feel wonderful. I didn't mean to fall asleep. I hope I didn't snore?" Brenda said, praying she didn't say or do anything sexual.

"What happens in our sessions stays in our sessions," the masseuse said as he gave her a big smile as though he knew what she was dreaming about. "I will leave you to get dressed. I hope you will come back and see me again. Here's my card. You can pay the cashier up front."

Lord, what is the matter with me? Why after all these years am I still dreaming about James? That man has probably moved on with a wife and five kids by now. Girl, you just need to get a grip and focus on the here and now. She was trying to convince herself that the dream didn't mean anything.

When she arrived home, a strong since of loneliness overcame her. She sat in the driveway staring at the house. Memories of her home back in Charleston replaced the vision of the place she called home with Ray. She remembered watching Momma Greene digging in her garden while talking to Ms. Liz about her secret for keeping the cats and raccoons out of her yard. Snapping herself out of her day dream, Brenda slowly opened the car door and breathed a big sigh of desperation and emptiness. Sounds of the television penetrated her eardrums as she turned the knob to enter.

She walked towards the den. Ray was lying across the couch with empty bottles of beer on the coffee table while a half consumed bottle hung from his lifeless fingers. She'd noticed his drinking had become more frequent over the last few months. Whenever she would mention it to him, he would dismiss it as just his way of relaxing after a hard day's work. Brenda turned off the television, cleaned up the mess, took her shower, and went to bed alone.

She lay there crying herself to sleep again, thinking about all she had given up to be in this marriage and how different things would have been had she just told James the truth and broke off her engagement with Ray.

She could hear her mother's voice: "Bre-Bre, you need

to save those tears for when you get married."

Momma Greene told her this whenever she would cry over something trivial like getting a B on her test when she felt she deserved an A.

Now I know what she meant. Lord help me, I can't go on like this. I can't live like this for the rest of my life. She banged her fist on the pillow.

Just then she heard a still small voice say, "***Weeping may endure for a night, but joy comes in the morning.***" She took a deep breath, wiped her tears, and drifted off to sleep.

Although most people would hate getting up at four in the morning, Brenda looked forward to leaving the house and keeping her mind occupied. She looked forward to going into the cancer ward and visiting the children and holding their hands while they took their chemo. She knew that most of the patients didn't have family that lived nearby, so she made an effort to make them feel welcome while they visited the hospital. One patient in particular, Ms. Betty Mae Cook, was her personal favorite because she reminded her so much of Momma Greene. Ms. Cook was known as Ms. Betty on the ward.

Ms. Betty was an eighty-year-old, heavy-set woman with a thick New York accent. She was diagnosed with ovarian cancer over ten months prior and had been coming in for experimental treatments. Her home was Brooklyn, New York by way of Beaufort, South Carolina, but she moved to Atlanta about ten years earlier to be close to her son who worked for a prestigious law firm that Ms. Betty could never seem to remember the name of.

Brenda enjoyed sitting and talking with Ms. Betty whenever she would get a break from the lab. She would laugh at all of her quirky sayings and remedies she'd had for curing everything from warts to athlete's foot and at how she would often reach for her wig and makeup whenever a man would enter the room.

She often told Brenda, "I don't care what you are going through, you need to keep yourself up and pamper yourself because life is too short."

Ms. Betty also liked to make passes at the younger male doctors and interns, then say little comments that would make Brenda blush. "Shoot, the bottom half of me may be out of commission but my main organ can still imagine," she'd remark.

Ms. Betty would doze off in the middle of the conversation but always woke up just before Brenda left to go back to work.

"Honey, you don't look so good. Why don't you tell Ms. Betty all about it?" she said with her eyes half open.

"It's nothing; I didn't get much sleep last night, that's all," Brenda said, looking down at her paper work so Ms. Betty couldn't read the expression on her face.

"Girl, don't lie to me. I've been on this planet long enough to know when a woman is having man troubles and when a woman has been crying over one. Shoot, I've done my share."

Brenda gave her a hug and a kiss on her forehead.

"You need to get some rest, and I'll check in on you tomorrow, okay?"

Just as she turned to walk towards the door, in came this tall, handsome man with a short neatly shaven Afro that connected to his nicely groomed mustache and beard. His eyes were dark brown and penetrated directly into Brenda's. He wore a nicely tailored grey suit. He looked like he stepped right of a GQ magazine.

Frozen in her tracks by the intoxicating aroma permeating from this man, she found herself sizing him up to see if he was wearing a wedding band.

"Hi, Momma. I just came to see how my favorite girl was feeling today." He looked directly into Brenda's eyes as he walked passed her to Ms. Betty's bedside.

"I'm doing just find now that my favorite son is here," she said, giving him a kiss on his cheek.

"I'm your only son."

"Well, then you know I'm telling the truth," she said as they both laughed.

"Brenda, this is my son, Jason Mathew Cook III, Attorney. Isn't he a good looking young man?" She was pinching his cheeks as though he were a five year old.

"Nice to meet you. I'm Brenda Greene. Your mother speaks very highly of you."

"Brenda works here at the hospital. What is it that you do again, sweetie?" Ms. Betty asked, adjusting her wig.

"I'm the head researcher in the cancer center."

"My, how fascinating. So you are the genius that's going to find a cure for this horrible disease that's trying to take my favorite lady from me," he said, smiling at Brenda and flashing his pearly whites.

"Well, I hope so. She is a fighter and so far she is responding well to the treatments. I should be getting back to work. It was nice to meet you."

As soon as Brenda turned to walk away, Jason called out to her.

"Do you mind if I have a word with you in the hall? Momma, I'll be right back."

Brenda felt a little uneasy, but she stepped outside the room with Jason anyway.

"I want to thank you for taking time out of your busy schedule to spend time with my mother. I work such long hours and don't get to visit as often as I'd like, and when I do come by she is so weak from the drugs and treatment she hardly knows I'm in the room. I worry about her so much." He was trying to man up as he held back the tears.

At that moment, Brenda wanted to put her arms around this tall statuette of a man, but she knew she wouldn't be able to reach. She empathized with his pain.

"It is my pleasure. Your mother reminds me so much of my momma. She was a character as well."

"Was?"

"Yes, my mother passed away years ago from liver cancer."

"I'm so sorry to hear that. I guess you really do understand what I'm going through. I know you have to get back to work. I hope we can talk again," Jason said, taking

Brenda's hand to shake it.

Ever since that day, whenever Brenda would visit Ms. Betty, Ms. Betty would talk about her son and how impressed he was with Brenda and how he would ask if Brenda came by to see her, and what time of day she would stop in.

Ms. Betty knew Brenda was married, and she told Brenda about Jason's soon to be ex-wife, Cynthia, who, in her opinion, was a low-down, gold-digging heifer who didn't like her, and about how Cynthia wanted to place her in a nursing home when her son told her she was coming to live with them.

One day after finishing her paperwork, she bumped into Jason in the parking garage. "Well, hello there, stranger. I thought I'd never see you again. How have you been?" He hugged her as if they were long lost friends. Brenda was a bit stunned by his display of affection to someone he had only met once.

"Hello, how are you? How is Ms. Betty doing today? I've been so swamped with paperwork I haven't had a chance see her in a few days," she said, looking straight into his eyes.

"Momma is coming along as well as to be expected. They said she may come home if things keep going the way they've been going with her treatment," he said, walking her to her car.

"Well, I'm sure she would be ecstatic about leaving the hospital and the food."

Before she knew, it they had talked for more than thirty minutes.

"I can't believe how late it is. I'm so sorry for keeping you from getting home. I'm sure your husband is waiting patiently for his lovely wife. I know I'd be pacing the floor," he said, smiling as he opened the car door for her.

If you only knew how wrong you are and how much I would rather stay in this garage talking to you, she said to herself, waving goodbye to him and starting the ignition.

Driving home, she couldn't believe how comfortable she felt with Jason. It was a strange but somehow familiar feeling. She knew that Jason was flirting with her, but she dared not think that it was anything more than his personality.

Again, the overwhelming feeling of frustration consumed her as she approached her street.

Lord help me! she thought, not knowing what she would find when she opened the door. *Maybe he won't be there and I can just zone out.*

When she pulled in the garage, Ray's car wasn't there. Brenda's countenance changed and she began to relax her shoulders then entered the house. She walked straight to the bathroom and began to fill the tub with hot water and prepared a nice bubble bath, lit some candles, and played some smooth jazz on the stereo. Once again, her imagination ran away with her. This time it wasn't James but Jason who consumed her thoughts.

Every day she would look forward to going to the hospital to see Ms. Betty. During each visit, she would mention her son and how much he was impressed with Brenda. Brenda would hang around hoping to run into Jason but often missed him because she'd arrive too late or leave to soon. After months of dealing with her frustrations about her marriage, she sought help from one of her coworkers, Sonya.

Brenda met Sonya five years ago when she first arrived at Emory. They worked closely with Administrators to raise money for cancer research. The two of them hit it off from the very beginning. Brenda felt that she was sent by God as a replacement for Shannon. Both of them had so much in common. Shannon was very out spoken and direct, and so was Sonya. Shannon had a no-nonsense approach when it came to men and so did Sonya. The only difference between the two of them was Sonya was a 45-year-old divorcee with three kids.

Unlike Shannon, Sonya didn't get the way she was until her husband left her for a white woman with five kids, no job, no shape, and no education.

Brenda enjoyed living vicariously through Sonya because she was now single and shared all her dating experiences with her. Sonya was proud of her new status and often told Brenda she was happy her husband left her before she got too old and everything went completely south.

Sonya was a short woman, about 4 feet 10 inches tall,

with pecan brown skin; she was a very pretty woman and had a nice curvy shape for a woman her age with three kids.

She had shown Brenda several pictures of her ex. The two of them were a strange pair. He was six feet four, with a slender build and fairly attractive. Brenda had her share of questions for Sonya when it came to how she ended up with a man that tall. She told her she had always dated tall men, then she'd laughed and comment on how true the rumors were about their hands and feet.

Sonya shared with Brenda how lonely she was for years in her marriage. She said her husband was a good provider and an excellent lover, but he just couldn't remain faithful to her. They were only married a year when she found him in her house with another woman. Being young and madly in love, she forgave him then he cheated on her again when she was pregnant with their second child, but she forgave him again because she didn't want her children to grow up without their father. The last time he cheated on her, she said she lost her mind because he gave her an STD and she was pregnant with her third child.

This time she found out about the affair when she went to her doctor's office for her checkup. She told the doctor she was having burning sensations when she urinated. When the doctor came back with the results, she leaped off of the table, almost forgetting to put on her clothes. She got dressed, picked up her kids, drove them to her mom's, went home, went under her side of the bed, and pulled out her loaded .45 and waited for him to come through the door. Sonya said she doesn't know how long she sat there, but it was about 11 p.m. when he opened the door and about 11:30 when the police showed up at her door and arrested her for attempted murder.

Her husband spent two weeks in the hospital after having been shot in his inner thigh two inches from his groin. She said her husband didn't press charges because he knew what he had done and he didn't want the mother of his children in prison. However, she did spend the night in jail and had to pay a $1,000 bail. They tried to work things out after the third child was born, but he hooked up with the hot mess he's with now after Sonya stopped sleeping with him.

Brenda shared with Sonya all the issues she was facing on in her marriage and how lonely and frustrated she'd become over the years.

"Sounds like he's got a chick on the side, honey," she said giving her that crooked smile she'd usually make with her face when she was certain about something.

Brenda didn't want to believe what Sonya said was true, but deep down inside knew it could be a possibility. She remembered how much Ray had hurt her in the past and promised that he would never break her heart that way again. In some strange way, she was hoping that it might be true because at least that would be a logical explanation for the way he was behaving. It would be better than not knowing if he was tired of her or using her for her money and contacts she had acquired for him over the years through the hospital's various parties and fundraisers they attended.

"Girl, why don't you go with me to the gym?" Sonya asked.

"When did you join a gym?" Brenda asked, looking her up and down.

"Yesterday. Girl, I'm not getting any younger and my kids are practically grown and out of the house. I need to keep my girlish figure before it all goes south for the winter, spring into menopause, summer flashes, and completely falls." Both of them fell out laughing. Brenda needed that. She agreed, but needed some workout clothes, so they went shopping.

When they arrived at the gym, Brenda felt so awkward. She had never worked out a day in her life. Sweating and showing agony in front of a bunch of strangers let alone a bunch of good looking, toned, men and women was not something she had ever wanted to do. Sonya approached the reception desk and showed her ID.

"This is my guest, Brenda Greene. She will be checking out your facility today," she said, retrieving her locker key from her bag.

Brenda was impressed with all of the amenities they offered for their members. She knew this was no ordinary club. This club was for the "well-to-dos," as Momma Greene would say. She wondered how Sonya was able to afford such an exclusive membership.

"Girl, how in the world could you afford a membership to this place?"

"Well, if you must know, I won this membership when we had the silent auction two weeks ago."

"I don't remember seeing a sheet for this facility on the display table."

"I know. I kept it way in the back out of view, and then I stayed close to the table so no one would be able to get to it."

"Girl, you know you were wrong for that."

"I know, right? God please forgive me, but I was desperate. Between the kids, bills, and the job, I just needed something to help me relax," she said holding up her hand as if God were giving her a high-five.

The gym was crowded with so-called "well-to-do" black folk who looked as though they'd been working out all their lives. Every female had on something short and tight showing off every detail of her toned curves. Women were lifting weights, running on the treadmills, and taking spin and yoga classes while the hot guys flexed their muscles, lifting 250lbs, wanting to impress. Fear overcame Brenda as she approached the only thing in the gym she felt she could control.

This looks like something I can start off with, she said to herself as she attempted to read the directions, punching in her weight.

"Do you need some help with the machine?" the young lady, asked watching Brenda struggle with the machine.

"Yes, thank you."

When she finally got the hang of it, she took out her book and began to read while walking at a steady flow. As soon as her heart rate began to build, she heard a familiar deep voice say, "Hello there, stranger…funny running into you here."

Slowly Brenda gazed up; there was Jason with a big

smile on his face looking excited to see her.

"I didn't know you worked out here. Isn't this a nice surprise?" His eyes were beaming up and down her figure.

"This is my first time coming here, or working out for that matter," she said, feeling awkward and smelly.

"Well, I hope this won't be your last. It would be nice if we could work out together sometime. Maybe I can be your personal trainer," he said laughing.

She got off of the treadmill in mid-motion and almost stumbled onto the floor. Jason stretched out his hand to catch her. Brenda fell gracefully into his arms.

Even with sweaty armpits this man smells good. It had been a long time since she had been held. It felt good. She needed the touch of a man, even if he wasn't hers.

Instead of continuing her workout, Brenda sat and talked in the cafe located on the second floor overlooking the entire facility. She could see Sonya flirting with two guys near the freestyle machine. Every now and then she would catch Sonya looking up at her and giving her the thumbs up.

Attempting to ignore her, she'd turn to Jason and continue her conversation.

"I was hoping I'd see you again. It's been a while since I've seen you at the hospital," he expressed, looking deep into her eyes.

"I haven't had a chance to visit your mother as much as I used to. I've been so busy."

"You need to relax and enjoy yourself. You work too hard. Say, I know a nice place right downtown that plays jazz; the manager and I are good friends. Why don't we go check it out?" he said as he grabbed her hand.

For a moment, Brenda was tempted. She was about to say yes until Jason slightly touched her hand and she saw her wedding ring.

"I'm here with my girlfriend."

"She can come along."

"I didn't bring anything nice to change into," she quickly expressed, hoping that this would be a good enough excuse.

"Did you come here in your workout clothes?"

"No, I changed out of my work clothes."

"No problem. It's a really casual place. Get your friend. Get freshened up and I'll meet you guys outside."

What just happened? She went down to get Sonya and filled her in on what had just taken place. Elated, Sonya agreed, broke away from the men she was flirting with, and ran to the showers.

"Okay girl, when we get to the car you remind me about all the planning we have to do for some big fundraiser for the hospital…okay?" she plotted, rushing to get dressed. Laughing, Sonya held the door for Brenda has she continued to get her exit strategy together.

"Sonya, I'm not playing. You know I can't go out with this man. I'm a married woman. You of all people shouldn't be encouraging me."

"I'm not encouraging you to do anything. I don't see what the harm is in having a little innocent fun with a friend," Sonya said, smirking.

"Friends? When did he and I become friends? I barely know the man," she said, trying to make her point. As they approached the lobby, Brenda's palms started to sweat. She continued to give Sonya the eye to remind her of the excuse they had collaborated together; however, Sonya was more focused on getting a better look at Jason.

"Are you beautiful ladies ready to paint the town?" he asked opening, the door of the gym to escort them outside to their cars.

"Well, aren't you charming?" Sonya responded as she gave Brenda the eye of approval. "We're more than ready!" Sonya bellowed out, forgetting what they had discussed.

"Sonya, aren't you forgetting something?" she asked, trying to prompt Sonya to remember her line.

"No."

"Didn't you tell me we had to work on the fundraiser coming up soon?" She hoped Sonya would play along this time.

"Girl, I forgot to tell you it was rescheduled, so we

have a little more time to work on it than I thought." Jason's face changed from disappointment to happy all in a matter of seconds.

They followed Jason to the club. Brenda questioned Sonya about her not sticking to the plan. She told Brenda she needed to step out of her comfort zone every once and awhile. Brenda agreed and decided to call Ray to let him know she wouldn't be home until late.

When he answered, it sounded as if she had awakened him out of a deep sleep. Not that concerned, he told her to have a good time and he would probably be gone when she got home because he had to leave on an early flight to Chicago for a couple of days. Feeling a bit disappointed that he didn't ask her to come home and spend time with him, she hung up the phone abruptly and decided she wasn't going to waste any more time thinking about Ray and how he was treating her. She was going to enjoy her life.

Brenda loved the band and the conversation she and Jason were having. He was funny and attentive; something

Brenda hadn't had from Ray in a long time. They were having such a good time that she almost forgot Sonya was even there.

"Brenda, I wish I could stay and hang out with you guys, but I need to be getting home. I got an early day tomorrow," she said smirking.

"Well, Jason, I guess that's my cue. I had a great time tonight. Thanks for inviting us," she said, preparing to leave with Sonya.

"Do you have to leave? I really enjoyed spending time with you tonight. I thought we could go get a bite to eat and talk about my mother's treatment," he asked, hoping she would agree.

"Girl, didn't you tell me you didn't have to work tomorrow and that Ray was out of town tonight? All you are going to do is sit at home and be depressed," Sonya said after pulling Brenda to the side.

"I can't hang out with this man like that. I'm married and so is he."

"Well, I don't see anything wrong with getting

something to eat and talking about his mothers' health concerns," Sonya said.

A bit perplexed, she looked at Jason. Thoughts of the conversation she had with Ray on the way to the club plus the way he had been treating her all rushed to her brain, and before she knew it, she agreed to let him take her out for a late supper.

Chapter 13

THE SEVENTH COMMANDMENT

After that night Brenda and Jason became really close friends. Whenever he'd stop by the hospital to visit his mother, he made sure he called Brenda beforehand to see if she was working so that they could have lunch. She really began to enjoy the time and attention Jason was giving her. She had not realized how much she missed having a man pay her compliments and treat her like she was special. To her, he was a breath of fresh air and she could finally exhale and relax without feeling like she was walking on egg shells.

He made her laugh and showed interest in what was going on in life. He was attentive and smart. Shc hadn't fclt this comfortable around another man since James.

Brenda listened as Jason talked about his wife and how unhappy he was in his marriage. She began to feel more like a therapist as she tried to convince Jason to work things out with her. She even invited him to visit her church and said maybe he could talk to her Pastor as well as suggested the two of them go to a marriage counselor. He just kept insisting that there was no hope for the two of them.

"We both want different things out of life," he explained. "I guess we just fell out of love a long time ago."

The longer she listened, the more she could relate to everything he said. The more time they spent together, the more Brenda looked forward to seeing Jason. Whenever she and Ray would have a disagreement, or he ignored her, she would pick up the phone and call Jason and instantly she would cheer up.

"Something must be wrong with that Negro. If I had you for my wife I would worship the ground you walked on. I would never leave you alone. The places I would take you. The things the two of us could do," he'd express.

Brenda found herself imagining herself with Jason traveling to all these places.

Snap out of it, girl. You can't go there with this man.

You are a married woman and he is a married man, she'd say to herself to try and get a grip on reality, but secretly she hoped it was possible.

More time went by, and finally Brenda started looking forward to getting up in the morning. She started attending the gym on a regular basis. She bought herself a whole new wardrobe. She changed her hairstyle and started scheduling weekly massages, manicures and pedicures, and Ray started to take notice in her behavior.

"What have you been up to lately?" he said, looking her up and down as she prepared dinner.

"Not much."

"What are you making?"

"A salad."

"Well, how about I take you out for dinner tonight? And maybe we could go to a movie," he said, reaching for her hand.

What's up with him? she thought to herself. It had been a while since they went to dinner and a movie. "Okay, just let me change."

"I'll see what's playing," he said as he opened the paper.

They enjoyed a nice meal at a local Chinese restaurant. Ray tried to strike up a conversation asking her about work. She could hear him talking but her mind was elsewhere.

"Brenda.....Brenda!"

"Huh?"

Ray became frustrated. "Where did you go? You've been doing that a lot lately," he said.

"Doing what?"

"Daydreaming, that's what. What's wrong? And don't tell me nothing!"

"I don't know what you're talking about. We probably should leave so we won't miss the beginning of the movie."

Ray was baffled. He knew Brenda was hiding something and he was determined to get to the bottom of it, but he knew if he pushed too hard she would shut down completely. He watched her as they drove to the movie and as they sat in the theater. She was closed off. This was unlike Brenda. *I'm losing her,* he thought.

They arrived home and Brenda went straight to her room to turn on the TV and got undressed. Ray walked into the bedroom. He stood against the door watching her. Brenda pretended not to notice him standing there. She knew if they began to talk, she would have to tell Ray how she really felt.

"Are you going to tell me what's wrong with you?"

"Please, Ray. I just don't feel like getting into it with you tonight."

"We don't have to get into anything. I'm trying to give you what you said you wanted and look at the way you're acting."

"Well, it's a day late and a dollar short," she said, getting a little upset.

"What are you trying to say?

"I'm saying that maybe we shouldn't be together anymore," she blurted out with tears in her eyes.

Stunned, Ray saw the intensity on her face. He knew that Brenda meant what she said. The last time they broke up, he almost lost her to James.

"Can we talk about this?"

"Talk? I've been trying to talk to you for years about our marriage, or should I say our so-called marriage, but you were too busy with work and lying around the house ignoring me."

"Ignoring you? So you think I'm ignoring you?"

"Lord Jesus, give me strength. Would you stop repeating me? I have tried everything I can think of to get us back on track, but I'm tired. If I am always alone in this relationship, then I might as well be." She turned away from him so that he wouldn't see her cry.

"I'm sorry I hurt you," he said as he turned and walked out the room.

Suddenly her cell phone rang. Wiping her face and clearing her throat, she answered.

It was Cathy, a nurse who rotated on the floor where

Ms. Betty was receiving her treatments.

"Hello, Brenda. I hate to disturb you at home but I know that you are very close to Ms. Betty and I thought you should know that she was back in the hospital. They don't expect her to make it through the night."

Immediately Brenda got up and put on her clothes, grabbed her purse, then keys, and headed towards the front door. Ray was in the living room reading his Bible when she came running into the living room.

"What's the matter? Where are you going this time of night?"

"I can't talk right now. I need to get to the hospital."

"Do you need me to go with you?"

"No!"

When she arrived at the hospital, she went to the 8th floor to the ICU where Cathy worked.

"Where is she? How is she doing?"

"You know how she is, trying to crack her jokes to make everyone feel comfortable," Cathy said.

When Brenda walked in the room, a familiar feeling came over her. She tried to suppress it, but it became stronger as she walked closer to Ms. Betty's bedside. Brenda barely recognized her. Her face was sunk in and her eyes were bulging out of her head. The cancer had taken a turn for the worse and Ms. Betty knew it.

Brenda took hold of Mrs. Betty's hand, then began to stroke her salt and pepper hair. As she watched Ms. Betty drift in and out of sleep, Brenda began to think of Momma Greene. She remembered that she wasn't able to be by her side when she passed away. The thought of loosing another person she cared for began to overwhelm her.

Just then Jason came into the room. He immediately grabbed Brenda and gave her a big hug. He squeezed her so tight.

"How is she doing?" he asked.

"She is resting right now. They gave her morphine for the pain and something to help her relax."

Brenda watched as Jason hugged and kissed his

mother.

“I didn’t know you were working tonight?” he asked.

“I wasn’t. I got a call telling me she was admitted and I rushed over here to see how she was doing.”

“Thanks for coming. I don’t think I can face losing her alone. You’re the only one that knows what I am going through.” Brenda took Jason’s hands.

“Let’s pray that God’s will be done.” Brenda took hold of Mrs. Betty’s hand and began to pray. After she prayed, the nurse came in.

“Why don’t the two you go down to the cafeteria and get some coffee or something to eat? I’ll call you if there is any change.”

They both started down to the cafeteria.

“Why don’t we get out of this stuffy old hospital for some fresh air?” Jason asked.

Brenda was hesitant.

“What if something happens and the nurse needs to reach you?”

"You heard her. She will call me if there are any changes. Besides, just like you said in your prayers, it is all in Gods' hands."

Brenda told Jason to drive to a quiet spot nearby where she liked to go and get away from everything just to regroup. The air was crisp. The moon was full. They talked and laughed about all the things Ms. Betty used to say and do. As they sat there, the time just seemed to stand still. Nothing seemed to matter. All of Brenda's issues with Ray didn't matter; in fact she didn't mention him at all.

Suddenly the air became quite chilly. She began to shiver.

"Are you cold?"

"Just a little," she said, rubbing her arms.

"Can't let my baby catch cold," he said as he put his arms around her and began rubbing her arms.

Baby? Where did that come from? she thought.

Brenda enjoyed being close to Jason. It had been a long time since anyone cared about how she felt, let alone wanted to do something about it. She melted under his touch. Before she knew it, her head was on his shoulder.

"It feels good to hold you like this," he said.

"It feels good to be held like this," she said. With that, he placed his hands on her chin, lifted her head, and they looked deep into one another's eyes. Then he kissed her.

What the heck am I doing? I'm a married woman and he is a married man, she thought, barely trying to push Jason away.

"We shouldn't…" she said, finally breaking free.

"Brenda, I want you to be mine. We could travel the world. I will give you anything your heart desires," he said with a dazed look on his face.

"That isn't possible and you know it," she replied.

Jason stood up from the bench. Frustrated, he pulled her close to him.

"Why are you fighting how you feel? We've been tap dancing around this for months now. Don't you think we should do something about it?"

Before Brenda could say anything, she was in his arms again giving him a more passionate kiss. His hands were all over her body. She began to reciprocate and melted into his arms.

She could hear a small voice speaking to her.

***Thou shall not commit adultery*.**

Trying to reason with God, she began to plead. *Lord, please help me. It has been so long since I've been touched like this or felt wanted. Please just this once let my body have what it wants.*

Just then Jason's cell phone rang. It was the nurse at the hospital telling him that his mother was awake and was asking for him. They composed themselves and headed back to the hospital.

When they arrived at her room, they were surprised to see Ms. Betty sitting up in the bed. She was wide awake. The nurse was taking her vitals and checking her IV.

"How's my best girl?" Jason asked.

Ms. Betty looked at him with a smile on her face.

“Hi son,” she said with a very shallow whisper.

“Momma, don’t try to talk…look who’s here..Brenda.”

Ms. Betty turned her head slowly in Brenda’s direction and smiled.

Brenda walked closer to her bedside. “Hello, Ms. Betty. It’s so good to see you sitting up and looking so beautiful,” she said, fighting back the tears.

Brenda gave her a kiss then sat down on one side of the bed while Jason sat on the other. Ms. Betty looked at the both of them, squeezed both of their hands, and smiled.

Jason looked over at Brenda. “I think she is trying to tell us something.”

Just at that moment, Ms. Betty let out a gasp for air. She looked at Jason and smiled with a tear falling from her eye, and then she slipped away. Jason kissed her on her forehead, said goodbye, and buzzed for the nurse.

Brenda wanted to cry but she didn’t want to make a scene. She was glad she was able to say goodbye to her friend, and she was happy that she was able to be there for Jason.

Deep down inside she wanted to give him a big hug and comfort him the way she knew he wanted her to. She could tell by the look in his eyes as he talked to the hospital staff that he was hurting more than he let on.

"I should be getting home," she said taking her keys from her purse.

"I'll walk you to your car," Jason said as he signed the last piece of paperwork.

"I can manage; handle what you need to handle here and I'll call you tomorrow."

"I've done all I can do for tonight," he said

Hand in hand and in silence, they walked to the parking lot.

"Here's my car. I know your mom is at peace now."

"Yes, she is, and it's comforting to know that she isn't suffering anymore."

"Well I should be going," she said as she attempted to open the car door. Just then Jason grabbed her, turned her around, pressed her up against the car, and gave her another passionate kiss.

Brenda was putty in his arms as he pressed up against her.

"Thank you for being here with me through all of this," he said, looking deeply into her eyes. "Goodnight."

Trying hard to get her head wrapped around everything that transpired minutes before, she drove home not realizing how she got there. Her mind raced trying to rationalize why she allowed another man to put his hands all over her, and more importantly why she allowed him to kiss her.

I hope Ray is asleep. The last thing I need is to get into it with him right now. Brenda pulled into her drive way. She tried to compose herself. When she looked around, she realized Ray wasn't home. His car wasn't in its usual spot. It was 1 a.m. in the morning. Normally, she would be upset, but tonight she was relieved.

Feeling strangely numb to everything, she decided to take a hot bubble bath to calm herself. While the water ran in the tub, Brenda undressed herself. Her mind began to race. She thought about Ms. Betty and how much she was going to miss talking and laughing with her. Slowly she glided her body into the hot water. As she soaked, her mind wandered to Jason. The more she tried not to think about him, the more she thought about him. Her body began to tingle with excitement as she remembered his touch and the way he held her. It was a war that she was too tired to fight.

Letting out the water and drying herself off, she stood in the mirror looking at her naked body. She saw someone she didn't recognize.

"Why did I let him touch me? I know better. He is a married man. I'm a married woman. Nothing can ever happen between us. Oh Lord, please forgive me," she said as she bawled her eyes out and collapsed on the bathroom floor.

Girl, stop acting like it's the end of the world. Ray drove you to it. A still, small voice sounding a lot like Shannon invaded her brain. *If he was doing what a husband is supposed to do, you wouldn't need someone else to fill that urge you've been having for years. Shoot, where is he at 1 a.m. in the morning? Sure not here with you, is he?"*

It was about two in the morning when Ray arrived home. He walked straight to the bedroom hoping to find Brenda asleep. When he noticed she wasn't in the bed, he began to look throughout the house. He began to panic. He knew her car was in the driveway. Finally he walked into the bathroom and found her lying naked on the floor fast asleep.

"What have I done?" he said as he lifted her up and carried her into the bedroom and placed her in the bed.

I'm so sorry I've hurt you. I wish I could be the man you need me to be. I know I don't deserve you, he thought to himself as he caressed her hair.

The next morning Brenda woke up to the smell of blueberry pancakes and bacon gliding up her nostrils. She could hear the gospel music playing and Ray attempting to sing. For a moment, Brenda thought she was dreaming. She knew she had a hard time last night but she didn't remember getting into bed nor did she remember when Ray came home. Her last thoughts were of Ms. Betty dying and Jason.

Drained and confused, she slowly sat up, covering her nude body with the sheets. Just then, Ray walked into the room with a tray of pancakes, bacon, eggs, orange juice, and a small vase holding a single flower.

"Good morning, babe. Are you hungry?" he said, placing the tray on her lap.

"I could eat," she said, pleasantly surprised at how appetizing everything looked.

She wanted to know where all this attention was coming from and why she didn't have on any clothes. The last thing she remembered was taking a bath.

He began cutting her pancakes into small bite size pieces as if she were a two year old. "After breakfast, I thought we could spend the day together."

While Brenda ate, Ray took hold of her foot and began to massage it.

What is up with him? The only time he ever shows me any type of attention is when he's done something wrong or when he knows he's on the way out, she thought to herself.

After breakfast, Brenda took a shower and got dressed while Ray washed the dishes. She was still curious but decided to go with the flow until he showed his true colors.

The day started off better than Brenda could have imagined. They went to the zoo, then to the museum and had a bite to eat. The day reminded her of when they first met, when she first fell in love with him.

"I know I've been neglecting you and I know we haven't been jiving, but I want to make things better between us," he said out of the blue.

Brenda just looked at him. He had said and done all the right things before and things just went sour afterwards.

"How do I know you really mean it this time? I'm not getting any younger and I don't want to waste my time loving someone who doesn't want me," she said, trying not to get emotional.

"I guess you have every right not to believe me. I've let you down before. Just don't give up on me. You're the only woman I've ever cared about and who has ever cared about me and I want to prove that to you."

The conversation at lunch got Brenda thinking about giving her marriage one more chance. Thoughts of the night before constantly bombarded her brain and she wanted to come clean with Ray, but she knew that would be a bad idea.

They finished lunch and decided to walk through the mall. They looked through several stores for trinkets and CDs. Ray wanted to check out his favorite men's store for a new suit for church, so Brenda continued to browse around until she decided to go into Victoria's Secret. She had never bought anything from them before, but was curious about some of the items they sold. Sonya told her about her many shopping sprees she'd taken in Victoria's Secret for her "special dates" and how effective the products were on her potential suitors. Scanning up and down each section, she decided to purchase perfume and bath oils.

As she began to sift through the clearance table, she heard a woman laughing quite loudly. She turned and saw a tall statuette woman holding a silk laced, red, thong in the face of a man that looked a lot like Jason.

Listening more intently, she moved closer to get a better look at the man's face.

"How do you think I would look in this on our trip to Jamaica?" she said, picking up the bra to match.

"You would look even better when I take it off," he said laughing. Just then, Brenda knew it was Jason. She didn't know what to do. Her hurt side told her to confront his lying, cheating, no good ass, but the other half said that she had no right to be angry because it could be his wife, and she was married as well, and that she was the no good cheating ass, so she had absolutely no right to be angry.

Trying to get out of the store without letting Jason see her and with her sanity intact, Brenda accidentally knock over a display located near the door way. Petrified, she closed her eyes and clinched her teeth.

Just great. All I need is for him to see me and have him think I'm stalking him, she thought, trying to place everything back. When she reached down to pick up the last pair of underwear, another hand was grabbing the same pair. When she looked up, she noticed it was Jason. Brenda saw how surprised he was to see her.

"Hello, Brenda. Funny running into you here. I was going to call you later to let you know the funeral will be tomorrow at 11 a.m. at my mom's church, St. Vincent United Methodist downtown. I've been so busy trying to take care of the funeral arrangements and contacting family and friends. You know how these things can be."

Before Brenda could say a word, the woman walked over.

"Jason, I need your card to pay for these items," she said, holding out her hand. Jason reached into his wallet and handed her the credit card.

"Why didn't you introduce me to your wife?" she said, knowing good and well that she didn't want to face the woman whose husband she made out with.

"Brenda, this is Liza. Liza, this is Brenda, a close personal friend of my mom's.

"Nice to meet you, Brenda," she said as she placed her

arm around his. "I'm going to check out the body oils then we can go to the jewelry store."

After Liza walked off, Brenda could hardly contain herself. "You must take me for the biggest fool ever," she said, trying not to get loud in the store.

"What are you talking about?" he said, trying to play dumb.

Before she could get a word out, Ray walked up behind her.

"So here you are. What did you buy for me?"

"Nothing. I was just sniffing some perfume, but I'm ready to go," she said as they headed for the door. She turned to look back at Jason and the mystery woman. Jason's eyes connected with hers. Giving him an evil look, she quickly turned her head in shame.

Anger began to overwhelm Brenda as she and Ray drove home from the mall.

How could I be so stupid? He was just trying to get into my pants. What the hell was I thinking? How did I fall for all his lies? she said to herself, trying not to scream out loud.

"I had a wonderful time today. Did you?" Ray asked as he caressed her arm.

Brenda could hear sounds coming from his mouth, but she couldn't understand what he was saying. She was too consumed with her own thoughts. Her mind went back to that evening she shared with Jason and all the things he said to her. Then it flipped to what she overheard in the store.

Why am I acting this way? I'm married. I'm a God-fearing woman. I should know better. Why did I let my guard down?

They finally arrived home. Ray opened the car door to let Brenda out, something he hadn't done since they first started dating. When they got to the doorstep, he opened the door and swept her off her feet to carry her into the house.

"Tonight I'm going to take care of you for a change," he said as he looked deep into her eyes.

This is what she had been waiting to hear from her husband for so long, yet she felt nothing.

Why? Why now? What made him want me all of a sudden? Did he somehow find out about my indiscretion with Jason? What am I thinking—how in the world could he possibly know about Jason? I don't know if I even care if he does. It's his fault in the first place that I fell prey to his advances.

As she continued to battle with her thoughts, Ray had already run her a bath and poured her a glass of wine.

"Why don't you go soak in the tub while I put on some music and build us a fire?"

She decided to forget about everything and enjoy being pampered for a change. After all, this is what she'd been praying for, for so long. God couldn't have answered her prayer at a better time, a time when she was about to give up on everything: her marriage, her sense of right and wrong, love…

Ray blindfolded her and escorted her into the bathroom. She could smell the scent of lavender permeating throughout the room. Slowly he undressed her then lifted her carefully into the tub filled with bubbles. Just then, Ray removed the blindfold from her eyes. Brenda was amazed to see candles lit around the tub, on the sink, and along the toilet bowl. Flabbergasted to say the least, she wanted to know what alien kidnapped her husband and took over his body. Whatever it was, she didn't care; she liked this new man.

While she soaked, her thoughts went back to her unfortunate encounter with Jason at the mall. Shame and betrayal were the emotions that engulfed her.

I wish I never met him. I should have never let him put his hands on me. How stupid could I be? I never want to see his lying, cheating face again, she said to herself as she slid down into the suds. Suddenly, she popped up out of the bubbles.

"I'm a cheater!" she yelled out. Just then Ray answered from the next room.

"I'll be right there," he said.

Brenda removed her hands from her mouth and sighed in relief because she realized he didn't hear what she said.

"Okay," she replied back as she sunk slowly back into the water.

Lord, please forgive me for being so weak. I promise I'll never see Jason again. Just please keep Ray like this or I may have a relapse with someone else.

Just then Ray walked into the bathroom with just a smile and a bow stuck to his chest next to his heart. He entered the tub and began kissing her.

"I'm giving you my heart for life," he said with a smile.

Promises flowed from his lips. Never would he hurt her again, never would he make her doubt his love for her. He wanted to be the husband she needed. He was ready to be a family man and tonight would be the night he wanted to create their beautiful child. Never had she felt so close to Ray.

At first she was afraid to let her guard down. Her heart couldn't stand another moment of disappointment and rejection. She wanted to believe him, to let go and enjoy the attention her soul had been longing for. Whatever he'd done in the past, she told herself, she would leave it in the past and start fresh.

Brenda had all but given up on the idea of having a family.

Nothing but separation and divorce ran through her mind for the last eight years; besides, Ray had never discussed children. He had never talked about his own family nor has she ever seen him around kids. No matter how the idea originated, for her it sounded like it could be a great start to a new beginning for them.

Perhaps he will settle down and spend more time at home, she thought. Finally, she relaxed in his arms and stopped thinking. Magically is how the evening ended.

Chapter 14

LAST RESPECTS

A glimpse of sunlight caught under the open crack in Brenda's eyelid. The night felt like a dream. She didn't want to wake up from it. Slowly she stretched her arms. Brenda was pleasantly surprised to feel his perfectly sculpted abs still lying next to her.

I can't believe he's still here with me. Usually he's out of bed at by 5 a.m. He never wants to stay and cuddle. He always says it's a waste of a perfectly good day. She opened her eyes only to find him staring at her.

"Good morning, Mrs. Jackson. Did you sleep well?

"Yes, I did."

"What's the plan for today? I cleared my schedule so we can spend the entire day together. Whatever you want to do—your wish is my command."

"I wish I could stay in bed all day but I have a funeral to

attend. Remember my friend Ms. Betty who was a patient at the hospital?"

"Oh, yeah. I kinda do remember you mentioning her to me a couple of times. I didn't realize how close you two really were."

"She wasn't just a patient and a friend; she reminded me a lot of my momma," she said with tears filling her eyes.

"Well, I'll go with you," he said as tried to comfort her.

Brenda wasn't prepared for that. As much as she loved the idea of him wanting to be by her side during this difficult time, she knew that Jason would be there and it would be awkward for the two of them to be in the same place at the same time with her. Besides, she didn't want to see Jason at all.

Later that morning they both got dressed and headed for the church. Brenda was surprised to see so many of the hospital staff's cars parked in front of the church; however, the only person she wanted to see was Sonya. She needed Sonya to be the buffer between her and Jason while she collected her thoughts and tried to keep her emotions intact.

I don't know why I can't seem to get it together. It's not like we slept together or we were talking about leaving our significant others for each other. Girl, you need to get a grip and stop tripping. I'm sure he's not sweating me right now.

The church was packed. Ray and Brenda took a seat in the middle row of the pew. She looked around and saw Sonya giving her a smile and silently mouthing the words, "Are you okay?" Brenda nodded once, yes. Ray took hold of her hand and gripped it tightly.

He whispered in her ear, "I got you, babe."

Lord, I don't know what's gotten into my husband, but whatever it is, please don't let it jump out, she prayed silently.

The preacher asked everyone to stand as the family walked in. Brenda turned around and saw Jason walking in with a woman who clearly wasn't the woman she saw him with in Victoria's Secret. To make matters worse, this woman looked to be about six months pregnant. *Maybe that's his sister or a cousin. This couldn't be his wife. He told me they were separated for a year and their divorce would be final in a few weeks,* she thought to herself.

As they walked passed her, Brenda noticed that Jason was wearing his wedding band. He looked straight ahead until he approached his seat. She couldn't help herself—she had to find out exactly who this woman was.

After the service they went to the burial. Ms. Betty was lowered into the ground as the preacher gave the benediction. Brenda took Ray's hand and they began to walk to the car.

"Aren't you going to pay your respects to the family before we leave?" he said, turning in the direction of Jason and the woman.

"I know you don't like this sort of thing. Besides, I already sent a card and some flowers from the both of us, and they seem a bit preoccupied with things at the moment," she said, noticing the woman's arms connected into Jason's.

"Don't be silly. It won't take but a moment. I'm sure her family would want to talk to you being that you two were very close. I know you think I don't understand your southern traditions, but I do," Ray said.

As they headed towards Jason, Brenda's heart began to race. Jason saw them approaching and greeted Brenda with a hug.

"I'm glad you were able to be here today," he said pretending as though nothing happened between the two of them.

"I wouldn't miss being here for the world," she said, looking into his eyes as if to say *who is this woman?*

"Honey, don't be rude. Introduce me to your friends," the woman said.

"Where are my manners? Brenda, this is my wife Cynthia. Cynthia, this is Brenda. She works at Emery University Hospital. She was really close to my mom," he said with a straight face.

"Nice to meet you. I'm sorry. I never got a chance to go by the hospital, but I have been having such a difficult pregnancy. The doctor had me on strict orders to relax. But my boo has been keeping me posted on everything that has been going on," she said as she gave him a kiss on the cheek.

Brenda wanted to slap the fake smile off of Jason's face. She felt so used and deceived that she could hardly stand to look at him.

"Hello, I'm Ray Jackson, Brenda's husband," Ray said, reaching out his hand to shake Jason and his wife's.

"Nice to meet you. Brenda has told me so much about you," he said, giving her a longing look.

"I think it's time for us to be leaving to get to the repast at the church," his wife stated. "We're paying the caterers by the hour. Nice to meet you."

Embarrassed, angry, used, furious, and hurt were just a few of the many emotions that downloaded into Brenda's brain cells. If she were a white woman, her entire face would have been beat red with rage. She couldn't wait to get home to wash the stupid off of her. However, for the moment she had to pretend that everything was cool.

Back and forth she played every word Jason had ever said in her head.

I can't believe I fell for his crap. Thank you, Holy Ghost, for keeping me. Help me to forgive myself and move on. With that, she and Ray went home, and they spent the day watching movies on the couch until they fell asleep.

Months went by and things between her and Ray were going great. They had been making progress in their relationship. He had begun spending more time at home with her and they were taking weekend getaways. They also started attending church together regularly. He began working with the youth again, and occasionally he and Pastor Benjamin would work late on special projects which kept her free to go work out with Sonya a few nights a week.

One evening, she and Sonya decided to go to the gym right after work. Ray had a big photo shoot out of town so they planned to work out then go out to dinner afterwards. The entire day, Brenda felt a little tired but she chalked it up to not getting enough rest. Ignoring her feelings, she decided to go anyway. When they arrived at the gym, they headed straight to the locker room to change. Just as Brenda walked out of the locker room, she saw Jason.

He was shirtless and washed down in sweat from lifting weights. She pretended not to notice him and tried to avoid him by walking in another direction to get to the treadmills.

"Brenda....Brenda!" he yelled as he followed her.

"Leave me alone!" she said, hurrying to get to the treadmills. She fumbled with the controls while Jason stood beside the machine trying to get her to listen to him.

"What! What in the hell could you possibly say to me that would make what you did be okay? No, let me rephrase that: what in the hell could you possibly say to me that would make what WE did be okay?" Brenda bellowed out as she sped up the pace on the machine, trying to walk off her rage.

"Can we go somewhere and talk about this?" he asked touching her arm.

"Negro, if you don't get your hands off of me, I'm going to slap all your lies out of your mouth. Who in the hell do you think I am? I'm not some dumb bitch you picked up off the street—I'm not a whore! I thought you were a real stand-up person who was deeply hurt by his mother's illness. I can't believe you would use my relationship with your mother to seduce me. What kind of a person would do such a thing?" she said screaming at the top of her lungs.

Everyone in the gym's eyes and ears were glued to them while they listened to their conversation.

"Brenda, calm down and let me explain. Can we go somewhere and talk about this, please?" he pleaded.

Unfortunately, Jason couldn't get a word in edgewise after that. Brenda chewed into him so hard all he could do was hold back blows while he tried to get her to calm down. Hearing the commotion, Sonya ran over to Brenda before she could pick up the five pound barbell to swing at Jason.

Before she could attack him, Brenda collapsed into Jason's arms. Sonya attempted to revive her but with very little success. She called for someone to get a wet cloth to put on Brenda's forehead. As luck would have it, there was a doctor working out near the Nortex machine. He had observed everything that had taken place.

They carried Brenda into a quiet room away from the crowd. Sonya and Jason stayed with Brenda until the doctor took her vitals.

Finally, Brenda opened her eyes and looked around the room. "What happened?" she asked. "Where am I?"

"You're at the gym. You fainted," Sonya said with a concerned look on her face.

"Brenda, are you alright? Is there anything I can get for you?" Jason asked with a guilty look on his face.

"Yes, get out of my sight!" she said with a serious look on her face.

"Miss, you need to calm down. Your pressure is elevated and you need to relax so it can go down," the doctor said as he checked her pulse.

Jason headed for the door. Before he walked out, he told Brenda he was sorry and he hoped she would forgive him. Brenda turned away.

After about thirty minutes, the doctor told Brenda she should go home, get something to eat, get some rest, and call her doctor in the morning.

After she arrived home, Sonya made her lie down on the couch and put her feet up while she prepared her something to eat.

"Girl, I've never seen you act like that before. What has gotten into you?" she said, handing her the food.

"I don't know. I've never acted like that before in my life. It's like the moment I saw him, all I wanted to do was scratch his eyes out," she said, taking a sip of soup.

"Well, I hope I never get on your bad side. Girl, you turned that place out today," Sonya said, laughing.

She fluffed a pillow for Brenda to put behind her head. "Well, I need to go home and get ready for my gentleman friend who is stopping by, unless you need me to stay?"

"No, you go ahead and enjoy your date," she said as she adjusted herself.

"Are you going to be alright? I don't mind. Gary can wait.

He thinks I'm going to give it up, but I've got news for him. I'm waiting on the ring," Sonya said, giggling as she gave Brenda a hug.

"I'll be just fine. Thanks for everything, girl. I don't know what I would do without you."

"Well call me if you need anything. Remember what the doctor said, and I'll see you tomorrow at work."

Brenda thought about everything that had transpired at the gym. She couldn't believe she behaved that way. It wasn't in her to attack someone, no matter how angry she was. When she got to work the next day, she decided she would take things a little slowly and keep her work load to a minimum. No more would she let her emotions dictate her actions and that included her outside distractions. From now on, she was going to focus on family, true friends, and her future.

She met Sonya for lunch in the cafeteria. She continued to tease Brenda about her outburst at the gym and filled her in on what transpired after she passed out. They finished lunch and started to head back to the office when suddenly Brenda felt light headed and stumbled, almost dropping the tray. Sonya noticed the sweat bursting out of her forehead and called for someone to bring her a wheelchair.

"Okay, there is definitely something wrong with you, and I don't want you to tell me that you're fine. You're going to let one of these doctors check you out today and I am not taking no for an answer," Sonya said with a worried look on her face.

Too weak to argue with Sonya, they headed to Dr. Fielding's office. She had been a long-time colleague of both Brenda and Sonya's. They had built up a good work relationship over the years and they knew that she would do a thorough job.

Sonya filled the doctor in on what had transpired the day before and what Brenda just experienced minutes before. Worried, Sonya asked Brenda if she wanted her to call Ray to let him know what was going on. She said no. She didn't want to worry him over nothing.

After about two hours of being poked and prodded, peeing in a small cup, and having almost what felt like a gallon of blood drawn from her arm, Brenda sat in the hospital gown on the table shivering from the cold air blowing directly on her exposed back and arms coming from the air conditioning vent directly overhead. Dr. Fielding finally came back into the room. She sat down behind her desk, flipping through the chart. Finally she spoke.

"Brenda, I need you to reduce your stress and get plenty of rest because your blood pressure is very high and you need to get it down. Also, your blood sugar is elevated. None of this is good for the baby," she said with a serious look on her face.

Brenda was shocked. Sonya jumped up out of the chair. "I knew it! That explains why you were flipping out," she said very excited.

"I'm pregnant?" Brenda said in shock.

"Yes, you are. I would say about two months. I take it this is good news?" Dr. Fielding asked.

"Yes, I hope so," she said, staring at her wedding band.

"What's wrong, Brenda? Why aren't you happy about having a baby? I thought you wanted to start a family?" Sonya asked.

“I’m happy. I’m just not sure if Ray will be,” she said as she headed back to her office.

“Why wouldn’t he be? Didn’t you say things were going good between the two of you lately and that he said he wanted to start a family?”

“Yes, things have been going good. But since that night he never mentioned having kids and I don’t want him to start acting strange again. I don’t think I can handle it right now,” she explained as she began to get emotional.

“I think you are worried about nothing. Give the man a chance. He might surprise you. When he gets home tonight, have a nice romantic dinner waiting for him with candles and soft music then tell him the good news.”

Chapter 15

THE TRUTH SHALL MAKE YOU FREE

Little did she know that night would be the last time she would see Ray alive and that her whole life would be played out before a group of strangers who would decide she was mentally unstable which caused her to murder her husband and Pastor. If it had not been for the testimony of psychiatrists and other mental health experts, she would be in a state prison serving a life sentence for double homicide.

It didn't help that she had a first time Public Defender who was young and inexperienced. She had tried on several occasions to hire a real attorney, but found that Ray had put most of their savings into his studio and other investments, of which she knew nothing about. Brenda thought there was at least $50, 000 in their account, but after checking with her bank, all that was left was $2,000. Most of that money went to cremate Ray and pay the funeral home.

The monies she saved to one day buy a home were gone, and the studio had two leans placed on it because of all the equipment and financial obligations Ray was caught up in so it went in to Foreclosure and everything was sold to pay off his debts. There was nothing left for her to do but pray and ask God for a miracle. If it weren't for Sonya, she wouldn't have anyone, and up until today she was her only visitor for seven months...

Now she stood mesmerized as she listened to Ms. Benjamin confessing to murdering the two men who once meant everything to her.

"Why did you let me take the blame for something we both did? I thought you were a woman of God? I always knew you didn't like me. I saw the way you looked at me whenever you saw me with Pastor Benjamin. I never thought in my wildest dreams that you would frame me for murder."

"Brenda, please calm down. It's not what you think at all. I never meant for you to ever spend a day in jail or in this facility. I had every intention of coming forth before the trial, but I became very ill and was hospitalized for over five months. After I was released, I knew my time was getting short, and I wanted to get my affairs in order and make things right before I left this earth..."

"Brenda, I want you to know that I've always admired how much you've grown into this strong, independent young woman since the first day I laid eyes on you. You've accomplished so much in such a short time, and I know it had to be hard since you lost your grandmother. I know she would have been so proud of all your achievements. Any woman would be proud to call you her daughter. I can tell that you were raised with values and morals by the way you carry yourself. You've always stayed focus on your goals no matter what you were going through, be it in your marriage or the death of your momma. She had to be with you even through all of this."

Brenda was speechless. Ever since the day she'd met Mrs. Benjamin, she had always felt the woman hated her. For all she knew, Mrs. Benjamin thought she was having an affair with her husband.

Mrs. Benjamin continued. “I can tell that you were loved and cared for as a child. It is so important for a girl to have a mother who loves and cares about her and is training her up in the fear and admonition of the Lord and that she never forgets the teaching of her mother...”

“You see, I was brought up the same way. I had a mother who loved me and taught me right from wrong. I was given a lot of love and wisdom from my parents. They worked hard to give me everything I needed. I was blessed with a wonderful stepfather who loved me as if I was his own. My dad and I were very close, and we did everything together until he became very ill...”

“Every night I would sit by his bed side and read verses from the Bible and beg God to heal him. I’d cry out night after night in Jesus’ name for God not to take him away from me and my momma. He died on my 15th birthday. I was never the same after that day. I became angry at God and I resented my mother for telling me all those years how God answered prayers and how God could heal the sick and raise the dead. How God did this and that..."

"My bitterness led to some really bad decisions that cost me a lot in my life. I started acting out at school, hanging out with the kids who drank, cut classes, and used drugs. My mother and I fought all the time. She would take me to church and have me stand in front of the church for prayer. She would try to 'beat the devil out of me.' But it didn't work. We went to counseling a few times, but I just didn't want anyone to tell me anything. The only thing I wanted was to get high and hang out with my friends. I became very promiscuous, and the next thing I knew, I was pregnant. Even then I didn't want to believe it. I was almost six months when my mother noticed how much my body was changing and made me go to the doctor..."

"I delivered my little girl on my sixteenth birthday. It was almost as if God was trying to replace the loss of my daddy—at least my momma felt that way. As for me, I didn't want the responsibility. Raising a baby at sixteen was hard and

I just couldn't do it, so I wrote my mother a note and left town with some friends of mine."

Brenda just sat there with her ears glued to every word coming from Mrs. Benjamin's lips.

"I always wrote letters or sent post cards to my mother to let her know I was safe and to check on my child. Throughout the years, I would call on our birthdays and my mother would send me pictures of her.

"Why didn't you come to visit your child or talk to her?" Brenda asked.

"Because I was ashamed of who I became. You see, I was addicted to crack and the drugs had priority over everything and everyone. I did a lot of things to get it. I stole, I prostituted myself, and I stripped in sleazy clubs. I wasn't what you would call 'Mother material...'

"After I finished dancing one night, I went to a motel with this John and he tried to stiff me out of my money and started hitting on me, so I pulled out the switch blade I always carried on me and I stabbed him five times in the stomach. I ran out the room not knowing whether he was dead or alive. The following morning, I was picked up by the police after the clerk at the motel identified me as the hooker who checked in with the guy."

"Was he dead?"

"No, but he was in critical condition. I heard he had to have some of his large intestines removed and he had to stay in the hospital for four months. Anyway, they charged me with attempted murder and solicitation. I served five years in State prison. While I was in jail, my mother had me sign over my parental rights so she could legally adopt my daughter. It was the right thing to do..."

"After I served my time, I went to a halfway house where I met Mr. Benjamin. He was a former addict, pimp, and convict who had been through a similar program, who turned his life around, and became a small time preacher at one of the shelters in the hood. Our relationship started out as teacher-student, then it grew into confidante, and then he became like the father-figure I so desperately missed. He told me he had developed feelings for me and wanted to take care of me. I knew I didn't love him the way a women should love her husband to be, but he was offering me something I hadn't had in a long time and I wanted a fresh start, so I said yes..."

"We got married and we did mission work through the Salvation Army and with some small churches in a few states, then he told me God was calling him to pastor, so we settled down here in Atlanta."

Brenda sat there wondering why Mrs. Benjamin decided to tell her life's story today of all days. This was the most she had ever spoken to Brenda in all the years they'd known each other.

"This is all interesting and everything, but I don't quite see what all this has to do with me sitting in this place with a murder rap hanging over my head while you're walking around Scott-free," Brenda said.

"I understand your frustration. It's just that from the day you walked into our church, I knew it was a sign from God," Mrs. Benjamin said, searching through her purse then pulling out a picture.

Mrs. Benjamin handed it to Brenda. It was a picture of a little girl about five years old sitting on a woman that looked a lot like a young Momma Greene. Before Brenda could say a word, Mrs. Benjamin handed her another picture of Brenda when she was sixteen years old dressed to go to her high-school prom.

"Where did you get these?" she asked.

"They're mine. My momma sent me a picture of you every year up until you graduated from high school…I'm your mother, Karen."

About to fall out of her seat, Brenda didn't know whether to cry and embrace this woman or slap the hell of her for ruining her life. This was not how she imagined this day would be when she finally met her biological mother.

She just sat there in shock, unable to speak a word; unable to move. Nothing but questions ran through her head. Questions only Mrs. Benjamin could answer, and no matter how disgusted she was with her, only her so-called mother could answer them.

"My mother? No, you are not my mother. A mother wouldn't abandon her only child and never try to contact her. A mother would never miss every important event in her daughter's life to run the streets with pimps and drug dealers. A mother would never sit up in the same church every Sunday for years and not once speak to her own daughter or let her know she was her birth mother. Nor would a mother kill her daughter's husband and let her child sit in a mental hospital for seven months and take the rap for it. No, lady, you are NOT MY MOTHER!" she yelled.

"I know you are angry with me and you have every right to be. No mother in her right mind would have done any of those things. That's why I let Momma adopt you and I stayed out of your life. I didn't know how to be a mother and I knew the way I was living back then was not suitable for a child. I know I did the right thing letting Momma raise you. That was me loving you."

Brenda knew she was right, but she wasn't going to let

her off the hook so easily.

"None of that should have kept you from calling or writing. Do you know how many nights I spent dreaming about you? I guess I should thank you for keeping your distance because maybe I would have turned out just as screwed up and selfish as you."

"I guess I deserved that. You don't know how much I wanted to reach out to you all those years. After I married Mr. Benjamin, I thought about coming to get you. I didn't tell him about you right away because I wasn't sure I was going to stay with him. He was a bit controlling and too ambitious. He starting talking about having children of our own once we settled down and started our first church, but after two years of trying, I found out I couldn't have any more children..."

"There has never been a time that I didn't think about you. I promise you, Brenda, I will fix this mess and you can get on with your life. I hope someday you can find it in your heart to forgive me."

Just then the orderly came to the door. "Time's up," he

said.

"Brenda, I know this is a lot for you to process right now. I promise you I will make things right." With tears streaming down her face, Karen waved goodbye.

Evening came and Brenda couldn't sleep. The days' event consumed her mind. Everything she thought she knew about the world somehow made no sense anymore. She couldn't believe that the people she had once loved and held in such high regard could be so selfish and deceiving. Everything she felt about Ray started to disintegrate. The once naive, giving person no longer existed. It was time for her to look out for herself. The life she'd once dreamed about having would never come to pass.

Is this what Joseph felt like when he was being persecuted by his brothers and thrown in prison for something he didn't do? she prayed. *Father, please help me. I know I've made mistakes in my life. I fell in love with the wrong man. I trusted the wrong people with my heart and my life. Help me clear my name and start over. Make me a much wiser and stronger person. I know there is more work out there for me to do and I promise I will serve you until the day I die. In Jesus' name I pray. Amen.*

With her heart at peace, she drifted off to sleep. Suddenly, she heard a still voice calling her name. Brenda thought it was the night orderly. She got up to look out the opening in the door. The orderly was at his station with his feet propped up on the desk leaning back in his chair reading a magazine.

"I could have sworn I heard someone calling me," she thought as she walked toward her bed.

Before she could drift off into a deep sleep, she heard the voice again. "***The truth shall make you free...***" This time, she snapped to attention and looked around the room.

"Who's there?" she yelled out, but there was no answer. "I must really be losing it. I have got to get it together."

Instead of going back to sleep, she pulled out her Bible. When she opened it, the pages fell open to John chapter eight. Her eyes went straight to the 32nd verse. "***Ye shall know the***

truth, and the truth shall make you free..."

Instantly, she felt a surge of peace. Fear and doubt no longer consumed her. This time, she knew things were going to work out for her good. God had heard her prayers. Somehow, someway, He was going to make this right and this nightmare would soon be over. Joy would come in the morning.

Chapter 16

JOY COMETH

Days, weeks, and months came and went, but there was not one word from Mrs. Benjamin. Not even her public defender came to visit her with news on her appeal. She contemplated why she should depend on this woman who perpetrated this fraud all these years. After all, she denied her all her life, so why should she trust her to come through for her now?

With no money, she couldn't hire a new attorney, therefore, Mrs. Benjamin was her only hope. She had all but given up, but she remembered what she read in her Bible, and she knew that she needed to keep the faith and not doubt. Just at that moment, the orderly knocked on her door.

"You have a visitor in the waiting area, Brenda."

Once again, the walk down the corridor to the visitor's lounge felt like an eternity. Could it be her attorney letting her know about her appeal or that she was free? Or perhaps Mrs. Benjamin to tell her she changed her mind and couldn't go through with it. Or perhaps it was Sonya coming by to bring her some much needed cheering up.

No, it wasn't Karen, nor was it her friend Sonya. There at the table sat a middle-aged Caucasian gentleman dressed in an expensive navy blue suit and checkered bow tie. On his wrist was an expensive gold diamond encrusted watch.

He couldn't possibly want to see me; maybe they made a mistake at the desk, she said to herself as she slowly approached the table.

"Good morning, my name is Edgar Boldman. I am your new attorney and I have some good news…the charges against you have been dropped and you are free to go."

Brenda couldn't believe her ears. Was this her guardian angel sent by God to deliver her the good news?

"I am? I don't understand. Are you my new Public Defender?"

"No, I was hired to represent you by a private source who

prefers to remain anonymous at this time. I have been looking over your case and reviewed the evidence against you and things just didn't add up. We also exhumed the body of Mr. Benjamin and discovered he had been drugged prior to being murdered. Also, Mrs. Benjamin confessed to poisoning and stabbing the two men.

Emotions began to overwhelm Brenda. On one hand, she was elated that she was freed of all charges and she could get out of this facility, but on the other hand she felt sorry for Karen. After all, she was her biological mother and she was also her only living relative. This was not how she pictured their reunion. Their relationship was far from how she dreamed. Hating her would be so easy, expected even. However, compassion and forgiveness dominated.

"Where is she? Is it possible for me to see her?"

"She's in the hospital suffering with complications from pneumonia. She has been in ICU for five and a half months—things have been touch and go for months," her attorney replied.

Somehow Brenda knew Karen was holding on to see her, and no matter what she had done to her in the past, she knew she couldn't let her leave this earth without letting her know how she felt.

While her attorney tied up the loose ends at the facility, Brenda went back to her room to get dressed. Looking around the room, she reflected on the past year. She had tried to break free, not just physically free, but mentally free, of all the mistakes she had made since she met Ray.

Today will be the beginning of a new chapter in my life. I will not look back. Thank you, God, for hearing and answering my prayers.

Sonya had been waiting outside in the lobby. She got a call from Mr. Boldman, who saw her number listed in Brenda's files as her emergency contact. They both embraced for what seemed like hours. With tears running down their faces, they tried to compose themselves.

"Girl, you don't know how glad I am to know you're getting out of this place."

Suddenly Brenda realized she had nowhere to go. She had lost her rental home months ago, and all her belongings had to be sold just to pay her back rent and all of her and Ray's debts. Truly, she was starting over from scratch. She was glad that her car was paid off before all this mess occurred, and thanks to Sonya's generosity, she had a place to stay until she got back on her feet.

Sonya's house was small but inviting. For Brenda, it was definitely better than being locked up in the facility. Today, she would make a fresh start. No more regrets. It was time to put on her big-girl panties and grow up. After she settled in, she ran a bubble bath. She sat in the tub, contemplating what her next move would be. Getting back her job at the institute seemed like the first step; however, she didn't want to be judged by her former colleagues.

Brenda knew it would be difficult to persuade people to donate money after she had been accused of murder, but she could work behind the scenes in the lab. A job is what she needed, and she knew fear of what people might say or think of her had to take a back seat.

"That bath surely hit the spot," Brenda said as she walked into the kitchen after drying off and getting dressed.

"What would you like to eat for dinner? We can have steak, chicken, or fish. I'm going to fix you a nice welcome back to freedom dinner, or we can go out to dinner and celebrate—my treat," Sonya said as she stood in front of the open refrigerator looking in the freezer.

"Thanks girl, but I really want to go to the hospital to check on Karen, to see how she's coming along."

"I don't understand how you could care about what happens to that woman after all she's done to you. First, she walks away from you when you were a baby, looks in your face for years while she plays first lady, turns around and kills your no-good-ass husband, then turns around and let you rot in that place for as long as you did."

"Everything you're saying is true. I should be angry with her, but all I feel right now is sorry for her. The average person wouldn't think twice about her after everything she's done, but I need to forgive her so that I can move on with my life. If there is one thing I've learned over the years, it's that no one can do anything to you unless God allows it, and whatever He allows is for my good."

"Do you need me to come with you?"

"No, I can manage. Thanks though. I will see you when I get back. Maybe we can watch a movie and veg out."

Brenda talked to herself all the way to the hospital, rehearsing what she would say to Karen. Even though Karen explained some of her reasons for abandoning her, Brenda still wanted to know why she stayed away after she got married to Pastor Benjamin and why she didn't call or come home after Momma Greene got ill or when she died. Anger began to resurface as Brenda reflected on how she felt so alone during those difficult times in her life. All she could see was Karen, then Mrs. Benjamin, not saying one word to her as she went before the church for prayer and marriage counseling with the Pastor.

Okay girl, you need to get a grip. You said you've

forgiven her, so you need to let it go before it eats you up inside, she thought as she approached the hospital.

When she walked through the doors of the hospital, the smell of disinfectant and urine almost took her breath away. The waiting room was filled with homeless men and women. Some were coughing and others were sleeping on the floor. Others were reading and drinking the free coffee and stale cookies left out on the counter. The nurses were either on the telephone or chatting amongst themselves, apparently unconcerned with their patients. She walked up to the desk to get a visitor's pass.

"I'm here to see Mrs. Karen Benjamin."

"She is not allowed to have visitors unless they are cleared through the department of correction and your name has to be on the list," the nurse stated with a sarcastic demeanor. "May I have your name, please?"

"Brenda Jackson."

"Sorry, I don't see a Brenda Jackson on the list."

"Maybe she has me under Brenda Greene."

"No, no Brenda Greene on the list either."

"I'm her daughter. Do they at least make exceptions for family?" she said practically in tears.

Just then Brenda's, attorney approached the desk.

"Mr. Boldman, hi. It's me, Brenda."

"Hello, Brenda. I'm glad you're here. You just saved me a call."

"I want to see my mother, but they won't let me because I'm not on the list."

"Nurse, she is with me. I'm Mrs. Benjamin's attorney," he said, showing his identification.

"She's in Room 249. You can take elevator D," the nurse directed.

"I've been meaning to contact you about your mother's wishes," he said, reaching into the inside of his suit jacket.

"Wishes? What wishes?" she asked.

"Her last will and testament. You must know her condition is very critical. She gave me this envelope to give to you in the event that she passed away."

When she got to the room, a police officer was sitting outside the door. Mr. Boldman flashed his badge.

"She's with me."

When they walked in the room, the first thing that grabbed her attention was how Karen looked. Tubes were in her nose, attached to her arms, and an oxygen mask was pressed securely on her face. The room showed decades of neglect. An old tattered curtain separated Karen from another patient in this semi-private room with dried blood stains scattered on certain areas of the floor.

Flashes of Momma Greene lying in the hospital bed dying from cancer penetrated her brain. *Not again, I can't do this again; Lord, please give me strength.*

Just then, Karen opened her eyes.

Brenda went closer to her bed side and held her hand. Karen tried to remove the oxygen mask from her face but she was too weak.

"No, don't try to talk."

After several failed attempts at trying to keep Karen

from removing the mask, she finally assisted her.

Her words were faint, but Brenda placed her ear close to her mouth. A tear left her eye and ran down her face. "I'm so sorry…love you don't ever doubt that. Please forgive me," she said as she took her last breath.

Just then all the machines started sounding off. The nurses came into to the room to check on Karen.

"She's gone," the nurse said, removing Karen's oxygen mask while another removed the tubes and turned off the machines.

Again her thoughts of losing another mother overwhelmed her. This time she didn't have James' shoulder to cry on.

"Do you need me to call someone for you, Mrs. Jackson?"

"No."

"Will you be alright? Perhaps I can drive you home? You can come back tomorrow and pick up your car."

"I'll be alright, thanks."

In disbelief, she walked out of the hospital to her car.

I can't believe this is happening to me again. There is nothing left that Satan can do to me. He's taken it all. James, Ray, my baby, my career, my money, and now both of my mommas.

When Brenda reached Sonya's apartment, she was in the kitchen preparing dinner. Sonya noticed the expression on Brenda's face and immediately greeted her at the door.

"Are you alright? Come sit down and I'll get you a glass of water," she asked, heading to the refrigerator to get the pitcher, then to the cabinet for a glass.

She handed Brenda a glass of water. "How is your mom? Has her condition changed?"

"Changed, yes it's changed; she passed away. Now I will never get to know the woman who gave birth to me. She wasn't what I imaged she would be, but she was all I had left," Brenda said.

Sonya could see how broken-hearted and hurt Brenda was. For years she saw this strong, confident young woman who had high expectations for herself. Now she was looking at a woman who was at her lowest point.

"Brenda, you are a fighter. You haven't lost everything. You've got your faith in God and I know you thought I haven't been listening, but you've always told me that He won't put more on you than you can bare. He will give you double for your trouble."

"In my head I know you're right, but my heart is another story. I think I'll go lie down for a while."

Just as she stood up, the envelope fell out of her purse.

"What's that?" Sonya asked.

"What?" Brenda asked, looking around the room.

"This envelope. It fell out of your purse."

"Oh, I forgot all about this. The attorney gave this to me and told me Mrs. Benjamin, I mean, Karen…I mean, my mother wanted me to read it after she passed."

"Well, go ahead and read it," Sonya insisted, waiting eagerly on the edge of the sofa like a child waiting to open their Christmas present.

Hesitant, Brenda slowly tore the letter open. As she

began to read, her eyes became filled.

My darling daughter,

I know I haven't been there for you like a mother should've, but I want you to know that I love you more that you could ever know. Lord only knows how much I wish I could change the past and make things right between us. There is no excuse for me staying out of your life all those years. I missed every precious moment of you growing up. I missed your first steps, your blessing, your first dance, your first boyfriend, and all the wonderful things that come with being your mother.

Know that all these years my heart ached for you, but I knew that Momma would take better care of you than I could. The day you walked into the church, I felt as though God was giving me another chance to be a part of your life, even if it was from afar. I knew that He wanted me to watch over you and protect you in some way. So, I called Momma and asked her to release my funds because I wanted you to have it some day when you would really need it.

Here is a key to a safety deposit box along with a bank account number in your name at First Trust National Bank. I know it won't make up for everything you've lost, but I hope this will give you a fresh start at a new life. I love you and I hope someday you can forgive me.

Karen.

"You hear her, Brenda. Let's jump in the car and get you to the bank," Sonya said, pulling Brenda to the door.

"Can you please give me a minute to gather my thoughts?"

"Sure, as long as you gather them on the way to the bank."

Brenda, still in shock, got up off the couch, picked up her keys, and headed for the door.

"Wait a minute. It's 10 o'clock at night—the bank isn't open," Brenda said as she sat back on the couch.

"Oh yeah, I forgot. I guess I got a little carried away." Sonya said.

"You think? We'll go first thing in the morning." Brenda

said as she put back her keys and purse.

All night long Brenda tossed and turned over what Karen had said in the letter. She wondered what could possibly be in the safety deposit box, and what did she leave for her in the bank account, and why did she keep all this a secret until her death. She knew none of her questions were going to be answered that night—maybe never.

The next morning before Brenda could open her eyes, Sonya was at the bedroom door knocking and singing.

"Money, money, money, money…MONEY!"

Still sleepy, Brenda pulled the covers over her head to drown out Sonya's annoying singing.

Sonya barged into the room and pulled the covers off of Brenda's head.

"Girl, its eight o'clock! The bank opens in an hour."

"Give me ten more minutes," she said, turning on to her stomach.

"It's Friday…that means if we don't get there early, the lines will be long and you know everyone and their mama gets paid on Friday. Now get up."

She knew that Sonya was not going to let up. Using what little energy she had, she dragged herself out of the bed then into the shower. As soon she got dressed, they drove down to the bank. Remembering the last time she went to the bank and found that Ray had depleted all their savings, she hesitantly walked up to the bank teller. Clenching her jaw, she handed the lady her ID and the bank card.

"Good morning, Mrs. Jackson. What can I do for you this fine day?" she asked.

"I'd like to see what's in this account and this safety deposit box, please," she said as she handed her the account number and key.

They watched the teller type in the numbers. Sonya clung to Brenda like they were waiting for a door prize to be revealed at a game show.

"I see that you have $120,215.27 available in your account."

"Say what!" Brenda and Sonya yelled out.

"Would you like to make a withdrawal?" Spellbound, she asked the teller to repeat what she said. After hearing the amount the second time, Brenda and Sonya attempted to compose themselves.

"Excuse me, but can you tell me who deposited this money into my account?"

She eagerly waited as if they were about to hear a drum roll.

"It looks as though this account was set up as a fund by a church in South Carolina."

Brenda couldn't believe her ears. After all these months of sitting in the crazy house feeling alone and abandoned by everyone she knew and loved, to hear that her church back in Charleston was not only praying for her but also supporting her completely overwhelmed her with love. They proceeded toward the bank-vault. She and the teller turned the key. The teller left and Brenda pulled out the box and set it on the table.

They took a deep breath. "Okay, girl. Let's see what else God has blessed you with," Sonya said.

There was a brown envelope inside along with pictures of a young Karen holding a baby. Written on the back was: *My two favorite girls, Karen and Bre-Bre.* The other picture was of Momma Green holding an infant. There was also a stack of papers and a letter with a set of keys. It was a deed to Momma's Greene's house. She opened the letter.

Brenda,

I purchased Momma's house after you put it up for sale and I am signing it over to you. Here are the keys. Everything is as she left it. The furniture is still in storage. I located the company and continued payment. I always hoped that one day I would be able to live in it again and start my life over with you and my grand-children being a part of it. Now that I won't be able to do that, I pray this can help you start a new life.

Love always,

Karen.

In disbelief Brenda asked Sonya to pinch her to see if what she was experiencing was real. Staring at the deed to her grandmother's house, she nearly passed out.

"Hallelujah! Thank you Jesus!" Sonya exclaimed. "Girl, God has given you a fresh start."

"I can't believe it. Why didn't she tell me she bought the house? Where did she get all that money to buy back the house and furniture and how come Momma Greene's attorney didn't tell me?"

Just before she could finish asking more questions, she saw a stack of letters wrapped in a rubber band addressed to the church. They were from people in Charleston who attended her home church, people she had worked with in Atlanta and back home. Opening letter after letter, she was surprised how much love and support they all gave her, and more shocking was the amount of money they had donated to her freedom fund set up at the bank.

As she continued through the box, she found a post office box key along with a note directing her to more letters.

Her heart was overwhelmed because when she got locked up, she thought that no one cared, and maybe they were disgusted that she allowed herself to be a Christian woman caught in such a horrible predicament. This made her decision much easier. Brenda knew what God wanted her to do. It was time for her to go back home.

Flying wasn't her favorite thing to do. In fact, she was terrified of the idea. However, she wanted to experience how she was feeling at the moment, and after all she'd been through over the past few years, nothing was going to rattle her nerves. The sooner she got back to Charleston, the sooner everything would feel like a bad dream that she could finally wake up from.

It was going to be difficult to say goodbye to Sonya. She'd been her rock in a hard place for quite a while and they had been through thick and thin. Brenda wanted to do something special for her friend before she left town, so she set up a day at the most exclusive spa in Atlanta. They had a wonderful day relaxing while they got their massages and mani-pedis. Suddenly with a serious look on her face, Brenda turned to Sonya.

"Sonya, I just want to thank you for all you've done for me while I've been going through all of this. You've been a great friend to me and I just want you to know I love you. You've given me food when I was hungry, clothes when I was naked, shelter when I was homeless, and you visited me when I was in prison. I know that the Lord put you in my life for a reason. You've been there when I had no one to turn to," she said, reaching to hold her hand.

After their pampering was over, Brenda pulled out an envelope and handed it to Sonya. Wiping her eyes with the sleeve of her spa robe, Sonya reached out to take it from her.

"What is this? Sonya asked.

"It is a small token of my appreciation and love for you. One day I hope to do more."

Curious, Sonya ripped open the envelope. It was a check for $5,000, the keys to her car and a ticket for a cruise to Jamaica.

Sonya was so excited, she jumped up and ran around the room. "Girl, you didn't have to do this, but I sure ain't gonna give it back to ya."

Brenda burst out laughing. "Girl, you know yo head is bad," she said in their pretend Gullah accent.

"All jokes aside, don't you need a car to get around?" Sonya said after she settled down in her chair.

"I will get a new one…Remember, I am starting fresh and that means getting rid of everything from my past," Brenda said.

"I'm gonna miss you, Brenda." Sonya said.

"I'm gonna miss you too, girl, but look at it this way. I'm only a phone call away and just a four and a half hour drive, so it won't be that bad. Besides, I'm going with you on the cruise."

Epilogue

DOUBLE FOR YOUR TROUBLE

God is awesome, she thought as she marveled at the cloud formation below the aircraft. *It's amazing how He holds this pile of steel in the air without it falling. I know He can hold me up through whatever comes my way. There is so much I need to do. I need to get the house together and then find me a job, but first I need to go back to church.*

It had been years since Brenda stepped foot in her home church. She didn't know if her church family would look at her with disgust or accept her back into the fold. She knew they had been aware of her situation. After all, they did start her legal fund.

When the plane landed, her heart fluttered as if it were full of bees. Brenda wasted no time. As soon as she departed the plane, she headed straight to the car rental desk, then to baggage claim. She located the storage company where all of her mother's items were and made arrangements to have everything delivered, and then she headed straight home.

Surreal is how it all felt as she drove down her street to Momma Greene's house.

Nothing's changed, she thought, pulling into the drive way.

As she climbed the stairs on to the porch, tears began to flow. Brenda knew that when she opened the door, her mother wasn't going to be on the other side, yet being back where she felt safe and secure brought about mixed emotions of sadness and gladness. She walked inside and stood in the living room for a while, then went into the kitchen. Each room brought back pleasant memories of her childhood and of every moment with Momma Greene. All the laughter, meals, and teachable moments flashed before her eyes.

Suddenly, memories of James eating dinner at the dining room table popped into her mind. At that moment, the movers pulled up at the house, interrupting her day dream. Brenda had turned on the lights and power prior to arriving in Charleston, which made it easy for her to settle in.

She spent most of the night and the entire weekend getting the house just the way she remembered it. Among the boxes of what-nots and pictures, Brenda found in an old Bible that belonged to Momma Greene. She took it as a sign that she needed to get back to church right away.

After weeks of being isolated, she started her job search. She knew it had been a while since she worked at MUSC in the laboratory or spoke to any of the doctors. However, she wanted the opportunity to work back at the place where it all began: the place where she was taught and trained, the place where she last spent time with Momma Greene, and the place where she met and fell in love with James.

She reflected on all the good times they all shared. She knew Momma Greene liked James and wanted them to be together. She remembered all the laughter and long discussions. She knew she had made the biggest mistake of her life when she let him get away.

If only things were different. If only I had listened to my true feelings and not my flesh. I was so young and stupid. How could I hurt the only man who truly loved me? My life would've turned out so differently. Time for me to snap out of it. No more could have, should haves. It's time to face reality and move on with my life. The past is the past and there's nothing I can do about it. James has moved on with his life and I need to move on with mine.

Sunday was here. Half-dressed with a bit of hesitation, Brenda sat on the edge of her bed trying to come up with an excuse not to follow through with the promise she made to herself. As much as she tried to stall, she could almost hear Momma Greene's voice yelling at her from downstairs

"Brenda, get a move on! The Lord don't need you, you need the Lord; He don't serve you, you serve him," she imagined.

Suddenly, she felt rejuvenated and more determined than ever to get there. With the last sweep of her eye shadow, she took one more glance in her full length mirror and headed out the door.

When she pulled up to the church, she noticed that it had been remodeled yet it still looked familiar in some ways. She was surprised how many cars were parked in front, and when she walked through the doors she was astonished by all the renovations. Nothing was quite as she remembered. The congregation had grown by leaps and bounds. Hoping to see a familiar face, she headed into the sanctuary. The usher met her at the door.

"Good morning, welcome. Please follow me."

Certainly things were not the way Brenda remembered. These weren't the ushers who welcomed members and visitors on Sunday morning back in her day. The ushers she remembered growing up were sometimes loud and mean. They never smiled unless you were an important guest or white.

When she took her seat her, eagerness grew stronger to hear the Word. The choir sang her favorite song "Broken but I'm Healed" by Byron Cage, and the praise dancers heightened her anticipation as they danced to the "Battle Is

Not Yours, It's the Lord's" by Yolanda Adams.

When her pastor approached the pulpit, Brenda pulled out her pad and pen and opened her mother's Bible. His words penetrated her very soul as if he spoke into her spirit.

"To all who mourn in Israel, he will give a crown of beauty for ashes, a joyous blessing instead of mourning, festive praise instead of despair. In their righteousness, they will be like great oaks that the LORD has planted for his own glory. Forget those things that are behind you and press towards the prize of the high calling in Christ Jesus. Because eye hath not seen, nor ear heard, neither have entered into the heart of man, the things which God hath prepared for them that love him."

Just then, she knew God was using him to speak of her past, present, and into her future. She knew it wasn't a mistake that she came back to Charleston, and she was able to move back into her mother's house and was now sitting in her home church. By the time the Pastor was done giving his message, Brenda knew what she had to do.

When the alter call was given, she walked down the aisle and rededicated her life back to the Lord. Before she knew it, all her old friends and church members walked up to her and gave her a hug and a kiss to welcome her back home. Some of them she remembered, others she only recognized their faces, but just the same they all welcomed her back to the family and that is what she needed more than anything: a family and somewhere to belong.

When the Pastor found out who she was, he came down off of the pulpit and publicly embraced her and whispered in her ear.

"God has work for you do child. He will give you the desires of your heart."

After the service, she felt more revived and determined to make a fresh start. Since her childhood deacon had passed away some years ago, Brenda was assigned Deacon Calvin Brown. He was a short man, well dressed, with a full beard, about 78 years of age. He prayed with her and inquired about her needs and concerns. No one had asked her what she needed in a long time, so she was taken back a bit by the question but finally she opened her mouth and blurted out, "A job!"

With a chuckle he reached into his pocket and pulled out his business card with his phone number.

"This is my card. I will be in prayer with my wife for God to open doors for you," he said.

Just then, a young lady walked up to her.

"Hello, Brenda. It's been a while, girl. How have you been?" the woman said.

It was her old friend Vanessa. They grew up in the church together but had lost touch when they graduated high school. Last she heard, Vanessa went into the military after college.

"Hi, Vanessa. It's been a long time. How've you been?" she asked, giving her a hug.

"It sure has. I've been fine, can't complain. God's been good. We've got to get together and catch up."

"That sounds like fun."

"Great! Give me your number and I call you before the

week is out. Maybe we can go out to dinner or something and shoot the breeze like back in the day," Vanessa said, pulling out her cell.

So far the day went better than she had hoped, and now it was time to go home, fix something to eat, and then get started with her job hunt. After such a motivating sermon, she was more determined than ever to get back to work.

Showered and dressed in her pj's with a bowl of her favorite ice cream, she pulled out her computer and started her search. After filling out applications at several hospitals and laboratories in the area she prayed and called it a day.

****

Weeks went by and there were no call backs from the six interviews she had at three of the top hospitals and laboratories in the area. While waiting, she became very active in her church on a couple of ministries and nonprofit organizations helping women who've been abused or in prison get back on their feet.

Vanessa and Brenda became close. More and more they shared their life experiences and found that they had a lot in common. Brenda missed having someone to confide in since it had been months since she heard a word from Sonya. The last time they spoke, Sonya had met up with an old flame and things were getting "hot and heavy." She knew Sonya had a one track mind and that man was the train she wanted to ride, and that meant she had no time for Brenda.

One day after a couple of days of throwing herself a pity party for one, she decided to turn on her favorite gospel music. Before she knew it, she was shouting and praising God for all he had done for her. The feeling of melancholy and despair had faded in the midst of her giving thanks and was replaced with hope and faith that God would supply all her needs has he had done in the past.

Suddenly the phone rang. It was Deacon Brown. "Hello Sister Jackson," he said with a cheerful tone.

"My wife and I are having a get-together with some

family and friends in a few weeks and we would love for you to come. My nephew is relocating back to Charleston after being away for a while, and we wanted him to get reacquainted with some of the people from the church. I hope you can join us. The two of you have so much in common."

"Sure, I'd love to come. Just let me know the date and time?" she replied, hoping that this wasn't a setup.

Meeting someone at this point in her life was not on her agenda. The last thing she needed was a man. She needed a job. That would make her feel accomplished and fulfilled. Besides, she wasn't ready to get back out there and explore her options. She knew her record in that department wasn't the best.

After weeks of not hearing anything, the telephone rang. It was her old instructor at MUSC. He had received Brenda's application and resume'. He offered her a position that just opened in his department for an Assistant in the Cancer Research Laboratory. It wasn't the high paying position with prestige she once had at Emory, but it was a job in her field of expertise and she needed to get back to doing what she loved and knew God called her to do.

It didn't take long for Brenda to get back into the swing of things. Within a matter of weeks, she was assisting the department head with special projects and training new lab technicians. Brenda felt her life was finally getting back on track. She was doing what she loved. She was home where she knew she belonged.

While she sat at her station, her mind began to wonder back to the last time she worked in the lab with James. She thought about the hours they spent working on special projects, the way his eyes squinted every time he laughed. The way his voice sounded when he said her name, how his lips felt next to hers.

"Brenda... Brenda." A voice called breaking her out of her deep day dream.

"Yes... yes sir what can I do for you?

"I heard a doctor will be coming in to give a lecture on new cancer research in a couple of weeks and I want our best lab technicians to attend. I heard he made great strides in this field and is relocating here to start up a new department. He is going to hand-pick his own people to work with him. I thought you might be interested." Her department head stated.

"Why of course! Thank you for considering me, sir. What is the name of the doctor?"

"I'm not quite sure. I didn't get all the details yet. I just got the memo this morning, but the department heads will be meeting in about two weeks and I will have all the details then. I just wanted to give my best worker a heads up because I want you to bring your A-game when you meet him."

Everyday Brenda prepared herself for the doctor's visit. She knew this was her opportunity to be a part of something revolutionary in the field of medicine. Ever since Momma Green's death, she promised herself that she would help find a cure for cancer, and this was her opportunity to work with the best even though she didn't know who he was. The last time she really felt she worked with someone of that caliber was when she assisted James.

Feelings of reminiscence began to engulf her mind. *Here I go again. Let it go, girl. The man is gone. Lord, how could I have been so stupid?*

Sunday arrived and Brenda couldn't wait to attend the service. She wanted to give God thanks for all he had brought her through and what he had done in her life since she moved back to South Carolina. She thanked him many times before at home, but being in the presence of other believers worshiping and hearing the sermon gave her the strength she needed to take the next step in her life.

She felt as though she was getting her marching orders straight from the Commander and Chief of her life. With His directions and the praise of the saints motivating her, she knew everything she would face from here on out would be a piece of cake.

After the service Deacon Brown and his wife approached her. "Praise the Lord, Sister Brenda. I'm so glad we ran into you. We wanted to let you know we are having our get-together this coming Saturday and I hope you're still going to come."

"Of course I wouldn't miss it. What would you like me to bring?"

"Nothing. Just bring yourself. My husband has been shopping since last month. He's so excited about our nephew moving back to town and staying with us that he's bought everything from grits to ox tails." Mrs. Brown said laughing.

"Me? My wife has gone crazy herself. She has redecorated the guest bedroom and bathroom."

"How long will he be living with you?" Brenda said, attempting to sound interested.

"Until he can get his beach house situated. He's had it rented out for years and the tenant's lease won't be up for a couple of months. He has some renovating he wants to do before he moves back in."

Brenda was intrigued. "A beach house? How nice. I'm sure he will love being back here. There is no place like home."

On the drive home she pondered on the conversation she

had with the Browns.

Not too many black men have beach houses in Charleston. The Brown's nephew must be well off.

Once again her thoughts ran to the time she spent at James' house on the beach. How they spent the night sleeping on his balcony under the stars, how they walked along the beach talking for hours picking up shells and laughing, and how he walked out of her life angry and hurt about her engagement to Ray.

When she arrived home, all she could do was cry uncontrollably. How different her life would have been had she just chosen James. If only she had let him love her...

≈

The week had come and gone and Saturday was finally here. She had gotten one last call from Deaconess Brown asking her to make her mother's famous banana pudding she'd heard the members rave about. They wanted all of their nephew's favorite southern dishes and she didn't know how to make banana pudding. Brenda agreed and followed Momma Greene's recipe to the letter. She got dressed and headed to the Brown's.

Having never visited their home before, Brenda attempted to follow the directions given to her by her Deacon. John's Island wasn't a place she frequented. The last time she was in the country, she was a young girl about six. Her grandmother took her to visit some friends of theirs. She remembered how long a drive it was from the city and how far apart the houses were from each other. Although she had fun playing outside with the kids until it got dark, she didn't like how far they had to walk to buy candy from the local grocer and that there were no sidewalks or the fact that there were no street lights when it got dark.

After several wrong turns on a couple of dirt roads and dead ends, she approached the two story brick house with a magnificent wooden porch, two old fashioned rocking chairs, beautiful hanging baskets surrounding the porches up and downstairs, and a marvelous view of the lake.

She saw all the cars parked on the lawn. It seemed to have been at least sixty cars and a few motorcycles. Driving a little further towards the house, she spotted Vanessa's car with an empty spot next to it. She parked her car, grabbed her dessert, and headed to the house. Before she could knock on the door, it opened and a young girl greeted her.

"Hello, welcome. My name is Cheryl. I'm the Brown's great-niece. Everyone is in the back of the house by the lake. Come on in and I'll take you back."

Brenda was amazed at how magnificently their home was decorated. She glimpsed the pictures of the Browns when they were much younger as well as all of the beautiful decor throughout the house. She could see love flourished there and everything was family-oriented and inviting. When she got to the backyard, everyone was laughing and having a great time. Deacon Brown was on the grill barbecuing and his wife was at the food table covering everything with foil to keep the flies away.

Brenda walked up to her and handed her the banana pudding. "Well I'm glad you made it here safely, sweetie. And thanks for the pudding—my nephew just loves this stuff. He bragged about once having it when he used to live here a while back and I promised him I would have some the next time he came to town. In fact, he should be back shortly. He had to check on his house to make sure everything is going smoothly with the renovations. He just called me and said he was in his car and heading back to the party. I can't wait for the two of you to meet. I just know you'll hit it off. Did I mention he's a doctor? I'll talk to you later, sweetie. I need to make sure my wonderful husband doesn't burn the meat."

Brenda began to mingle with the rest of the guest from the church. She and Vanessa took a short stroll around the property in awe of how much there was of it. As they sat by the lake talking, they heard a bell ringing from the house.

"Time to eat! The guest of honor has arrived," Deacon Brown yelled.

When they approached the house, the line was long.

They saw everyone who had already gotten their plate of food stop for a few seconds to talk to a gentleman standing next to the Browns as though they were in a receiving line greeting royalty.

"Girl, I can't see the guy's face, but I sure hope he's fine and single. We could sure use some fresh meat in our singles ministry at the church. Everyone has run through the guys we have now and they ain't worth two cents," Vanessa blurted out.

The closer they got, the more she began to smell a familiar smell. It was the scent of cologne that once stirred up unholy emotions and thoughts that she had to repent for, time and time again. At last they approached the table of food. She removed a paper plate from the pile and began to prepare her food when suddenly one of the guests behind her accidentally bumped into her knocking her food to the floor. As she nervously began to clean up the mess, she heard a familiar voice.

"Let me help you with that," the man said reaching to

pick up the food.

Both of their hands touched and a sparks began to shoot up Brenda's arm. As she slowly looked up at the body that belonged to the scent that caught her nostrils earlier in the evening, their eyes met.

"Hello Brenda," he said with a big smile on his face.

Brenda was paralyzed as if she was lost in time. She could hardly believe her eyes. Could this really be? Before she could snap out of her trance, Deacon and Deaconess Brown interrupted them.

"I see the two of you found each other. Brenda, this is my nephew, Dr. James Powers. James, this is Brenda; she's a member of our church. I'm so glad the two of you finally got to meet one another," her deacon said.

Still in shock, Brenda just stood there dumbfounded.

"Brenda and I have met before, Unc."

"You have?"

"Yes, I was her mother's doctor when I lived here."

"Well, I'll be! Isn't this a small world?" Deaconess

Brown said.

"It sure is, and getting smaller by the minute," Vanessa said butting in.

Brenda's thoughts consumed her.

Could this really be? Is James really standing in front of me, or am I still sitting by the lake day dreaming about him?

"You look as beautiful as I remembered," he said.

"Thank you, so do you…I mean you look exactly as I remembered you."

"Well, it looks like the two of them have a lot of catching up to do. We're going to just leave you two to get reacquainted," Deaconess Brown said. "Why don't you take your food and go down by the lake where it's nice and quiet and we'll entertain the rest of our guests."

"Honey, that sounds like a plan!" Deacon Brown exclaimed, knowing that this was their strategy the entire time.

Her heart began to beat fast. This was what she had been praying for: another chance with James. She had so much she wanted to say, but the words just couldn't come out.

He looks as fine as I remembered, she thought.

"Shall we?" he said, taking her hand leading the way.

They sat down on the bench by the lake. Brenda could feel his eyes looking her up and down.

"I was hoping get to see you."

"You were?"

"Yes, actually I have a confession to make."

"You do."

"Yes, I asked my aunt and uncle to throw this party. I told them to invite the church members hoping that you would come."

"How did you know I was back at the church or back in Charleston for that matter?" she asked with a puzzled look on her face.

"Well, I have known for quite some time that you moved back to Charleston and since my aunt and uncle settled down here after they retired; I decided to come back here," he said while looking deep into her eyes again.

"I don't mean to be too forward, Brenda, but it's just that I never got over you. I hope I'm not freaking you out, but I just feel that we've wasted so much time already and I just don't want to waste another second or waste this opportunity to tell you how I feel."

The things James was saying to her were like music to her ears. He was never one to mince words or hide his feelings. That was her downfall, but not anymore. She wasn't going to miss out on this chance that God was giving her for true happiness.

"James, there is just so much you don't know about my life since we last saw each other." Before she could open her mouth, James leaned in and gave her a long passionate kiss. Brenda's body completely dissolved in his arms.

"I know about all of it," he said as he pulled her closer to him.

"You do? How could you?" she asked looking up at him.

"I know about Ray, the time you spent in the institution, and your biological mother." Brenda was dumbfounded.

"But how could you know everything?" she said feeling a

bit embarrassed.

"Your girlfriend Shannon contacted me after she found out you was arrested," he said.

"But I haven't heard from Shannon in years."

"All I know is I got a call out of the blue one evening..."

"She told me who she was and that she couldn't get back to the states, but told me to find your birth mother. So, I hired some private investigators, contacted the Pastor of the church here about setting up a fund for you, and the rest is history. I did have the opportunity to speak with your biological mother, however. She told me that she was going to straighten everything out. It was surprising to find out that your pastor's wife was your mom. We met and she filled me in on what really happened, so then I found you a new lawyer. The reason everything took so long was because your mom was getting worse and couldn't give a statement to the district attorney."

All this information threw Brenda for a loop. The entire time she was locked away thinking that no one cared about her, that her best friend had abandoned her, that she would never see James or the outside world again and felt God had abandoned her, He was working everything out for her good behind the scenes using the very people she loved and cared about.

Brenda broke down in James' arms. She had never felt so safe. After that evening they were inseparable.

Another week came and Brenda was excited to get to work. This was the day she would meet the new department head and she was eager to make a good impression. In the back of her mind she thought about the wonderful weekend she'd just spent with James. She was still pinching herself to see if she was dreaming. It was as though no time had passed and they'd picked up right where they left off all those years prior. James had listened as she'd filled him in on all she went through in her marriage and he had told her about his life. They had made plans to meet for dinner after work. Brenda couldn't wait, but right then she had to focus on meeting the new department head.

Anxiously she entered the lecture hall where she found a

seat directly in the front. Straightening her lab coat, she organized her resume' and other credentials as she eagerly awaited his arrival. Suddenly, her boss along with a few other department heads walked in and stood before her. Then came the moment she had been waiting for.

"I would like to introduce the Director of our new Cancer Research Facility, Dr. James Powers," Dr. Black said.

Brenda nearly fell out of her seat. When James walked on to the stage, she could not believe her eyes. James was standing there in is long white coat with a big grin on his face.

Why didn't he tell me? she thought.

Just then, the department heads gave their recommendations as to who they felt would best work in his department. As each name rolled off their lips, Brenda waited for her boss to stand and give his. Finally they called the last name, but Brenda's wasn't it. She was devastated but tried her best not to show it. Nor did she make eye contact with James.

After the presentation, the department heads exited the stage. She could see James smiling at her. Brenda gave him a slanted smile as her boss approached her.

"Brenda, I know you are wondering why I didn't call your name."

"Yes, sir. I must say I was quite confused when you didn't."

"Well, there's a good reason for that. Dr. Powers, can you come here please?" Dr. Black said as he motioned for James to come over.

"Dr. Powers here tells me that the two of you worked together before and has personally requested you to work alongside him in heading his research department."

Wanting to kiss James and run around the facility, she tried to compose herself. Choosing to be professional, she settled for a hand shake and a "thank you, sir."

After the hall cleared, she and James stood there talking about his plans for the department and what Brenda's roll would be in it. This was a dream come true for her. More and more she saw God's hand moving in her life and how He was helping her obtain her purpose. Deep inside she felt unworthy of it all, but she was thankful He was willing to trust her, not just with the job of her dreams but with the man of her dreams.

That night James picked her up for dinner. He complimented her on how beautiful she looked in the dress she was wearing. It had been a long time since she had been treated like a woman and she was going to enjoy every minute of it. He kept it a surprise as to where they were going until they drove up to his completely renovated home on the beach. Thoughts of the last time she was there flashed across her mind.

When they approached the dining room, she saw a man standing next to a nicely decorated table and a saxophonist playing. The two of them sat down to a delicious meal as the sax player played all her favorite tunes.

"May I have this dance?" he asked, extending his hand for hers.

"Of course you may."

As they slowly swayed to the music, they caressed one

another. James took her hand and escorted her out to the balcony. hey looked out at the stars.

"Brenda, I've loved you for as long as I can remember and these past few days have been the happiest I've been in a long time. I know your mother is smiling down on us right now and she would kick my butt if I let you get away from me again so tonight I have a very important question to ask you," he said as he got down on his right knee and pulled a black velvet box out of his sports coat.

With trembling hands he said,

"Brenda Jackson, will you be my wife, my partner, my best friend, and the mother of my children? Will you marry me?

Elated, she began to cry as she looked deep into his green eyes and exclaimed, "Yes, a thousand times yes! I will be all you need and want me to be!"

That night they held each other until the sun came up. The next morning they drove to James' aunt and uncle's home to break the news. Ecstatic, Deaconess Brown began making wedding plans. Before Brenda knew it, she was making arrangements with the Pastor and contacting florist and a wedding planner. Before the week ended, she had everything planned.

Within six months everything was complete and the wedding day was approaching. Brenda's and James' working and personal relationships were blossoming. James knew Brenda was feeling a bit apprehensive about having a big wedding. He knew she had no family to sit on her side of the church, so they decided to keep the wedding simple but elegant with just a few close friends and family at their church with a nice reception on the beach under a tent at James' home where they planned to live.

Brenda decided to open Momma Greene's home to families whose loved ones were going through treatment. Things were falling into place and the Cancer Research Center was up and running and well on its way to breaking strides in the fight against cancer.

The big day had finally arrived, the day she would

become Mrs. James Powers, M.D. Everything was neatly set aside for the big moment. Sonya flew in from Atlanta to be her maid of honor. Even Shannon came from overseas with her husband and two children to share this special day with her as her matron of honor. Her heart was overjoyed and yet somehow deeply saddened as she stared in the mirror.

Momma, I wish you were here to see your prayers answered. I know this is what you've wanted for me all along and it's about to happen in a few hours. Momma, I miss you. I always thought you would be here to help me pick out my wedding dress and cook some of your famous dishes for the reception. As much as I want to walk down that isle and marry James, I don't know if I can stand not seeing you sitting there watching me as I say my vows, she said to herself trying not to cry and mess up her makeup.

Before she could get into to a serious crying fest, Shannon, Sonya, Samantha, and Vanessa burst into her room singing, "Here Comes the Bride." They saw the tears and immediately began to console her. Before she knew it, they were laughing and joking about her wedding night and letting her know that her mother and grandmother were watching over her.

The time had finally arrived. She was dressed and ready to enter the church. When the door opened, she began to walk down the aisle. She saw James standing at the altar looking dashing in his tux with a huge smile on his face. As she continued to look around, her eyes glanced up toward the video monitor where she saw Momma Greene's smiling face staring down at her. Brenda could hardly believe her eyes. It was as if her grandmother was there with her watching her marry the man of her dreams. Her heart was overjoyed as she proceeded down the aisle.

Finally, she was next to him and everything she had been through to get there seemed trivial and worth it. They said their vows. James' eyes became watery and his words were heartfelt as he choked backed the tears.

Everyone enjoyed the reception. Shannon and James' brother, who was the best man, made their toasts. James' aunt and uncle welcomed Brenda into the family. They took on the role of raising James and his younger brother after their parents, who were both doctors, died in a plane crash on a hospital mission to help aid Africans when they were teenagers.

Deacon and Deaconess Brown insisted she call them Mom and Dad. All in all, it was an excellent day and one Brenda would never forget. Now that they'd had their first dance, the bouquet had been thrown, and the cake had been cut, all they wanted was to be alone in each other's arms. They said their goodbyes then left their love ones to start their honeymoon.

He swept her up off her feet and carried her up to the beach house. There were candles all around the bedroom; rose petals led towards the bed where more were patterned in a heart shape. Champagne was on ice while Will Downing played softly on the stereo. The mood was set for romance and love, and that was what they made.

His arms were strong and he was tender and passionate. For years they'd wanted and wondered and waited, but no more. It was everything and more than she had hoped or even dreamed. The way he touched her made her forget all about Ray. Tonight she knew this is where she belonged all along. Momma really knew best and he was the best.

"I love you, Mrs. Powers."

"I love you too, Mr. Powers."

They spent their honeymoon in Hawaii and spent two weeks enjoying each other day and night. When they returned home, they began their life as Dr. and Mrs. Powers, living and working together. This was the life Brenda had dreamed about and she wanted to be the best wife she could be. Their working relationship also thrived. They continued to bring awareness to the community with fundraisers and parties. They even started a scholarship in honor of her grandmother, Mrs. Elnora Mae Greene. Within two years, their accomplishments were well known. James had written several journals and given lectures in three countries with Brenda right by his side.

Things had been quite busy, so busy that Brenda didn't

realize that she had missed several periods. For weeks, she had been light headed and sluggish but chalked it up to being overworked, even though the last time she felt this way she found out she was pregnant.

Could I be pregnant? That would be so wonderful.

She didn't want to get her hopes up nor tell James because she didn't want it to be a false alarm, so she made an appointment with her gynecologist.

While she sat on the exam table waiting for her test results, she remembered the last time she found out she was expecting and how happy she was only to lose her baby on the worst day of her life.

No, this time will be different. I won't let you do this to me Satan! I won't bring that old mess into my new life, she said as she rebuked every evil thought from her mind.

Finally the doctor returned with her results.

"Well, Brenda, I have some great news. You are pregnant, about four months I should say, based on your last cycle," she said, holding the results in her hand. "I think we should do an ultra sound to make sure and to see how the baby is progressing since you have had one miscarriage."

The doctor placed the gel on her belly. She rolled it around on her stomach. Brenda listened with anticipation for the heartbeat. Suddenly she heard a faint sound.

"Is that the heartbeat, Dr. Miller?"

"Yes, I believe it is," she said, continuing to listen further.

Continuing to roll around, the heartbeat became stronger and louder.

"Wow, is that our baby?" Brenda asked.

"Yes, it is, and he or she sounds healthy," Dr. Miller continued until she heard something.

"What's wrong doctor? What's wrong? Is my baby okay? Tell me!" Brenda asked getting upset.

"Everything is fine; as a matter of fact it is twice as fine," Dr. Miller said, smiling at Brenda.

Confused, she asked, "What do you mean twice as fine?"

"Brenda, I hear two heart beats. You are having twins."

About to pass out she exclaimed, "Twins!"

"Are you okay? Would you like a glass of water?"

"Yes thank you. Can you tell what sex they are?"

"Yes, are you sure you want to know? I can give you a picture of the two of them," she said, handing Brenda the picture of the ultrasound.

Brenda looked at the ultrasound and was overjoyed. When she arrived home, she called James to make sure he was going to be home by eight.

She prepared dinner and set the table for a romantic evening. By seven the house was well lit with candles, the table looked beautiful, the music was softly playing and the Jacuzzi was hot and bubbling. Brenda slipped into to something comfortable as she waited for James to arrive. Just then his car pulled up and entered the garage. When he opened the door, she was waiting with a glass of wine, adorned in a see through negligee.

James was pleasantly aroused by his wife's greeting. "Wow, I need to come home early more often," he said as he dropped his briefcase to give her a passionate kiss.

"Slow ya roll, big daddy, in due time. Let's enjoy a nice dinner first," she said, pulling his hands off of her.

"You know you can't get me all worked up and then tell me to go eat."

"True, but I have some good news and I want you to enjoy the meal I prepared first."

As they ate Brenda could feel James undressing her with his eyes. She knew he had one thing on his mind and that dessert was going to be her. If she was going to tell him, it would have to be now before he choked from stuffing his food down his throat too fast. She handed him the ultrasound.

"What is this?" he asked.

"It's an ultrasound of our babies," she said, waiting for his reaction.

In mid chew, the food spewed out of his mouth. "Babies?"

"Yes, babies, our babies. I'm pregnant with twins."

He jumped up from the table over to Brenda and kissed her. He placed his hands on her stomach then knelt down to listen to her belly for the heartbeats.

"We're going to be parents?"

"Yes! God has blessed us with twins."

"Baby, you've made me the happiest man in the world."

"No, you've made me the happiest woman in the world."

"How far along are you?"

"Only four months."

"Well, we better be careful. I don't want to hurt our bundles of joy or you," he said as he carried her off into the bedroom.

"You'll never hurt me or our babies," she said as she submissively laid her head into his shoulder.

****

Five months later, Brenda gave birth to a healthy baby boy and girl. The first thing she did when the doctor placed them on her chest was check their foreheads.

"Whew...thank you Lord." She said.

"What's the matter, babe?" James asked.

"I was just checking."

"Checking what?"

"To see if they had a peak," she said.

"Brenda, you know that it's only an old wives tale. You shouldn't take it seriously," he said as he picked up his son.

"I know. You're right, because in spite of everything that's happened in my life, the Lord has blessed me, peak and all."

They named the twins Elnora and Sam after her grandparents.

Six months later, James and Brenda invited their close friends and family to the babies' blessings at their church. Both Sonya and Shannon came with their new spouses and children. Life had finally come full circle for Brenda. She finally understood what Momma Greene meant when she said,

"***Bre-Bre, I don't care how difficult life gets. When you trust and serve the Lord in spirit and in truth, He will give you double for your trouble.***"

The following Mother's day she and James and their children went to visit Momma Greene's grave. They had Karen's body brought back to Charleston and buried next to her parents. Now they were all together again.

As they stood there with her past and present in one location, her heart became overwhelmed with joy.

"Momma, you were right, it all did work together for my good."

THE END

About The Author

Ella D. Fleming is a native of Charleston, SC, where she grew up on the projects and attended public schools. She writes a blog (Ella's Midnight Inspirations) as well as short stories and enjoys acting, writing songs, books, and plays, that help explain and simplify the complexities of everyday life.

She believes that great lessons can be learned through a simple story. She brings to the country the story-telling traditions of the wise elders and the culture of the people of Charleston where she still resides. She has performed her poetry and monologues at several local venues, churches, and organizations. Her passion is working to inspire others with her gifts.

She is a member of two writing groups and the Director of The Children of the Promise Royal Puppeteers at her church, Royal Missionary Baptist Church in North Charleston, SC.

She is a retired state of South Carolina employee where she worked as an Administrative Assistant for over 16 years. She is a graduate of Burke High School, Trident Technical College,

La Parisianne Cosmetology Institute, and Morris College Extension School of Religion. She is married, a mother of two, and grandmother of two.